THE

A GUILTY PARTIES NOVEL

ACQUITTAL

BY

PAT SIMMONS

Edited by Karen R. Thomas/Editorial Consultant
Proofread by Karen McCollum Rodgers/Critiqueyourbook.com
Cover design: Tywebbin Creations, LLC
Cover images: Bigstock 50999, 4899193, 29960207; istock 0000183
Author Photo: Naum Furman

ISBN: 1-4800-9482-X
ISBN-13: 9781480094826

DEDICATION:

"There is neither Jew nor Greek, there is neither bond nor free, there is neither male nor female: for ye are all one in Christ Jesus."

KJV Galatians 3:28

PRAISES FOR PAT SIMMONS

Simmons has laid it all out on the line in this installment of the Jamieson legacy. This is pure Christian romance with a touch of heritage. There were moments in the middle that I wanted them to get it together but it turned out better than expected. The personal touch of genealogy is wonderful and will make you think about your own family heritage. Wanted to see more Grandma BB but loved the new character development. Simmons is on top of her genre ...

Reviewed by M. Bruner "Deltareviewer" on *Free from Guilt*

Free from Guilt may be listed as Christian fiction, but it's so much more. You read about family history, romance and transformation. This is a great read and leaves the reader wanting more, with that being said I'm looking forward to the next Guilty installment.

Reviewed by Melody Vernor-Bartel for Reader's Paradise

I enjoyed reading The Guilt Trip because it shares a strong male storyline and family values. I recommend this book to anyone who enjoys family and redemption stories.

Reviewed by Sharel E. Gordon-Love for APOOO BookClub

The Guilt Trip is about understanding the meaning of family and learning to forgive. The power of prayer and family support can change a person's life. The main character's revelation that every woman is not out to trap him and the realization that he is not his father was touching. The author does a wonderful job including powerful messages within her writing. I look forward to more from this series.

Reviewed by Teresa Beasley for A&RBC Reviews

I am so loving "Guilty by Association!" Girl, you went all out!!!! When I thought there could not be a man to compare to Parke, you created "Kidd!" WOW is all I can say ... No, I take that back, WOW! WOW! WOW! The love .... WOW! The relationship blossoming ... WOW! The man .... WOW!

Darlene Mitchell, Virginia Guilty captain

*Crowning Glory...*voted best Christian fiction for 2011 by O.O.S.A. Online Book club and best Inspirational Romance of the Year (2011)

ACKNOWLEDGEMENT

Dear readers,

Akwaaba (welcome in Twi)

Thanks to all who have followed the Jamiesons since book one. As my ninth Christian novel, I would like to introduce you to this spinoff of the Guilty series, the Guilty Parties. Although the main characters may not be Jamiesons, they are connected through kinship or friendship.

The Acquittal would not have been possible without the Lord placing special people in my path to guide me along the way:

Professor Albion Mends (originally from Ghana, West Africa) with the Center for Religious Studies Faculty at University of Central Missouri. He gave my Ghanaian characters life. Professor Mends tirelessly answered each email, sent links to articles to me, directed me to YouTube videos and so much more.

To Missionary Avery Segal who shared his Ghana photos with the world through his blog and answered my questions.

Special thanks to the Ghana West Africa Missions, out of Searcy, AR for their service.

I hope you are swept away to the sights and sounds of Ghana, play under the tropical sun and dance to the African drum beat. *Akwaaba* to Ghana.

I have to send a shout out to my husband, Kerry—whew! Thank you for giving me space to talk to my characters. I love and appreciate you. To my son and daughter—I am blessed. To my old and new friends, including the Guilty captains, thank you for your support!!!

To the many book clubs, readers, and bookstores, thanks for promoting my work.

To Bethesda Temple Church and Bishop James A. Johnson and First Lady Juana Johnson, thank you for being Shepherds for Christ. I love you, Bishop!

To the descendants of Minerva Jordan Wade; Marshall Cole and Laura Brown; Joseph and Nellie Palmer Wafford Brown; Thomas Carter and Love Ann Shepard; Ned and Priscilla Brownlee; John Wilkinson and Artie Jamison/Charlotte Jamison, and others who were tracked down on the 1800s censuses and other documents; and my in-laws: Simmons, Sinkfield, Croft, Sturdivant, Strickland, Downers…and the list goes on.

Chapter 1

I never should've let her go, Dr. Rainey Reynolds scolded himself for the umpteenth time since Josephine Abena Yaa Amoah's departure—as if he could've stopped her.

Come home to Africa and ride on our crocodiles, play with our monkeys, walk above the trees in our rainforest, dance on our many beaches...Come to Ghana with me, and taste the freshest pineapples and papayas in the world, or delicious domedo...Come with me... Josephine's enticing whispers faded in his mind.

Her appeal had been so strong that Rainey had felt compelled to pack and program his GPS to that destination.

Tall and elegant, Josephine didn't just walk into a room. She moved like a dancer as if the rhythm of Africa's drums played in her head. The day she beckoned to him, Josephine's clothes were wrapped around her body like melted wax. Her rich brown sugar complexion glowed. Simply put, Josephine was a majestic woman, created to be noticed, from her husky African accent to her expressive brown eyes—and her hair—not one strand out of place. He remembered every detail, even the scent of her toothpaste.

However, despite Rainey's attraction, Josephine possessed one irritating attribute. The woman hadn't seen eye to eye with him on practically anything while she was a graduate exchange student at the University of Missouri at St. Louis.

"So..." Dr. Shane Maxwell said as he tapped his fingers on their table, interrupting Rainey's musing. "Let me get this straight. Where did this idea of doing missionary work suddenly come from, and of all places Ghana?"

Both had attended a day-long conference of the St. Louis Chapter of American Association of Orthodontists, the elite and highly competitive professionals of the dental field. With the lectures finished, they had just placed their orders at the Yia Yia Euro Café.

Rainey squinted at his colleague and childhood friend. Growing up, they had been inseparable. Easygoing until provoked, their memories rarely faded. Each possessed striking looks and an athletic body. They had their pick of women, especially when it was made known that "doctor" was part of their title.

Shane grunted when Rainey hesitated. "Wait a minute. Isn't that where the woman who thought she was too good for you hails from? What was her name? You two didn't even get along."

"Josephine Abena Yaa Amoah." Her name flowed easily as Rainey tried to duplicate the Ghanaian accent. "Granted, our personalities clashed most of the time, but there was a mutual attraction. Plus, she did invite me to her homeland."

"No, if I recall correctly—and trust me, I do—you told me this Josephine lady was conducting story hour at a library to a bunch of kindergarteners. It wasn't a personal invitation. You just so happened to be there because you were meeting your twin sister for lunch."

As Rainey tried to defend himself, Shane held up his hand. "Somehow you felt compelled to accept her indirect offer from how long again? It's been almost a year! You can't be serious? Desperation doesn't suit you. Let it go, man. Let her go, please."

And that was the problem; no matter how hard Rainey tried he couldn't erase her memory. "Dr. Maxwell," Rainey addressed him professionally just to annoy him. "As you know, it's not unusual for our colleagues to volunteer their services in any manner we chose, especially in underdeveloped countries. As a matter of fact, two groups recently returned from Central America, and did you know some children in Honduras had never seen a toothbrush?"

Rainey shivered at the thought of gum disease lurking in the hidden crevices. "Can you imagine? So I thought to myself..." he shrugged. "Why not give back? I contacted Dentists Without Borders and there just so happened to be a need in Peru and Ghana. I requested Ghana."

"What a coincidence," Shane said sarcastically before stroking his beard. "That's another oversight. We're not dentists, Rainey. We did not agonize three years in post-grad to specialize in orthodontics to pull teeth." The joke between them was all anyone needed was sewing thread. "In case you forgot, we're not licensed to extract teeth."

This was not the time for Rainey's friend to play the devil's advocate. "Just go with my flow. For the fun of it, I mailed my application to the organization, along with a copy of my credentials."

"What? If you were wearing braces, I would say they were too tight. Rain, listen to me, man." Shane leaned across the table. "We give back by donating thousands of dollars each year to charities. You and I serve on several boards, volunteer occasionally at Big Brothers Big Sisters, we sponsor little leagues at Herbert Hoover Boys Clubs...Write a check." Shane reached inside his suit pocket and pulled out his checkbook. "I'll even match you dollar for dollar, or donate supplies since you're feeling charitable." He poised a nearby pen to write out the amount.

"It's not all about the money this time." It was about seeing Josephine, her fantastic smile and experiencing the sparks between them that continued to simmer even in her absence. Neither time nor distance had smothered his attraction.

They paused when their meals were placed in front of them. Each silently said grace before they draped napkins on their laps. Although there was a lull in their discussion as they savored their selections, Rainey's mind continued to play a matinee of his life. He needed a sabbatical to escape his dysfunctional family.

The honorable Dr. Roland Reynolds had a flawless reputation in the medical profession and community as an OB/GYN practitioner. His father would tell his children stories about near death experiences during deliveries, but how by his skill and expertise, the babies had arrived safely into the world.

The illusion of the great and powerful doctor was shattered when he confessed to an old hit-and-run case that killed a man. For almost a year in his father's absence, Rainey, the only son, had played big brother to his older sister and head of his mother's home.

Only in a twist of fate did the victim's widow unknowingly become close friends with his sister, Cheney. His father was tried, convicted and sentenced to two years in the Algoa Correctional Center in Jefferson City, Missouri. Twenty-four months, seven hundred and thirty days seemed like an eternity to his family.

Rainey refocused on the present as he helped himself to another bite of roasted chicken. A few seconds later, he wiped his mouth. "I know what you're thinking."

"Oh, I doubt it."

"This is bigger than Josephine," he countered, almost convincing himself of that. Shane folded his arms. Reading his friend's suspicious expression, Rainey trumped the imaginary deck of cards they were silently playing. "Go ahead. Say it."

"Thanks for permission. Didn't this woman say, quote 'I'm not the woman who broke your heart; therefore, I'm not responsible to mend it', and added some nonsense about 'That's where God steps in' end quote? When you told me that, instantly I didn't like her. I still don't and I don't want to meet her, not even to see her brilliant smile you described. What type of woman turns down a Black man with money?"

Shane's memory retention was unprecedented. "Evidently, she does. Why do you always remember the things I would rather you forget? Okay, man. Yes, she did say it."

This was not the time for Shane to serve as Rainey's voice of reason. Pick any of Josephine's assets and Rainey was attracted to it. His stubbornness allowed her to slip away, because he refused to admit she had been right about her assessment of him.

It had been one year—no thirteen months—since Josephine flew back to Africa, with a goodbye to everyone except him. Pride kept him from contacting her. Then, to add insult to an already self-inflicted wound, no other woman since her had made Rainey forget about Josephine.

Josephine's presence had begun to melt his heart, and he liked the feel of it. He used every mental and physical constraint not to like her, but she had gotten under his skin, and if curiosity killed that cat, he would die meowing in the Motherland. Josephine had hypnotized him with her beauty, wisdom and saucy accent, but the timing of their meeting had not been under the best circumstances. Rainey was struggling with his own past regrets. When an ex-girlfriend announced she was pregnant, she demanded all of him—commitment and marriage.

Rainey's mistake was taunting the woman, whom he didn't love, with nothing but child support. Marriage wasn't an option. In the end, she terminated her pregnancy at four or five months and walked away. He couldn't quench the rage within whenever he heard about a woman aborting her baby. Rainey never knew that he could hate so strongly.

After all, his father had been in the profession of saving lives, not destroying them—at least that was his belief before the manslaughter conviction.

To further complicate matters, Rainey overheard that Cheney Reynolds Jamieson, daughter of an OB/GYN doctor, had committed the same unthinkable act with no remorse—or so he thought—while away at college. Shane didn't know about that, which added to Rainey's idyllic world being nothing but a lie.

Although he recognized it had been her personal choice, Rainey still confronted his twin. She had cited that God's forgiveness set her free years after she was guilty of that incident while decades after his father's act landed him behind bars. Despite Dr. Roland Reynolds's repentance, God had not set his father free. Wasn't God's forgiveness supposed to be across the board without favoritism? At this point in his life, Rainey could honestly say he was faithless.

"I've got to get away, Shane." The missionary work not only gave him a purpose, but a cover to escape.

Glancing around the café, Shane exchanged nods with other colleagues who had attended the conference. Rainey snickered at Shane's expression, one he sometimes mirrored: twisting his mouth before pulling on the strands of his mustache as he prepared to state something unpleasant.

"You've had a silver pacifier in your mouth since you took your first breath. We both graduated from Harvard, but your father pulled strings for you to work alongside Dr. Guggenheim. I, on the flipside, had to accept Locum Tenens assignments as an on-call contractor to gain experience.

"When Guggenheim retired a couple of years ago, you and your father bought out his practice. Now, Dr. Rainey T. Reynolds is the most sought after orthodontist in two states. So help me to understand this impoverished mission attitude."

Rainey hated when Shane used the "privileged-old money" monologue on him, but what he said was true. The Reynolds name was once considered among the elite in African-American society. That's why his father's blemish stung. He grunted to shake the bad memories that overpowered the good times he had shared with his father.

"Let me flip this script, my brotha." Rainey purposely used slang as he leaned forward. "Whether I had a family connection or not, we both earned our way to rank one and two in our classes. There were no strings my father could pull for me to be admitted to the best orthodontist school in the country.

"Since we represent the less than one percent of ten-thousand orthodontists who are African-Americans, I say our futures remain bright." Rainey checked him and sat back. At one time Rainey wanted to follow in his father's footsteps to make him proud. For Shane, it was all about starting a money trail where Rainey already had one started for him. "Tell me how volunteering in Africa is supposed to be a bad thing?"

"I know you've been under pressure since your dad's conviction, but if you need to talk to someone... How about that super-fine psychologist, Tierra Blake? I'm sure she would rework her patient load to fit you in for a private appointment." Shane wiggled a brow.

If anybody was going to soothe his broken spirit, he wanted Josephine to be in charge of his treatment plan. "I'm not going there. After one date, Tierra made it plain she wanted a husband. I made it plain I had no intentions of offering to be her 'Mr.'"

Shane snickered. "That's your problem, you and your blunt honesty with women. You missed out. If you want to get away, take a trip to Aruba or visit Mexico. You don't have to go to another continent," Shane paused, then took another bite of his vegetable medley.

"You can't talk me out of this. Besides," he said, grinning, "I've already been approved, renewed my passport, and applied for a visa to Ghana...I've started getting vaccinations."

"Incredible. Here, I thought you were just thinking about this foolishness, but it's a done deal." Shane fanned his hand in the air. "Man, you are messed up in the head. This trip has Josephine's name stamped all over your passport. I just hope she doesn't whisper subliminal messages for you to stay in Africa."

"This is a mission trip, remember? I'm not looking to relocate or build a summer home near the infamous slave castles." Rainey reminded his friend.

"Famous last words. It's you who needs to remember it's a trip to help the needy, not to become needy for a woman." Shane held both hands up. "Why am I wasting my time? We both know you're already whipped."

છઠ

As they were accustomed to doing on Sunday afternoons since his father's incarceration, Rainey and his two siblings with their spouses and their children met at his parents' palatial home for dinner. Saturdays were reserved to visit their father, according to a schedule set up by Gayle Reynolds—his mother.

Between bites, Rainey broke the news.

"You're what?" Janae's fork dropped on her plate. "Now is not the time to go in search of your roots, and I'm not referring to the movie either. How insensitive of you to want a pleasure trip while we're still in the middle of a crisis? Can't you hold off until Dad is released—I mean comes home?" It wasn't a question, but an unveiled demand.

"This is a *working* trip, Janae," Rainey emphasized.

"I'm so jealous. I think that's great," Cheney said with genuine delight. "Parke and I have been talking about visiting his ancestral home of Côte d'Ivoire, which borders Ghana. You know he's documented ten generations back to Paki Kokumuo Jaja, the chief prince of the Diomande tribe … "

Janae cut her eyes at Rainey's younger twin by three minutes. "Humph. Of course, you would." She pointed a manicured nail.

Rainey could say with certainty, his older sister's attitude was bestowed on her at birth. She mirrored their mother's snooty qualms. The shortest of them at five-seven and very nice-looking, Janae developed a "short woman's syndrome" when he and Cheney outgrew her by five and eight inches, respectively. That didn't stop Janae from demanding their respect and the last word as children and now as adults.

Older by three years, Janae was all about looks. Her flawless hair, makeup and clothes spoke volumes about her status in society that she wanted to maintain. Even after their father's past deeds were revealed, she was in self-denial in her self-righteous frame of mind; she insisted on a display of spotless appearance.

"I've never thought about a vacation in Africa, but a safari adventure sounds like something to look forward to." His mother's mouth hinted of a smile, but the castaway look in her eyes reflected sadness. "When I spoke to Roland this week, he sounded upbeat as we counted down eleven months, three weeks and four days until he comes home."

"Great, now you're upsetting mother with this nonsense," Janae ranted as she threw down her napkin on the table. Her husband, Bryce, tried to hush her, but to no avail.

He could do without the drama. *My poor brother-in-law.* For the last fifteen or so years of their marriage, Bryce had pampered his wife. In reality, they all were guilty of creating Janae, the Diva-zilla.

"Janae Reynolds Allen, if my son wants to go on this goodwill trip, he has my blessings and I'm sure his father would agree."

"While you're there, make sure you see Josephine," Cheney said with a wink.

"Josephine? Oh, so that's what this is all about, that high-minded African woman who lived with Grandma BB?" Janae lifted an arched brow.

Ignoring her snide remark, Rainey acted as nonchalant as possible. "If I have time, I'll try."

"Make time," Cheney said. "I'll give you her email address and phone number."

Yes! Rainey lifted an imaginary fist in the air as he forked another piece of lasagna and slipped it into his mouth. "Hmmmmm. Mother, this is exceptionally tasty."

Chapter 2

Monday morning, Josephine wasted precious time signing into her email account instead of coordinating her wardrobe for work. For the past few days, she had anticipated seeing a wedding gown picture from her oldest of two sisters, Madeline, who lived in London. Madeline's renewal ceremony was a few months away. Nothing—again. Josephine was about to log out when an email from her friend in the United States caught her eye.

The latest gossip from the Jamiesons was in the subject line. She smiled. That meant a praise report. Not long ago, Cheney's eleven-year-old daughter, Kami, received the gift of the Holy Ghost. Josephine had her own private praise party for the one soul snagged from the devil's hit list and added to the Lord's kingdom.

Unfortunately, she did not have time to read what appeared to be another lengthy Cheney email. Although curious, Josephine shut down her computer and hurried to shower. Hopefully, somebody left her enough hot water.

With her salary as a researcher, she could afford to live on her own and closer to her job, but Josephine preferred making her home with her parents and her younger sister, Abigail.

She dressed in record time. Unfortunately, in the kitchen no one had prepared breakfast this morning, not even baguette-like tea bread for her to nibble on.

Thanks, in part, to the daily hawkers milling through the intersections, pedaling everything from toiletries to fresh fruits and vegetables, Josephine wouldn't starve. They were mostly female entrepreneurs selling their wares to bring in family income. She respected that as her stomach growled. Grabbing her things, Josephine headed out the door to begin her work week.

The semi-organized public transportation system that Josephine and countless others depended upon was trotros. They could be anything from small Nissan buses to minivans or converted pick-up trucks. Joining others in the crowd, it was the norm for lines to swell as commuters waited for the Conductors or "mates" to step off the vehicle and yell the driver's destination to parts all over the city.

Before paying the mate her fare, Josephine patronized a hawker. The woman practically forced her to buy an *ankaa*. Sipping from a straw protruding out of the orange that was actually green in her country, Josephine savored the sweet juice. Next, she paid for a *koo-ko*. The hot mixture of liquid corn meal flavored with ginger and other spices in a plastic bag also sucked through a straw would satisfy her immediate hunger.

Throughout the bumpy ride—largely due to unattended massive potholes and the lack of regular maintenance on the trotro—Josephine thought about Cheney again. There were so many fond memories of America, particularly St. Louis. Her host family consisted of one person, a seventy-something eccentric childless widow that went by the handle Grandma BB.

Grandma didn't sound affectionate enough, so Josephine called her Grandmother B. The woman was always at odds with her young, vibrant and sassy next-door neighbor, Imani Segall. The interaction between the two was most times comical.

That's how Josephine became acquainted with Cheney—Grandma BB introduced her as a god-granddaughter. Josephine had heard of the terms god-daughter and grand-daughter. She had yet to locate that word in any dictionary. Cheney's twin, Rainey, was pleasing to the eyes, but Josephine hadn't dared to stare, not wanting his charm to hold her captive. Although she admitted to herself the chemistry was there, they were worlds apart, spiritually, mentally and yes, physically.

She had arrived in America right in the middle of chaos. Grandma BB was on trial for firing a weapon at Rainey's dad to even the score after learning that Roland Reynolds killed her husband.

Appalled at her host's eye-for-an-eye revenge, Josephine thought perhaps the Lord had sent her to the U.S. to lead Grandma BB to Christ.

The trotro came to a screeching halt because of a traffic jam. Thanks to reckless drivers and too many vehicles on the road, her ten-mile commute to the university would result in an unnecessary hour plus road trip.

The delay only caused Josephine to continue conjuring up images of the first day she met Rainey. He had followed her onto the elevator in the courthouse. At five feet-ten inches, Rainey definitely towered over her, whether she wore heels or not. He would never know his masculinity made her feel cornered and powerless.

At six-three, six-four—six foot-something, Rainey had a regal air about him. He was handsome with his thick, wavy curls, and lips outlined with a trimmed mustache and a goatee. Rainey's looks could only be described as breathtaking, heartstopping, and eye-bucking distinguished.

Josephine didn't exhale until she reached her floor and exited the close quarters. His intoxicating cologne continued to drug her, as it seemed to seep into her skin. She had guessed his identity even as he introduced himself. His eyes, nose and mouth reminded her of Cheney. Where his twin was fair skinned like a lemon, Rainey's coloring reminded her of the cocoa produced in her homeland.

"I'm Rainey Reynolds." His voice was strong and deep as he offered his hand.

Lifting her chin, Josephine accepted his strong, but gentle shake. "Ah. Correction, you're Doctor Rainey Reynolds, Cheney's twin. The only son of murder suspect, Dr. Roland Reynolds."

Of course, Rainey gritted his teeth, then snarled. "Watch it, lady. In my country, my father is innocent until proven guilty…"

Closing her eyes, Josephine groaned at her bluntness. Surely, she could have phrased that better, but once the words were out, Josephine couldn't retrieve them. She had deserved his response.

Their trotro had finagled around the jam only to stumble across not one, but two more accidents. It was just another day in the Ghanaian landscape.

Finally, when Josephine arrived at work, she and others disembarked quickly. She hurried across the campus of the University of Ghana at Legon, boasted as the most prestigious school in West Africa. As one of three researchers for several professors at the Graduate School of Nuclear and Applied Sciences at the Ghana Atomic Energy Commission, Josephine wanted to utilize the wealth of information she gained in America to advance her country's status in the world.

Inside her building, she greeted all who crossed her path as she headed to her station. Once settled, Josephine checked her workload for the day. Confident that she could meet her dead-lines, she signed into her email and opened Cheney's message.

Praise the Lord, Josephine!

I hope this email finds you absolutely abundantly blessed. Let me tell you what Jesus has done again. I'm four weeks pregnant! Can you believe it? We'll be adding another Jamieson to the fold. Parke is ecstatic. Of course, he won't be throwing up, eating everything in sight, or carry-ing extra body fat before going through twelve hours of labor.

She muffled her giggle to make sure she didn't rouse the attention of her colleagues. Without a doubt, Cheney was just as excited as her husband. The woman had a true testimony, consid-ering the doctors said she wouldn't have any children.

When Josephine met Cheney, she and Parke had adopted one of their foster children, Kami, and were in a legal battle to reverse the adoption of Parke's biological son, Pace, to another family.

During this time, Cheney had become pregnant twice. She miscarried one child, then delivered a stillborn son. Through it all, the couple had learned to trust Jesus. Finally, after the last pregnancy, Cheney delivered a happy, healthy, and hyper little boy. Eager to know more, Josephine continued reading.

My sister-in-law, Hali, is also expecting—I know… it must be something in the water. LOL. And Grandma BB—of course she's not pregnant, but stranger things have happened with surrogate mothers in demand, but she is as stubborn as ever. If you saw her, you would never know she had a stroke unless she's tired, then her speech might slur.

Grandma BB's recovery was indeed good news. Josephine had returned home a few months earlier when she got the news about her host suffering a stroke. Praise God for His mercy and grace, and that Grandma BB was a fighter.

Oh, and there's one last bit of news that may surprise you. Rainey is going to Ghana. Please continue to pray for him. Rainey says it's a missionary trip. Only God knows. Hopefully, you'll get a chance to see him. Be nice. :) Anyway, I better go. My house is too quiet with the children at home.

Love, your sister in Christ,
Cheney

Josephine's jaw dropped, then she blinked. She reread the line about Rainey. He's coming to Ghana—her homeland, a country she loved patriotically—for missionary work? Rainey? Had the impeccable, gorgeous and arrogant man undergone a spiritual metamorphosis and surrendered to Jesus? Surely Cheney would have mentioned that in one of her praise reports.

Questions swarmed in her head as she signed out of her email. Josephine's heart fluttered at the thought of seeing Rainey again.

When she left the States, they weren't on speaking terms. Yet the time and distance had not dulled her memory of him. His convictions—right or wrong—were tighter than matted hair, which was why they could never work as a couple.

Despite Rainey's cockiness, glimpses of his broken spirit bled through. His family crisis had taken a toll on him, as well as some emotional haunting some woman had done on him to break his heart.

Josephine didn't want to be party to a rebound relationship, and with an unbeliever. Of course, after Josephine returned to Ghana, Jesus chastened her about hesitating to intervene when it came to someone's soul.

Transitioning to work mode, or trying, Josephine researched information for two professors and conversed with her coworkers about new projects. While she focused on extracting scientific data from research data, Josephine couldn't banish more thoughts of Rainey.

She glanced out of the window nearest her workstation until she heard her name called. Turning around, she faced fellow researcher, Kim Ayew.

"What is going on with you? You've separated yourself from others most of the day."

Josephine stuttered to get the words out. "I just learned that my friend's brother from the United States is coming here on a mission trip."

"How exciting!" Kim smiled and then frowned at Josephine's blank expression. "That is a good thing, *yo?*

Josephine didn't answer. She couldn't answer.

Kim eyed her. "Hmm. You will marry him, *yo?*"

Where did that question come from? "No." Josephine had a ready answer. As a young newlywed, Kim thought whenever anyone mentioned a man, a ceremony to pronounce a couple husband and wife was not far off. Kim was on the plump side—a healthy attribute in Ghana. She had flawless very dark skin with beautiful features and a short afro; sometimes Kim wore twists.

"That is not an option to consider. Our differences are too great. Rainey is American, I had hoped for a Ghanaian mate."

Her colleague shook her head furiously. "You should not limit your happiness. If there is attraction, don't fight it," Kim scolded.

Fight? If Josephine said something was black, he would argue it was bleach white. "That's all we did, fight." Josephine tried not to grin, but a giggle slipped out anyway.

Kim's eyes widened in suspicion. She refused to go back to work until Josephine shared her thoughts.

Josephine shivered. "It's something about Dr. Rainey Reynolds that triggered my intolerance for arrogance. He is one of the most irritating and complex men I ever met. When he asked me out, I did my best to ignore him." Josephine *tsk*ed. "It is difficult to discount a handsome man dressed in all black attire and wearing a mischievous glint in his eyes."

"Oooh." Kim sighed and disappeared. She returned, dragging her workstation chair from on the other side to Josephine's desk. "How did you resist this magnetism?" Kim asked with her hands folded as an obedient student trying to soak in a lesson.

Taking a deep breath, Josephine closed her eyes and retrieved the flashback. "I was conducting a children's story hour at the small library where I was assigned work-study. Rainey's unexpected appearance distracted me."

"Good ploy," Kim approved.

"Wait...then I compromised my composure and flirted." She relived the moment, divulging more details.

"Listen, I know we didn't get off to a good start—" Rainey said once she gave him her full attention.

"Which was a result of your bad manners," Josephine had teased with a straight face.

"I remember it as your sassy mouth starting it, but what..."

She had whispered, "I'm on duty here. We'll have to trade character assessments at another time."

"Another time means you've agreed to let me take you out and we can exchange compliments." Folding his buffed arms, Rainey smirked as if he had scored the winning point.

"Only if I am properly asked." She slowly lifted a shoulder in a slight shrug, enjoying the power of flirtation.

"Go out with me. You won't regret it ... " Josephine finished the story.

Kim clapped her hands as she stood. "There has to be a part two between you and Rainey. It didn't sound like the end to me," her coworker stated with confidence. She walked away, pulling her chair.

As far as Josephine was concerned when she boarded the plane, it was 'the end'. For the remainder of the afternoon, Josephine wondered, *Do I regret the growing feelings I still have for him?*

Later that evening after Josephine returned home from work, she hoped there would be no power outages, so she could email Cheney for more details. Inconsistent electricity was a way of life for Ghanaians who summarized it as another casualty of local government's red tape. Last week, most of her neighborhood had lost power twice.

When she left the United States, Josephine made it clear that she didn't want Cheney feeding her any information about her stubborn twin. Her friend called her just as stubborn. Maybe she had been too quick to judge Rainey, especially since he was coming for missionary work. It wouldn't be the first time, according to her father, Gyasi.

On her computer, Josephine typed in the subject line, *This was very entertaining.*

Taking a deep breath, Josephine exhaled and asked the question that had been nagging her: *Has Rainey been involved in community service since I've been gone?*

What she wanted to ask was whether Rainey chose Ghana, or did Ghana choose him? To inquire would reveal too much about her lingering rebellious feelings. Josephine clicked SEND before she wrote another word.

Anchoring her elbow on the table, Josephine rested her chin in the palm of her hand as she stared at the computer screen. Ghana was five hours ahead of Central Standard Time. How long would it take for Cheney to respond? One thing for sure, she wasn't going to starve to death waiting.

Coming out of her bedroom, she followed her parents' and Abigail's voices in the kitchen. Her younger sister, who was a university student, had returned home early and prepared a dinner of smoked fish and banku. The cooked, fermented corn dough was one of Josephine's favorites.

Joining them, Josephine waited her turn as they washed their hands in a warm bowl of water on the table in preparation for eating. Her father, Gyasi Yaw Amoah was from the Akan tribe—the majority ethnic group in West Africa. Her mother, Fafa, was an ethnic Ewe. The two had been married thirty-three years. According to her father, Fafa was still as elegant and lovely as the day he married her.

After her father said the blessings, Josephine participated in the dinner conversation while they ate, but her mind wasn't far away from Cheney's reply.

Of course, she could always phone her friend, but calling overseas was expensive, even using an international calling card. So Josephine went through the motions of a regular evening at home. She prepared her clothes for work the next day and read a few chapters of a science journal for work. When Josephine's patience had grown impatient, she hurried to her computer and signed into her email account. Cheney had written her back! Her heart pounded.

Hi honey,

The only thing I can say about my brother is he's a man on a mission with Dentist Without Borders and nothing will deter his decision. He didn't ask, but I gave him your email address and phone number. I hope that was okay. He'll be there on February 17th for ten days and will stay with a host family in Abaka Lapaz. His flight information is...

No mention of Rainey asking for her contact number? He didn't ask for it? Josephine's heart dropped. He had no intention of seeing her at all. When she arrogantly told him that she didn't intend to be some clean-up woman, she meant it. After a few attempts to change her mind, he moved on—to her relief and slight disappointment. Her pride said she was worth the chase.

Josephine, I know my brother. Rainey has seemed restless. He hasn't attended church that I know about, yet he's more receptive when I talk about Jesus, so that's a start. He's soul searching. This mission trip is the most focused he's been about something in a while. I know that's information you didn't ask for, since you two weren't exactly on speaking terms when you returned to your country, but I threatened him to make sure he sees you before coming back here. Please be nice to Rainey when you see him. Let's pray that whatever he's searching for, God gives him the desires of his heart.

Much love, your sister in Christ,

Cheney

Threatened? If Rainey does reach out to her, it will only be because he was threatened. "Great. Thanks a lot, sister," Josephine mumbled, twisting her mouth in frustration. With a heavy sigh, she whispered, *Amen*, to Cheney's prayer and signed off.

On her knees, Josephine said her own list of prayers before slowly climbing into bed. She hoped Rainey would contact her voluntarily. If he didn't, she would have learned a lesson on the consequences of not holding her tongue.

Chapter 3

A month later, Rainey was ready to escape February's bitter cold temperatures. He was about to do something he had never done before—go after a woman who didn't want him.

"You know, it's not too late to back out," Shane advised, steering his Lexus toward the St. Louis airport.

Stopping by his condo earlier in the week, Shane didn't believe he was leaving until he witnessed Rainey packing. He quizzed Rainey on whether he had gotten enough travel insurance, travelers' cheques, malaria drugs, mosquito repellant spray, and a yellow fever immunization. The list seemed endless. Even now, Shane threw out anything he could dream up to make Rainey see going to Africa wasn't worth it.

"I'm looking forward to some warm weather. Besides, I can't get my money back."

Shane barked out a laugh. "This isn't about the money. We've wasted more on the gambling boat, and you didn't buck." He paused. "We both know this is under the pretense of a missionary trip. There is Skype, email, Facebook and international calling. This is an expensive house call."

Rainey fazed him out as he glanced at the road sign, indicating Lambert Airport was straight ahead.

"Nothing to say, huh? I just think you're going through a lot of trouble for a woman you're pining over. God help me never to be in your shoes."

"Dr. Rainey Reynolds does not pine. Let's say I'm intrigued." He shifted in his seat.

Shane released a mocking laugh. "Man, I hoped you would've overcome this obsession … whatever this thing is you have for this African woman. She whooped you with some serious voodoo stuff."

"From what I'm told, Ghana is a majority Christian country, so the only thing she and my sister dabble in is this Holy Ghost-holy living phenomenon. Besides, she rejected me. Isn't voodoo supposed to make someone your sex slave?"

"You could be someone's sex slave without crossing the ocean, so cancel the trip."

They battled wills back and forth until Shane exited the interstate and pulled into a space marked for departures. He forced his gear into park and faced Rainey. "I still think you are so making a big mistake, going after this woman."

"It won't be the first time I'm wrong about a woman," Rainey mumbled under his breath, thinking about his sister and ex again. Although his former girlfriend's betrayal happened long ago when he was still in undergraduate studies, that moment always stayed with him.

Releasing their seatbelts, both men stepped out of the car. Shane gave Rainey an overall inspection before patting him on the shoulders. "Never say I didn't try. At least promise me you won't drink the water and bring back some ungodly disease that has no cure!"

"You got it." This trip would cure whatever was ailing him about Josephine. He shook Shane's hand. "See you in ten days. Thanks for giving me a lift before going into your office."

At curbside, Rainey checked his luggage, including the fifty-pound box stuffed with toiletries from his mother and donations from colleagues. The most valuable item he carried was stored in his wallet—Josephine's contact information, along with an international calling card.

Once he cleared security, with two hours before his flight, Rainey detoured to the sports bar. When it was time to board, Rainey headed to his assigned gate. Once there, he recognized the mission team leaders, David and Frances Yancey, from their pictures on the website.

Both were dentists who were spearheading the mission trip under Dentists Without Borders. The couple had provided aid to Ghana numerous times in the past. Unfortunately, as David introduced the others in their small group, Rainey forgot their names just as fast. His mind was elsewhere.

Although Rainey was accustomed to flying non-stop, he needed every minute of the agonizing twenty-five hour flight, including two layovers, to rehearse what he would say to Josephine. After settling into his business class seat, Rainey fastened his seatbelt and glanced out the window, then for some odd reason felt the need to perform a character assessment on himself.

At thirty-six, Rainey was known for making calculated decisions with unwavering confidence. His handsome looks were a combination of both parents, while his height surpassed his father's by a few inches.

With the Reynolds' name, he and his siblings were destined for success. Yet, a twinge of doubt nagged at him. Would Josephine be glad to see him or would she shoot him down with her sassy mouth?

Stretching his legs, Rainey was glad the seat next to him remained unclaimed as the flight attendants welcomed passengers, and then demonstrated airplane safety instructions.

As the aircraft took flight, Rainey reached into the breast pocket of his lightweight linen blazer, glad to be rid of his wool trench coat, which he folded and stored overhead. He wouldn't need it with eighty-degree temperatures in Ghana.

When Rainey first contemplated the trip, he discussed it with his father during a prison visit. He didn't mention Josephine. Pulling out a recent letter from Algoa Correctional Center, he noticed his father's handwriting had improved. Gone was the infamous scribble doctors had a reputation for using that only nurses, assistants, and pharmacists could decode. These days, Dr. Roland Reynolds's missives were legible and rambled long. There were no short and sweet or rushed messages as if he had to tend to another appointment. Rainey unfolded the two sheets of lined paper.

Son,

I know you're excited about your upcoming trip to Africa. A change of scenery will do you good. I commend you for having a desire to do more. There is so much I want to say, but some things are better said face-to-face, so the sincerity can be seen. When you and Gayle visited me last time, I reiterated that I want better for you and your mother. Your sisters have husbands to lean on, although, I don't know how my son-in-law deals with Janae. I spoiled her rotten, but I know Bryce will take care of her. Cheney truly has a prince with Parke ... but who do you have, son? It's time for you to settle down.

You haven't let a woman get close to you in a while. You need that special someone, too. Although I have failed you and disappointed my family, my wife has stood by me, and together we will pick up my broken pieces. I'm praying you find that special someone. When you do, don't let pride keep you from her—pride has a way of destroying all things dear. I know. I was a hypocrite.

His father had always encouraged him to let his heart lead him. Rainey swallowed the lump in his throat. Even after all this time, he couldn't accept that his father, his hero, his best friend—the man who gave him unconditional support was capable of the cowardly act that had put him in prison. Although he was in good spirits, his father had become grayer and thinner.

His father and Cheney were two of the most important people in his life. Even though they hadn't done anything directly against him, Rainey had to forgive them for the pedestal he had put him on. But he couldn't forget, which caused a vicious circle of forgiving and then remembering.

Enough psychoanalyzing my family. Rainey refolded the letter as his mind returned to Josephine. Taking the emotional fight from his American backyard, he planned to end the stalemate on her African turf.

He couldn't wait to test the theory 'distance makes the heart grow fonder'. With a satisfying groan, Rainey closed his eyes just at the same time someone moved beside him.

"Hi." An annoying voice forced him to open one eye and turn his head. A blond, blue-eyed young man smiled. "It's cool you can afford business class. The rest of us are in coach. I'm thankful that I scrounged up enough money between two fundraisers and a part time job," the young man rambled on.

"And you are again?" Rainey prompted, wondering if he should feel ashamed for simply writing a check to participate.

"Thomas Green, I'm a third year dental student at SIU Alton." Rainey understood the acronym to mean Southern Illinois University at Alton, a campus across the Mississippi River from St. Louis. The volunteer's enthusiasm was apparent as he pumped Rainey's hand.

He and Thomas would be the Yanceys' assistants along with two hygienists. They would join forces with another team in Accra for their humanitarian effort.

"Is this your first missionary trip?" Thomas didn't wait for an answer. "It's my second one."

In two words, Thomas was high strung. "It is and I'm looking forward to it." Rainey tried to match Thomas' passion; condemnation hit him, instead, for the half-truth. But he came bearing dental aid to the villages. Rainey hoped that would be enough. "I'm also hoping to connect with one of my sister's friends. She's a native."

Thomas's eyes bucked and he became animated. "Insult 101. Never call Ghanaians natives. That's an American term. They prefer city dwellers, locals, or villagers."

Although Rainey learned a few common phrases, there remained a lot about the culture he didn't know. "I stand corrected."

"You'll catch on. That's why we mingle with villagers after we provide service to get to know them and learn their culture." Thomas made himself comfortable as if a third fundraiser paid for his business class seat. "Believe me, to avoid Insult 101-A, speak to everyone—and I mean everybody—children, babies, blind folks. Ghanaians like to get to know people..." Thomas then ran down his checklist of B, C and D of culture violations.

The crash course was fine, but Rainey planned to clock in his committed community dental service hours, and then he would contact Josephine. Nodding at intervals, Rainey's mind refocused on Josephine. Despite the sparks flying from their spats, the sparks also ignited the chemistry between them. Josephine might not want to address it, but she would now.

"I grew up in a single parent home. People helped my mom and me, so I'm giving back … I want to work in communities that lack sufficient dental options." Thomas seemed to be enjoying hearing himself as he started another conversation mid-sentence.

Whether Rainey wanted to connect with Thomas or not, he tried to look interested, remembering his own excitement at the possibility of practicing his profession once he graduated. But he wasn't in the mood to talk shop.

"Hmm, this really is spacious." Thomas whistled as he looked around, rubbing the seat's armrests. "Wow. I've never ridden in business class before."

Gritting his teeth, Rainey braced for what was coming next.

"Since no one is sitting here, do you mind—?"

"You may stay," Rainey begrudgingly invited him with a condition, "as long as you don't disturb my sleep."

Thomas's eyes widened and the gratitude was written all over his face before he even said thank you. "Oh, that's not a problem, Dr. Reynolds. I'll grab my books and catch up on some reading." He disappeared down the aisle. Within minutes, Thomas returned with a thick book bag.

For a second time, Rainey tried to surrender into sub-consciousness where images of Josephine could mesmerize him and whispers of "Come to Africa" beckoned to him. Soon his mind visualized her.

His nostrils flared as he held Josephine's face in the palms of his hands and coaxed her closer for a kiss—something that he regretted them never sharing. Their lips touched, but instead of the expected sparks, Josephine made a snorting sound.

Jerking himself awake, Rainey shook his head, and then blinked to focus. The party crasher was his seatmate. Thomas was knocked out and his jaw slacked so wide, that Rainey could have performed a dental examination, and wired his jaw together for good measure. Rainey sighed. It was going to be a long trip. The best he could hope for was that Josephine would make it worthwhile.

Chapter 4

Josephine's family and some friends gathered around the dining room table to enjoy a sumptuous meal after attending church services earlier. Between the laughter and stuffing her mouth, Josephine waited for her father's inquisition of his single daughters. At least he had for the last four Sundays.

He enjoyed regaling about Madeline's not too long ago Ghanaian ceremony.

Now, the family looked forward to Madeline and the British businessman, Dennis Harper, to exchange vows in a traditional Western-style wedding. The affair would take place next month in Dennis' homeland, which was the reason for Madeline's constant emails about her gown.

Initially, their father had been resistant to Madeline marrying an Obruni—a not so flattering term villagers called foreigners. Of course, they were not called that to their faces. Gyasi was concerned about his eldest daughter relocating, but somehow, Dennis had captured Madeline's heart, then wooed the Amoahs with lavish gifts as a show that he had the means to provide for his wife—impressive, indeed.

Josephine gave Dennis kudos. He had successfully won over her sister with the Word of God. Madeline had been the last holdout in the family to submit to the power of the Holy Ghost.

Talk about stubbornness, Madeline had a double dose. Probably the most stubborn person she knew, then Rainey's handsome face resurfaced in her mind. It was a tie between her sister and Dr. Reynolds.

"It won't be long before we prepare to visit your sister for another celebration. Exciting news!" Gyasi stated, then helped himself to another tasty *omo tuo,* rice ball and soup.

"*Yo,*" Josephine agreed in their ethnic Ewe tongue, which was one of the ten languages she and others could speak, including the Queen's English. That came courtesy of centuries of British colonization. But locals spoke Twi as their common language.

"Yet, I find myself with two remaining, lovely daughters without husbands ... " He shook his head.

A husband? Right. With Rainey's pending visit, Josephine had thought about him often, wondering if he could have been a suitable candidate. Except for Abigail, Josephine hadn't mentioned him to anyone.

Abigail cleared her voice and skirted the issue. "Papa, Evangelist Pastor Tanya Brown preached until everyone in the building was on their feet."

Helping himself to a second serving of *kenkey* prepared with hot peppers and fried fish, their father seemed to take the bait. "*Yo,* God's anointing was present this morning during worship service. She had actually traveled to the 'witch camps' and encouraged some to attend service. The Holy Ghost seemed to consume those demonic spirits as they repented of their acts."

While some truly dabbled with dark spirits that could overcome a person without the power of the Holy Ghost to fight the spiritual warfare, not everyone in the witch camps practiced "juju" and sorcery. Whether guilty or not, a woman could be banned from her village by a mere accusation of black magic. In a few instances, midwives who couldn't save the life of a child during delivery were removed and placed in the witch camps.

Continuing the diversion, Abigail then switched the subject to the country's beloved past-time, soccer, Black Stars. Her extended family with one set of grandparents, cousins and aunts had an opinion about the rival Nigerian team and Ebusua Dwarfs, their football team.

When there was a lull in the debating, many announced they were about to leave and thanked her mother for an excellent meal. Josephine exhaled while their parents walked their guests to the door. "We dodged the bullet again."

"Maybe not, with Rainey coming; he may be your bullet full of a love portion," Abigail whispered with a mischievous glint in her eyes and a magnificent smile, bearing a slight gap that added to her beauty.

Gyasi returned to the kitchen with their mother. He picked up the conversation, "Josephine, I have no qualms about offering a dowry to make you happy and to make sure you are cared for. You are twenty-seven. Abigail is twenty-three. Although I would not want to see another daughter leave me, I'd give you my blessings if he were a good man."

"Do not fret for my marriage." Josephine gave her father a tender smile. "God has already arranged it. Either with a groom on this earth or with Jesus in heaven—the ultimate Groom. I'll be all right."

Fafa didn't look convinced and challenged her. "There is no one your heart longs for?"

"Mum, you ask too many questions," seemed like a safe reply. She definitely couldn't count the brief one date she shared with Rainey under the backdrop of fireworks. Not from an explosive kiss, but the Fourth of July celebration at the St. Louis Arch. After that night she ignored that moment where she felt in sync with him.

"That's the only way I can get answers." Fafa smiled.

"It's all in God's timing, *yo?* When the Lord sends me a husband, my heart will know." Josephine quickly made her escape into the next room.

❧❧

Rainey's body survived the first layover the previous night in London and then the even longer one in Germany. He needed a bed. Not soon enough, the flight crew welcomed the passengers to Kotoka Airport in Accra, Ghana, the Gateway to Africa. *Interesting similarity.* St. Louis was referred to as the Gateway to the West.

Instead of their aircraft taxiing to a designated gate, the pilot landed on a tarmac. Rainey felt like the President of the United States jogging down the metal stairs when he arrived in foreign countries. The brightness of the sun almost blinded him. The tropical ninety-degree temperature was a heat wave compared to the frigid low twenties weather back home.

Yellow buses waited to whisk passengers to the baggage claim. Once he retrieved his luggage, Rainey stood in line for a Customs agent to check his passport and forego a request to search his bags. Once he was cleared, Rainey and others walked down a steep winding corridor until it opened up to a waiting area that Rainey could only describe as an outdoor covered pavilion minus a park ground.

His first order of business: call his mother. Rainey reached for his phone, then it dawned on him that he couldn't get service.

"Dr. Reynolds, that won't work here," Thomas said, coming from behind him. "There's a shop around here where we can purchase a pay-as-you go phone and a SIM card."

The team leaders approached, overhearing their conversation. Frances pointed in the direction of a tiny store. The entire group made the detour.

"You need two phones," the clerk pressed. *Suspect.* Rainey firmly declined.

Once everyone had their purchases, they filed deeper into the open pavilion area. Frances waved at a young man who was holding a sign that read "Dentists Without Borders St. Louis."

The man's dark skin glistened under a white short-sleeved shirt. *"Akwaaba! Akwaaba!"* he welcomed them.

An unfamiliar sensation came over Rainey. Tuning the man out, Rainey scanned the crowd as if he could identify the source. Standing not far from the sign bearer, stood a regal creature.

"Josephine." His heart beat excitedly beholding the object of his affection. Rainey smirked. Cheney must have told her. He would kiss his twin later for unknowingly aiding in his plan. Suddenly, the bustle of the travelers around him seemed out of focus; voices faded.

Once their eyes connected, Rainey felt powerless. Before he could take one cocky step toward her, a nudge on his shoulder foiled his mission. "Wow. Do you see that babe over there in the gold dress?"

Rainey harmlessly backslapped Thomas in the stomach in retaliation for interfering with his detour. "That babe is mine, so whatever fantasies you're conjuring up, forget it. I've been there and done it."

As if he was under a trance, Rainey carved the shortest path. His mind counted the steps it took to get to Josephine. She watched him. Rainey's nostrils flared as he invaded her personal space. Speechless, he stared. Her long braided hair was swept up into a ball on the top of her head, accenting her African features. Her skin glowed and her brown eyes sparkled.

"*Akwaaba! Akwaaba* to my country, Dr. Rainey Reynolds."

"Is that all you have to say?" *Or do?* Cocky, Rainey lifted a brow.

"I am being nice," she taunted him, "since you stated that I have too much sass in my mouth."

Already, she was testing his will. Rainey snickered. *Oh yeah.* They were about to pick up where they left off in America. He dropped his luggage and with the swiftness of a feline cat catching a country mouse, he slid one arm around her small waist and lifted her off the ground.

Closing his eyes, Rainey inhaled the summer moisture on her neck. The sweetness of a light fragrance tickled his nose. "You haven't changed a bit, but I have…"

"I am Badu, I'll be one of your interpreters during your visit to our wonderful country … " the sign-holding man interrupted their private moment. Rainey hadn't realized his mission team was on his trail.

Annoyed, Rainey reluctantly lowered Josephine back to her feet. Badu didn't know that the woman in front of him was Rainey's mission. Frankly, now that he saw her, his mission was accomplished—well, sort of.

Rainey couldn't decipher the emotions that played on Josephine's face. Stunned, a fleeting moment of embarrassment, then she blushed. She recovered quickly and exchanged greetings with everyone in his group, then Badu in their native tongue. It was as if she was stalling to look him in the eyes.

"Go. I know you're here for the mission work. I wouldn't be a proper Ghanaian and friend if I did not personally welcome you." She rumbled through her purse, pulled out a card, and handed it to him.

"I know you're on a schedule, but I would love to give you a tour of my beautiful country." Standing on her toes, Josephine brushed a kiss on his cheek. Was it his imagination or did she linger?

Didn't she know that little kiss made him want more? She shooed him away and then waved at the others. Rainey watched her body move with the lightness of a dancer as she disappeared into the crowd.

Oh yeah, they had unfinished business. Josephine didn't know it yet. As soon as he got some rest and regrouped, he would call her and then it was on.

Chapter 5

Have I lost my mind? I can't believe I did that! With as much finesse as possible, Josephine hurried away from Rainey as if she was in control of the situation and her emotions—she wasn't. She didn't exhale until she was confident that she was far away from Rainey's eyesight.

Then Josephine awakened from her trance. Was she crazy? Yes, number one to take such liberty to kiss him. It didn't matter whether it was his cheeks, lips, or forehead—a kiss is a kiss, and number two, in a public setting.

To make sure she wouldn't face Rainey and his group outside, Josephine stalled leaving the airport by heading to a snack bar and scanning the menu. She ordered a chichinga. While waiting for her order, Josephine rewound the scene earlier. In the months that she had been gone, Rainey seemed more handsome, taller, more muscular—basically larger than life, and more temptation than a single saved woman should have to endure.

She fought shivering under the intensity of his piercing eyes. Josephine thought she would faint when Rainey lifted her off the ground. His signature cologne made her woozy and Josephine liked it. All it took was one touch and she couldn't remember her name. The distance and time had not extinguished that small ember within her.

"Meda wo ase," she thanked the merchant, prayed over her food and savored the first bite. Not bad, but a beef kabob she purchased from street vendors in Accra tasted better.

Her musings continued. Rainey didn't come searching for her. It was she who compromised her dignity to chase down a man at the airport.

She shook her head in disbelief. Finishing her snack, Josephine headed outside to negotiate the fare with a taxi to the campus. Then she would fire off an email to Cheney and simply say that she greeted Rainey and his group at the airport and he looked well. Nothing more.

Cheney had said Rainey's mission trip was only ten days and he had already used one, or so traveling there. Josephine gnawed on her lips. The big question was would he call?

ॐ ॐ

Outside, Rainey and the team were heading to a line of parked vehicles when Badu, the Dentist Without Borders tour guide/interpreter, led them in another direction. "We will ride the trotros, our public transportation. Traffic is a maze."

Rainey's mind was still on Josephine until it registered that Badu had just called what he was staring at the transportation. "You've got to be kidding me," he mumbled. Several minibuses reminded Rainey of recycled minivans. The taxi car appeared as if it had excessive miles or had been a vehicle off a used dealer's lot.

Badu described a man as "mate" who helped them store their luggage and supplies in a minibus. Once they were nestled—more like packed—in their seats, the driver floored the piece of metal, giving its passengers a rollercoaster ride.

"Dr. Reynolds, you and another volunteer will stay at host families' homes as a way to fast track you learning the culture.

The rest of us will lodge at the school building that is also serving as our makeshift clinic," Francis reminded him.

For three days, the St. Louis team would work side by side with another missions group, then head to the Handi Children Outreach Home orphanage for the last day.

Most gasped as the driver negotiated near misses with motorists who didn't bother to respect the lights at intersections. Rainey panicked as he imagined the headlines of his demise: *St. Louis Doctor Killed in Trotro Crash.* To calm his nerves, he thought about Josephine's surprise visit. As his breathing returned to normal, he admired the passing scenery.

While the team leaders made small talk about their assignment, Rainey half listened. He preferred reliving that brief second he touched Josephine. Now, he craved more. Yes, he had definitely made the right decision coming to Africa. Did Josephine's presence and offering her number mean more than face value? Rainey couldn't wait to find out.

The short drive to their destination turned more into an hour plus ride, because the roads were akin to uncharted terrain.

Rainey's host family was the first stop. Getting out with his luggage, he scanned the yellow one-story home. Although he didn't know what to expect, he was thankful that his accommodations were not under the thatched roof of a mud hut. Then he chided himself for accepting stereotypes that the American media painted of Africa.

His hosts were a young couple, Chad and Nana Ofehe— he guessed about twenty-seven years old, with two small boys who appeared too young for school. After the introductions were made, they showed him to his room and where to store his things. It was small, clean—and had a bed. It was inviting, even if it was a twin size.

Sleep was on his mind when his hosts announced they had prepared a mid-day snack.

"We feared you might desire food after this long journey," Chad said.

Not wanting to be rude, Rainey accepted. Then came to realize he was hungry.

The table was already set and Nana waited for Chad to take his seat before she sat next to him. Then Chad offered Rainey a chair between the boys. Bowing his head, Chad said grace.

"This is one of our native dishes, groundnut stew. I hope you enjoy it," Nana said, once Chad was finished with the blessing.

"I'm sure I will." Before Rainey could swallow his first bite, the stew lit a trail of destruction as it sizzled on his lips and continued down his esophagus to what he thought he had—an iron stomach. He gasped for air.

"I'm sorry. I tried to go light on the crushed chiles and cayenne pepper." Nana frowned, clearly embarrassed.

Standing, Chad handed him two bottled waters from the refrigerator. "You'll adjust. Ghanaian dishes are spicy. The peppers help cool the body by releasing impurities. This was mild."

Wiping the sweat from above his lip, Rainey begged to differ about the peppers' ability to cool anything as his mouth and chest throbbed. What he wouldn't give for two tablespoons of Mylanta. Forcing down what was left on his plate, as his parents instructed him as a child, Rainey declined seconds, citing his desire for a nap. It was time for his iron stomach to live up to its reputation and neutralize the stinging attack.

Thanking them for the meal, Rainey retraced his steps to the guest bedroom. He couldn't pop open his mosquito net kit fast enough. Rainey wasn't about to take any chances with donating his blood to any female mosquitoes. Although malaria was eradicated in the U.S., he had started taking his malaria drugs before leaving home.

Chad stuck his head in the room minutes later to check on him. The expression on his face was one of surprise as he eyed the net. "There is no need for that. This is the dry season with less mosquito activity," he said to assure Rainey.

Less didn't mean zero. Plus, with two kids in the home, Rainey assumed they probably ran in and out of the house all day. He wasn't taking any chances.

Once Chad closed the bedroom door, Rainey rubbed bug repellant on his body for good measure. Lying down, Rainey zipped himself inside a screened tent-shaped net. Fatigue consumed him. Sleep descended on his lids, but not before his lips uttered, "Josephine, nothing will keep me from calling you as soon as I wake." He drifted off.

Chapter 6

Rainey was disoriented when his lids fluttered open hours later. Glancing around the room from within his netted cage, his mind registered his temporary lodging. He was in Africa—Ghana—and the high sun didn't appear as if it had moved from its position. Maybe the country's daylight was longer than in America.

Once he climbed out of the constraint of his protective contraption, he stretched, then eyed the tent as the source of his stiff bones. Could he tolerate eight more nights? As a boy scout, Rainey had been excited about sleeping in "the wild" in tents at campsites.

Reaching for his watch, Rainey's eyes bucked. "What?" He had slept through the afternoon, evening, night and now it was the next morning? "You've got to be kidding me." He was still drained.

Rainey collected his toiletries for a shower and a shave. He opened the bedroom door and sniffed. The aroma of breakfast reminded him that he had missed at least two meals. Deciding food was more important, Rainey hurriedly washed his face and thoroughly brushed his teeth in the small bathroom down the hall, then met them in the kitchen.

Chad glanced up with a smile. "Good morning, Dr. Reynolds. We didn't want to disturb you."

"*Makyeoo*," Rainey practiced his Twi. "Sorry, I must have overslept. I'll shower and be ready in minutes."

"Wash quickly, Dr. Reynolds," Chad's oldest son, Michael, said with a wide grin. Rainey noted the child's magnificent teeth alignment. "Sometimes, we run out of water."

He had heard stories about Africans walking miles to a well for water. He assumed that was strictly remote areas, not in populated cities like this one. Rainey hoped that wasn't the case. His expression must have shown his confusion.

Nana gave an apologetic shrug. "It's one of our inconveniences. Ghanaians blame it on politicians who are ill-prepared to handle the demands of city dwellers."

Chad agreed. "I suggest you hurry. Sometimes it's a hit-and-miss."

Rainey took heed to their warning. Twenty minutes later, he returned to the kitchen rejuvenated. Dressed in a lightweight shirt and pants, Rainey was ready to start and finish his first day of community service, so he could see Josephine.

Nana laid serving bowls and platters on the table. There were no individual place settings like the previous day. Chad and the children sat at the table washing their hands out of a large bowl of water.

Hmm. Rainey felt somewhat ashamed that he had spent too much time in probably their only bathroom or maybe they were prepared in case they did run out of water. Before Rainey could apologize, he spied breakfast. It appeared to be identifiable as eggs, rice and fruit. He relaxed, noting nothing that should require seasoning.

Chad offered him a seat and once Nana joined them, Chad said grace. "Jesus, we thank You for this opportunity to sit with our brother and break bread. Let us bless him. We ask that You sanctify our food and make a way for the nourishment of our brothers and sisters who are hungry..."

The prayer seemed endless as Rainey's stomach growled. "In Jesus' name," Chad said as if he heard it, too.

Famished, Rainey was ready to dig in when he noticed the absence of utensils. Everybody scooped food out of the serving bowls with their hands.

Rainey did his best to remain expressionless. True, he had read about this communal eating custom. Again, he assumed it was done in rural villages, not in progressive neighborhoods.

"This is communal eating. Free feel to participate any time, Dr. Reynolds," Chad encouraged.

Rainey watched their eating ritual with interest. It was orderly and with such skill that not one morsel spilled. Clearing his throat, he also remembered that it was not considered offensive to ask for silverware, which he did. Nana complied and gave him a fork, knife, and spoon.

"Medase," Rainey said his thank you in Twi. After one bite, he learned that appearances were deceiving. Even breakfast food was cooked in rich spices.

It was a smart move on the team leaders' part for placing him with a host family to learn more about his African brothers and sisters. It was because of his country's stereotypes of other nations, he assumed Africans ate with their hands because they were poor, starving and couldn't wait for utensils. Rainey couldn't hide his ignorance.

Their youngest son, Albert, scrutinized Rainey's every moment. He seemed more curious about why he wasn't eating as them. Albert had bright intelligent eyes and a smile, judging from some crowding among his lower teeth, which could be improved with braces.

"Are you married to a pretty wife and have children for us to play with?" he asked with a hopeful expression, which reminded Rainey of his nephews.

"Sadly, not yet."

The children seemed as crestfallen as him. In the past, when anyone inquired whether he had children, Rainey flashbacked to his aborted child, cheating him out of an offspring. But things might change soon. That was why he was there in Accra, but the only person who knew that was Shane.

Chad and his wife chuckled. "Those two are always looking for playmates as if they do not have each other."

"Do you want more children?" Rainey asked Chad.

"If the Lord would promise me another son, but Nana wants a daughter. Little girls are expensive, *yo?*"

Rainey snickered. He thought about his mother and two sisters. Out of all three, Janae had the diva instincts. "Yes, they are."

"Are you rich? All Obrunis are rich?" Albert peppered Rainey with another question.

Nana scolded her son. "Dr. Reynolds is not a foreigner. He is considered our brother." She then apologized. "Obruni is a foreigner, usually White and we've heard and seen on TV that many are rich in America." She blushed with a curious expression, too.

"It appears that television has deceived many Africans and African-Americans. This should be a learning experience for both of us." Rainey paused. "To answer Albert's question, no I'm not rich, but neither am I in need of anything. The reason I'm not poor is because I attended school for many years to become a doctor in my field. School is very important."

Because thou sayest, I am rich, and increased with goods, and have need of nothing; and knowest not that thou art wretched, and miserable, and poor, and blind, and naked, God whispered, startling Rainey.

Rainey chewed slower, digesting God's fleeting words. He might not be a regular churchgoer, but he had started to read his Bible. Well, every now and then, because he was curious about his twin's peace of mind. He had seen rebuke mentioned in Revelation or somewhere in the Scriptures.

"Agreed. We are glad you are here, Dr. Reynolds, so we can learn from one another," Chad said, oblivious to what Rainey just experienced.

For the next half hour, Rainey fielded more inquiries about America than he could ask about Africa. But he also questioned whether he was being boastful. It was one thing for a person to call him prideful, but there was no doubt God had called him out while eavesdropping on Rainey's conversation.

Finally, Chad announced that it was time for him to drop Rainey off at the building. Rainey made sure he didn't leave a crumble on his plate, then thanked them for breakfast. Minutes later, Chad drove away on the smooth streets of his neighborhood. The landscape began to change rather extremely as Chad turned on uneven half paved roadways.

He classified a few clusters of dwelling places as communities. Other homes were in the middle of nowhere. One village reminded Rainey of some sort of compound. Caught up in the scenery, Rainey suddenly remembered Josephine. "Oh no." Angry with himself, Rainey bounced his fist on his thigh.

Startled, Chad braked. "Is something the matter?"

"Yes, I forgot to call my lady friend who lives here."

"Would you like to use my cellular?" Chad offered.

Rainey declined the offer. "I purchased a disposable one yesterday at the airport." Besides, he needed privacy.

Resuming his speed, Chad grinned. "Did the merchant try and sell you two of them?"

"As a matter of fact, he did. How did you know?" Whipping his head around, Rainey blinked. Was that a chicken walking out the front door of somebody's home? Maybe his mind was playing tricks on him.

"For men that are unfaithful to their wives, the second phone is to use for girlfriends."

"What?" After the incident with his ex-girlfriend almost fifteen years ago, Rainey learned the price of unfaithfulness.

In the distance, a thick line had formed in a bare field. Chad slowed before turning off the gravel road and onto a dirt road heading toward the crowd. A building was up ahead.

"These people are waiting for us?" Rainey asked in awe.

"Yes."

"Incredible. In the States, a line like this usually means the latest electronic game, computer or flat screen TV is about to go on sale." Where did all these people come from? "How did they know the dental clinic was coming?"

"Word of mouth."

As Chad drove alongside, villagers' faces came into focus. Some had tortured features that hinted at the magnitude of their pain. The expectant hope in their eyes tore through him since he couldn't legally extract anything from their mouths to alleviate their sufferings.

"*Medase*," Rainey said when Chad stopped the car and he stepped out. Before driving off, the team leader advised Chad that Rainey wouldn't need a ride to Chad's home, but would be dropped off. Then it seemed as if all eyes were on Rainey as he made his way to the front of the line to the building's entrance. Some, even in their painful state, wanted to engage him in conversation. He remembered Thomas's warning to exchange a greeting.

"Glad you can make it Dr. Reynolds. Let's get started," Badu, the interpreter said in his proper English, glancing at his watch. He switched to Twi to instruct the crowd.

On the second floor of the makeshift clinic, those seeking treatment were mostly orderly. At least three or four wept silently as Badu assisted them with a questionnaire to gauge their pain level and history before the dentists could see them. Rainey's assignment was to assist Badu in answering questions.

Rainey determined some diagnoses from the foul breath, gum discoloration and yellowed teeth. As an orthodontist, he appreciated his patients with healthy teeth. Once the tedious paperwork was complete, Rainey steered the patient into a line where portable x-ray machines were set up.

Following a consultation with the dentist, local anesthesia was administered, then the extraction. The service was done in an assembly line fashion. In a few instances Rainey had to hold onto old men's hands during their cleaning and flossing procedures. He cringed at children's piercing cries.

Tears spilled from a young boy's eyes as the hygienist picked the plaque from his teeth before eventually applying sealant. Rainey guessed him to be about eight or nine. The child would be thankful years later for healthy teeth.

Reaching out, Rainey held the child's hand and squeezed it. His mind drifted back to a grade school classmate who had a serious case of crowded teeth. Some students had teased him unmercifully, calling him monster mouth. Jonathan, the victim of their bullying, never cried, but Rainey knew the remarks hurt his feelings.

Maybe it was pity or trying to be a hero, but Rainey befriended that classmate. Once Rainey told his father what Jonathan had suffered, Roland and a few of his close colleagues made sure Jonathan received treatment, including braces and follow up care at no cost. By the time Jonathan graduated from high school, his self-esteemed had improved and so did the attention from the girls. Fast forward ten plus years, and Jonathan was making a career in the marines.

That situation had also changed Rainey's career aspirations. Instead of following in his father's footsteps as a medical doctor, Rainey chose the dental field. He wanted to do more than extracting teeth, filing cavities and fitting caps. Rainey wanted to change lives and give people confidence with a single smile.

Rainey had forgotten about Jonathan until he looked into the face of the young boy. Dentists Without Borders was making a difference like his father had. He became teary eyed as he thought about all the good his father had done in his life, only to be overshadowed by the hit-and-run accident.

In hindsight, his father said he wished he had done the right thing, so did Rainey and the rest of the family. But a man had died and Rainey understood the debt had to be paid, but why hadn't God spared his father from serving time from a deed done so long ago?

"Dr. Reynolds...Dr. Reynolds," the hygienist called his name.

He hadn't realized he had zoned out.

"We're finished. You can let go of Jonathan's hand now."

Jonathan? Rainey blinked and stared into the boy's eyes. Although the tears were gone, the boy wasn't smiling. What were the odds of Rainey thinking about an old friend only to meet another boy with the same name? What a coincidence.

When Jonathan stood, Rainey personally escorted him to the table where donated toys were displayed for the children. He was starting to feel good about being a part of this trip. It had been a while since he was in the trenches. And just think, he had colleagues who donated their services for people in need all the time.

It was a pity that some could stand to benefit from his orthodontic services, however, to manipulate their jaws to function better would be counter-productive. Besides the cost of the prosthesis, patients would need regular appointments for their braces to be adjusted.

With renewed energy, Rainey kept pace with the other volunteers to keep the line moving. He couldn't believe the number of children that had come alone. A couple of times, he had mistaken girls for boys because of their short hair.

Upon further inspection, he noted the girls' soft features: long lashes, eyes that would capture a man's heart, lips that would pucker soon enough, baby doll shaped faces, their medium and dark brown skin complexion was void of marring. Rainey chided himself, thinking hair didn't make them beautiful.

He tried to imagine Josephine as a little girl who had grown into a wonderful, seductive heartbreaker. Rainey had to speak with her. The glimpse at the airport was doing him in.

He had planned on calling her the previous evening. That didn't happen and neither again this morning. Now it was late afternoon and the teams' potty breaks were few. At times, Rainey's patience wore thin, whereas Badu's had dissipated after a few hours. Quitting time couldn't come soon enough.

"How's it going?" Thomas walked up next to him carrying more sterile instruments for extractions.

"Overwhelmed." As the line snaked out the building, the body heat sweltered in the confined quarters. "I'm looking forward to four so we can get some rest, and these folks can go back home—"

"They won't." Thomas shook his head. "Many live too far to return to their villages, so they'll camp out here all night."

"All night?" The thought made him want to share his mosquito net. As the day progressed to late afternoon, Rainey craved some down time with Josephine. After all, wasn't she the reason why he came? After one day on the dental battlefield, Rainey wasn't so sure.

❧

It had been two days and Josephine had not heard from Rainey. "How foolish of me? *Ugh.*" Josephine clenched her fist. "I can't believe I went to that airport and practically threw my desperation at him," she mumbled to herself.

Clearly, Dr. Reynolds wasn't interested in resolving any misunderstandings between them. Shaking her head to erase the memories, Josephine stared out of her bedroom window as she watched the orange sky of the African sunset.

"Maybe it's a test," Abigail stated as she stood, leaning against the doorpost.

Josephine jumped, startled. "Would you stop sneaking up on me?!"

"It's in your eyes, Abena," Abigail said, using Josephine's Akan birth name for a girl born on Tuesday. "Mum and papa have noticed something, too. I just told them your man friend is here...okay, I said boyfriend."

"You what!" Josephine was livid. She could hear her parents discussing details of another engagement ceremony. "Remind me to pay you back in the future."

"I'll do no such thing." Abigail flopped on the bed and rested her head on Josephine's shoulder. "When do we meet him?"

"He's not here for me, remember?" Pouting was beneath Josephine, but she wanted to.

"He asked for your number to call."

Gritting her teeth, Josephine closed her eyes before admitting her misstep. "No, I gave it to him."

Abigail sighed. "He has it in his possession. If it were me, I would make him be here for me. You told me he hugged you and you kissed him. I want to meet my future brother-in-law."

Opening her eyes, Josephine lightly pinched her sister. She had divulged details to Abigail the day she learned about Rainey's trip. She purposely had not mentioned it to her parents for fear that they would gather the wrong ideas.

"You do not have to remind me of my ill judgment. I have been introduced to many men, but how was I to know that meeting Rainey would be memorable? I guess it serves me right. I had no mercy on the wounds he was trying to heal. It is the Lord making me reap the unfriendliness I sowed."

"If you are haunted with remorse, then seek him out and apologize. At least God will acquit you of your guilt. I wish I was a mosquito on the wall to hear that exchange." Standing, Abigail folded her arms and *tsk*ed. "You and Madeline have explored the world and entertained American and British men. Me? The only country I've visited is Nigeria and that's on the same continent. I am told that love never dies, it only grows stronger. Your anguish is proof of that Abena. I would marry him."

What is wrong with everybody? Who mentioned marriage or *love*? One date, one lunch and many disagreements sound like a prerequisite for a happily ever after? What she felt for Rainey was attraction only. That was all. "I would marry a Ghanaian brother if he loves me. Unless Rainey is willing to apply for dual citizenship, I am not adding to this madness. My family is here and so is my life."

"Be careful what you speak, sister. The Lord's ear is always close. It seems your heart and mind are at war. Let's pray God's will," Abigail advised.

Josephine scrunched her nose. "I'm older and supposed to be wiser."

"You are. Who do you think has been my teacher?"

"I was in the United States for sixteen months. I returned to implement my newfound knowledge to help my country. If anything was going to happen between Rainey and me, it should have happened then. The door of opportunity may never open again. I doubt if a short mission trip can patch up our differences to open another door."

"Sister, as the saying goes, 'If you make one step, God will make two'. Rainey's making waves. You're wasting time. Get out in the boat and row to save him. Now, you've said he has been here two days?"

"*Yo.*"

"I will pray God's will with you, but no matter what, I would go and apologize." Abigail added an American slang. "I'm just sayin'."

They laughed, but Josephine added nothing. She recalled a portion of Cheney's email: *You know God's plan of salvation is always bigger than us.*

Josephine would pray that she wouldn't make a fool out of herself or find heartache.

Chapter 7

Rainey tried clawing his way out of the pit, but he couldn't. He was gasping for air. The heat from the flames was beginning to consume his flesh. The pain was excruciating. That's when he realized he wasn't the only one on fire, everything and everybody—the entire earth was engulfed in flames.

"Jesus!" Rainey screamed. "Help me. I don't want to die like this. *Ahhhhhh.* Help!"

"Dr. Reynolds, Dr. Reynolds. Are you all right? Wake up." Someone gently shook him.

Panting for air, Rainey's eyes popped open. A man's face came into focus—Chad. Rainey began to calm down. Scanning the doorway, Nana backed away, looking concerned.

"Let's get you out of this nonsense," he said, unzipping the tent. "You are safe."

Rainey couldn't untangle himself fast enough. Freed, he stood and then sat on the bed. He rubbed his head and then linked his hands behind his neck. "It was so real. It was so real that I still smell something burning."

Chad inhaled, then sniffed again. "I do not smell anything ablaze." He took a seat across from him.

Rainey relayed the nightmare. Wiping the sweat from his face as evidence of what he just endured.

Without interrupting, Chad listened until Rainey finished, then left the room. He returned with a bottle of water.

"Dr. Reynolds, are you taking Lariam for malaria? It could be the source of your nightmare."

"I am. Ughh. I don't know which is worse: taking that drug, or letting your females bite me, then dying of malaria. How do you all handle it?"

"We don't give it much thought." Chad rubbed his chin. "It would be hard to find anti-malaria medication here. Our chemists—or pharmacists as you call them—will tell you to come back when you have malaria."

Either Rainey was crazy for being in Sub-Saharan Africa or the countrymen were in denial. Chad must have read his confused expression. Did the Ghanaians not know that malaria kills one child each minute in Africa? Rainey knew what he was going to send them for Christmas.

"We make sure we have good screens on our windows and check them periodically to make sure there are no holes. We keep the ceiling fans operating at all times. The wind distracts them from body scents. Not all female mosquito bites will infect you with malaria. In addition to using bug repellant, be sure to wear long sleeves, pants and socks, the pests like ankles and feet."

Rainey nodded, but his mind was still on the vivid, horrific, fiery images. The flames had been so real; the singe of burnt flesh would stay with him for a long time. Rainey shivered to shake away the horror, but it clung to him.

"Rubbing spray repellant with DEET is excellent. You may also apply Permethrin spray on your clothes. It's potent enough to kill or stun insects that come in contact with the fabric. Permethrin will remain in your fabric for at least six washings." He stood and patted Rainey on the shoulder. His touch sent a cooling sensation throughout his body. "You'll be fine. Get some rest. We have many hours before we all must arise."

Sleep? Both he and Chad needed to see a psych doctor. Rainey climbed back in his protective net covering. *How could Josephine live like this?* He wondered.

Once considered fearless, Rainey was too terrified to close his eyes. There might be a part two awaiting him. He had never, ever experienced anything like that in his life—not even as a child. And if he did, Rainey would run to his hero—his father.

That was then. This is now. Rainey was grown, educated and in a strange land. It wasn't as if he could pick up the phone and speak to his father at will. Most of Roland's weekly calls were reserved for his mother. Rainey preferred visiting his father, anyway. After that awkward first visit, he couldn't wait to bring his dad up to speed on home and to see how he was faring in confinement.

Cheney was a great source of encouragement and accessible by phone any time. Of course, he would have to get past her bulldog husband who wouldn't allow anyone, including him, to disturb her with anything like this in her condition. He didn't blame Parke's possessiveness. Every time his sister got pregnant, Rainey rooted for her to have a safe delivery. Who else could he talk to?

You have Me.

The Voice was subtle, but there was no doubt Rainey wasn't dreaming. There was no forceful rebuke, but a compassionate reminder. He held his breath, unsure what to do.

Pray in My name and I will do it, God spoke. *Come home to Me.*

Come home. Those were the same words Josephine spoke that drew him to Africa. What did God mean? He just didn't get the same results from praying as others like his sister did. When Cheney finished praying, it was as if she had taken a swig of happy juice. His father was more reflective, but Rainey's prayers were akin to repetitious words that had no life. Yet, he felt obligated to say them because that's what society expected from him.

But the Lord just told him to pray. Rainey opened his mouth to recite the same prayers, but the words that spilled out were unrecognizable, then he understood them. "You are the God of Abraham, Isaac, and Jacob, and You are my savior. Remove me from this emotional torture and show me the purpose of my being here... in Jesus' name. Amen."

I will give you rest, God spoke a portion of Matthew 11:28.

Suddenly, a peace descended upon Rainey and he dozed off. When he woke again later that morning, he felt refreshed. Nana passed the bowl of warm water again for everyone to wash their hands. Rainey declined and was given eating utensils upon request. Breakfast had become an experiment for his taste buds, but he was starting to enjoy the spices. Neither of his hosts mentioned the overnight incident. However, there was no doubt in Rainey's mind what he experienced was real.

Within a half hour, Rainey had showered, dressed and was en route to the makeshift clinic. He and Chad engaged in healthy banter about their countries' sports, men and relationships. He confided about crossing the ocean to see Josephine.

"For months since she left St. Louis, I couldn't stop thinking about her. I've been here three days..." Rainey grimaced, "yet she seems farther out of my reach. It's not her fault, but mine. She gave me her number and I thought about her during that episode last night. I doubted she would have welcomed my call that early."

"Next time, call." Chad smirked. "Women are flattered when you think of them. Maybe you should call Josephine and invite her over for dinner, *yo?*"

"No. Don't take this the wrong way, man, but I need to spend some alone time with her, just Josephine and me, then I can bring her to dinner."

Chad didn't respond right away. "Excellent!"

Once they were on the familiar road to the building, Rainey was amazed to see the larger crowd, waiting for services. Once Chad parked, Rainey braced for another repetitive day.

◈◈

Josephine stepped from the taxi in front of the old school building where the mission team had set up camp. Her heart pounded with excitement and fear. Again, her actions were out of her character: to be absent from work, to hunt down a man who she hadn't convinced her sister or her heart that she didn't like, contrary to her surprise visit at the airport. Even though Abigail was all for Josephine's covert mission, Josephine had yet to tell her parents about Rainey, and they hadn't asked.

Now what? *God, I'm out of my comfort zone here.* Taking a deep breath, Josephine exhaled as she walked slowly, exchanging greetings with others along the way. Then she saw him. There was no mistaking Rainey in a crowd, his proud stance, his hidden muscles under nondescript casual light-colored shirt and pants. She could see him donating money to charities, but to remove his designer clothes for a mission trip, this had to be God's doing.

Yes, he outshined those around him. Josephine paused in her conversation just so she could observe him, cataloging his movements frame by frame. His mannerisms and smiles with the villagers spoke volumes, whether the locals understood English or not.

Rainey was laughing when he casually glanced over his shoulder. Their eyes connected immediately. Turning completely around, he used one hand to shield his eyes as he squinted. Josephine swallowed. Her heart pounded in apprehension. Would Rainey view her presence as desperate?

His eyes brightened as he shoved the paperwork in a young man's arms and headed her way. Dr. Rainey Reynolds' signature swag could not be duplicated. "Josephine."

"Hi." Her words jammed in her head. "I hope I'm not interrupting because I know you're here on a mission."

"And you're part of it." Rainey didn't blink. "I came for you."

"Pardon me?" *If I fainted because of what I thought I heard, would you catch me?* Not knowing the answer, Josephine stood erect.

"We need to talk, sooner rather than later. I wanted to call you, but my energy is zapped at the end of the day. And since this is our last day here before we go to the orphanage, where the line is even longer, thank you for coming to me. God knows I've been trying to get to you." He paused and stared. "I want to kiss you," he admitted.

Okay, so maybe this was a good idea. Rainey was still attracted to her, even though it was bad timing. "I sense that."

"I see your saucy mouth hasn't changed."

She blushed under his stare. Josephine would never admit she wanted him to kiss her. "Neither has my honesty. The feelings are mutual, but you may not kiss me. Too much public affection is considered inappropriate in my country. Do you need any help?"

"I'll say yes just for you to stay here. Are you sure I'm not supposed to touch you." He grabbed her hand and she didn't fight him—a first.

"Certainly," she answered amused. "Dr. Rainey Reynolds, you've changed. You speak freely."

"I came here to be set free." His voice was low; his piercing eyes held sincerity.

God can set anybody free from wherever they are, she thought, but held her tongue.

"Badu has been one of our interpreters, but I'd much rather have you." Rainey interrupted her musing. "You're much prettier. You do speak Twi," he teased.

She shoved him. "Twi, Ewe, and nine other native languages."

"Beauty and brains that come naturally." Rainey tugged her alongside him. "Is hand holding permissible?"

"Men, women, adults, and children hold hands as a custom signifying friendship," Josephine replied, wondering if he would buck at the idea of men walking down the street holding hands. Then she would have to explain it had nothing to do with homosexuality.

"Starting as friends is good and then we can accelerate from there." Rainey winked.

Josephine did everything to keep from fanning herself, even if she could claim it was from the heat. Instead, she quietly awaited his instructions.

ॐॐ

God, thank You for sending Josephine to me. Maybe it was the benefit of doing this selfless task. Rainey couldn't withhold his grin.

She was more beautiful than he could ever remember as he admired how she engaged the children and the elders. Their eyes twinkled as she spoke rapidly and softly. In hindsight, Rainey could've kicked himself for wasting so much time indulging in spats when she lived in St. Louis, instead of defying their differences and getting to know each other.

Thomas strolled up next to him. "Dr. Reynolds, if you don't mind, we need your ...Whoa." His eyes practically bucked as his mouth seemed to salivate. Rainey immediately reached out and claimed Josephine's hand. "She's taken, remember?"

Josephine lifted her brow. "No one has taken me," she defended in her classic Ghanaian sharpness.

Somehow her defiance was attractive. But he wasn't about to let her get away with that. As Rainey was about to challenge Josephine, Thomas cleared his throat.

"Dr. Reynolds, should we count you in with the team going sightseeing?" Thomas eyed him and then Josephine.

"You should not. Whatever sights I need to see, I hope she could wow me with anything about Ghana." She nodded.

"Lucky," Thomas mumbled and walked away as Badu approached them.

"We could use your assistance in passing out supplies." Badu turned to Josephine and exchanged greetings in their native tongue, then waved for them to follow him upstairs.

Badu stationed them at the give-away table where he and Josephine gave out dental kits after the hygienists applied sealants. "You were right about one thing," Rainey said, stealing a private moment.

"Just one thing?" She teased and scrunched her nose in jest.

Although he enjoyed their tit-for-tat, Rainey had to say this. "You were right to say that since you didn't break my heart, I shouldn't expect you to repair it—"

"I am sorry. I should have never said that." Cringing, she glanced away. When she nervously faced him, the shame was apparent.

"*Shhh*," he whispered, wanting to place a finger on her full lips. Actually, he was thinking of a kiss. Unfortunately, he wasn't fond of Ghana's no public affection rule. "You've been mending it, without either of us knowing it, since the first day we met."

Josephine shook her head in denial. "I didn't want be in a rebound relationship—although temporary, because I had no plans to remain in the Unites States—where a man like you guarded your heart." She paused as if she was debating if she should say more.

Granted it wasn't the ideal setting to discuss personal matters, but Rainey prompted her to continue. "Don't hold back, please."

"Well, I was confused and appalled by your lack of warmth toward your sister—twin—because Cheney made a bad decision and God forgave her."

"I was wrong for that and Cheney accepted my apology. Our relationship is back on track."

"Excellent." Josephine's face lit up. "No one wants to fellowship with an unforgiving person."

Rainey reached out to touch her face, then paused. Restraint when he wanted something was not his strong point. "Your honesty liberates me. No other woman has been as blunt."

"God's truth is the only thing that sets a person free." She playfully bumped him.

Before he could nudge her back, it seemed as if in a coordinated effort, everybody flocked to their table for free dental kits. When some had questions, Rainey listened to the dialogue until Josephine translated it.

Classy, passionate, and a woman Rainey wanted in his life. He had been so wrong about her. Rainey would never confuse Josephine's confidence as stuck up again.

While caught up in his musing, she asked him to verify the answer to a villager's question before she responded in Twi.

He snapped out of it. "Yes, soft foods for the remainder of the day."

"My apology comes after God chastened me when I returned home. Jesus let me know that I should have been there for you as a sister in Christ," she said out of nowhere in between patients.

Although Rainey appreciated God working on his behalf, he felt he didn't really need Him on this one. "My attraction for you is stronger than what I feel toward my sisters or church."

"I can't be separated from God. We're a package deal. That's the only way we can move forward."

She was serious. Rainey felt it. Josephine Abena Yaa Amoah wasn't going to budge. But he came this far and he wasn't about to go home empty-handed or heart empty. "I'm ready."

"Are you?" Josephine folded her arms and lifted a brow in a seductive challenge. Rainey had the disappointing feeling that she wasn't teasing him. "Definitely." That was the last word before they were swamped again.

Chapter 8

Rainey had hoped Josephine would spend the remainder of the evening with him. He was disappointed that she had a previous engagement that evening, but she assured him they would talk later. "We will spend the entire day together tomorrow," were her closing remarks after leaving him at the makeshift clinic.

The next morning, Rainey prayed for his safety as he clutched his seatbelt and braced for impact at any second. Between the vehicles and people, the streets of Accra were an obstacle course as Chad expertly guided his car through traffic as they inched closer to downtown.

With the blessings from his team leaders for his absence, the only mission work Rainey would do that day was to spend time studying what made Josephine tick. And she was waiting to take him sightseeing. He didn't want anything to get in his way to make that happen.

When the cars slowed or a traffic light snagged them, vendors invaded the roadway. Like a swarm of bees, they were going car to car, selling their wares.

"How do they do that?" Rainey pointed. He had meant to ask when he first saw them. One woman's glide reminded him of Josephine's strut. The posture was the same: erect, confident and no nonsense as she balanced a platter artistically stacked with various fruits on her head.

Chad shrugged. "It's as normal as walking. It's an acquired skill that's learned as a toddler. Impressive, yo? Believe me, they can carry more on their heads than in their arms."

Rainey did his best to avoid eye contact with any of them, or he would empty his pockets to the handfuls of child hawkers. The peddlers were demanding his attention as one female hawker yelled, "Yess", "puuure" and "plantain".

The bustle was a stark contrast from the remote villages. Accra, the capitol of Ghana, could rival New York City. As a matter of fact, the madness reminded him of Branson, Missouri, where at one time the infrastructure couldn't handle the workers, residents and tourists as the city expanded, rapidly building theaters for live shows and other attractions. The real shocker for Rainey was the modern, progressive city and locals littering their sidewalks as if they were trash cans. *Unbelievable.*

"Here we are. Barclays Bank of Ghana." Chad honked to warn pedestrians his intent to pull over to the curb.

"Medase." Rainey stepped out of the car onto the crowded sidewalk. Hawkers rushed him, attempting to block his path. Vendors called out to him. Making eye contact, he spoke, but shook his head in response to their goods. *"Dabi meda ase."*

Using a fraction of his strength, Rainey forced them out of his way. Evidently, no thanks wasn't acceptable as they tried to entice him with anything from fresh fruit, to a bar of soap, to bottled water. Through the haze of the street vendors and pedestrians, Josephine came into focus as she leaned against the building watching for him.

An older woman with missing teeth, but kind eyes waved flowers in front of him. "How much?" Chad had explained during one of their dinner conversations that Ghanaians enjoyed the art of negotiation when selling their wares.

"Six cedis," she said.

Rainey tried to do the conversion, but couldn't fast enough. It was probably only three dollars or so in U.S. currency, and to him that wasn't bad—he guessed. He didn't want to keep Josephine waiting.

He slipped the Ghanaian dollars out of his pocket, foregoing the bargaining, took the flowers and continued on his way.

Standing near the bank entrance, Josephine looked in the opposite direction. A warm breeze teased her loose micro-braids as she tilted her face upward toward the sun. Orange, brown, and green colors were streaked throughout her sundress that danced with a slight breeze.

Her poise prompted a flashback. It had been late June when Rainey was standing outside the Ferguson Library in St. Louis. He wanted to surprise her with a boxed lunch in an attempt to woo her. Funny, he was still trying to woo her. This time, he had progressed from the box lunch to an airline ticket.

Back then, like now, Josephine hadn't noticed him, so Rainey admired her carefree bounce down the street. She had been unaware of the attention she garnered from passers-by. Several times, as today, she had lifted her face to the sun as if she expected a kiss.

Any photographer would be in awe of her natural beauty then and now. As if sensing his presence through the crowd, she turned and wowed him with an engaging smile. It was a force that pulled him until he was within a few feet from her. Street venders tried to intercept, but Rainey wasn't having it.

They stared at each other. Her skin and face were flawless. Without saying a word, she was alluring. The "look, but don't touch" rule was increasingly becoming an annoyance. Giving her the flowers, Josephine smiled while he brushed a kiss on her fore-head.

He preferred her lips, but he was mindful of the public display of affection ordinance. It didn't matter. Before returning home, Rainey was determined to get his kiss, hug, and her commitment.

"Did you sleep well?" She slipped her fingers through his. Squeezing them, Josephine guided him through pedestrian traffic with ease.

"Like a baby, after you sang me that African lullaby last night."

"Very well. I've already secured a car. If you were with me, they would have overcharged you at least thirty cedis. To Ghanaians, all foreigners from the United States are rich."

"Where do they get that idea?"

"Mostly television shows and YouTube."

Surprised, Rainey shook his head. "Granted, I'm not very dark, but how can someone determine that I'm a foreigner."

"You cannot judge a man by his skin color. Ghanaians come in all shades, too. Attribute it to the shenanigans of Colonial Masters and others, but who knows? It's your confident walk of a man in charge—powerful and good-looking—that draws attention."

Rainey would comment about the good-looking part later, but currently he wished he were in control of his life. Keeping their hands linked as they wandered down the busy sidewalk proved challenging, but he wasn't letting go of her. Suddenly, Rainey heard what could be...two people kissing. Josephine pulled him closer before he could turn around.

A man sped by them on a bike. Rainey frowned. "Do you have beautiful eyes in the back of your head? I didn't hear anyone yell watch out."

"The kissing sound is a polite way to say pardon me instead of yelling."

Why did the woman mention kissing when that's what he wanted since he learned her name? But Rainey had to take it slow while being in a hurry. He only had a few more days in Ghana. "What impresses you?"

"There are always things about a person that impress and disappoint," she said as they turned a corner where cars for hire, basically rentals, and taxis were lined up. Josephine pointed to medium size black car at the end.

"I didn't ask a general question. I was very specific, Miss Yaa Amoah."

Josephine seemed thoughtful. If his money, profession and looks didn't impress her, the only other hindrance he could think of had to be…"Let me guess, church." Rainey waited for the confirmation.

"The wellbeing and strength of the family is important to Ghanaians. As far as the Lord, going to church on Sundays is not a substitute for daily devotion. A person has to be attracted to God to want to spend time with Him."

What attracted him to Josephine was her unpredictability. Unfortunately, the Reynolds family wouldn't be stronger until his father returned home. Releasing his hold on Josephine, Rainey stuffed both hands in his pants pockets. He had no defense for the argument about God. He never viewed a relationship with God as an attraction. Until the other night, Rainey wasn't a hundred percent sure that He really paid attention to him.

When Josephine touched his arm, he flexed his bicep. "God is ready to open doors in your life. The only thing you have to do is unlock your heart to receive it."

Through hooded lashes, he stared at her. He wished he could seduce her mind. "Are you in tune to my thoughts, or something?"

She giggled. "No. God is."

"I have a thing about letting a woman drive when we're going out," Rainey switched the conversation as they stopped at the end of the row of cars. "If you'll be my GPS, I'll get behind the wheel. Where are we going, anyway?"

"African-Americans' number one tourist destination when they're in search of their heritage—Elmira Slave Castle. Afterward, we'll grab a bite to eat before heading to Kakum National Park." Standing at the driver's side, Rainey slowly opened her door, getting another whiff of her fragrance.

"If you were to have even a minor accident as a foreigner, it would become a catastrophic event. One look at you and they would try to sue you for as much money as possible. Don't worry. Our travel is no farther than one hundred and forty-five kilometers."

Mentally calculating the conversion, Rainey guessed ninety miles wasn't bad. "They really have it in for us foreigners." Once she gathered the hem of her dress for him to close the door, Rainey rounded the car and got in.

Finally, they were alone, shutting out prying eyes, no invading hawkers, or racecar drivers on a busy street. Rainey exhaled and reached for her hand.

"I don't. Believe me. I'm pulling for you, Dr. Rainey Reynolds. God knows I am."

A cheerleader or one-person fan club, coming from Josephine, he would take it. After performing a brief head check, Josephine jerked forward into traffic. A whiplash might be a serious concern for Rainey later on. He double-checked that his seatbelt was secure.

Once she was at a steady speed. Rainey relaxed and stretched his legs. "I don't think there's been a day since you left that I haven't thought about you. Although we said we couldn't get along—" he paused, "I know before you say it that it was my fault, and of course you're right. But I've never longed for a woman—your presence, even for a trivial disagreement—like this ever before." Rainey wasn't there to play games, so he put it out there.

Tilting her head, Josephine squinted, deep in thought. "You are a complex man."

"Only you broke my code." He was ready to go deeper, but when she didn't respond, Rainey changed the subject. "I've tried to pick up certain words since I've been here, but Ghanaians speak too fast and forceful. Not you. Your words are soft, but just as passionate." He smiled. "Tell me something in Twi."

"*)yɛ me dɛ sɛ WO w) ha,* which means, I'm glad you are here."

Pleased by her declaration, Rainey asked, "How do you say you are beautiful?"

"*Woho yɛ fɛw.*" Yes, her words were like a caress.

It was as if Rainey could inhale the passion, and at that moment he knew, their language and culture would not be a hindrance. "Yes, you truly are. We can make a relationship work."

Josephine seemed pleased, but didn't comment. It didn't matter because he enjoyed her presence. Glancing out the window, he noted his surroundings. As they drove farther away from the bustle into residential areas, the palm tree-lined streets re-minded him of any low-income neighborhood in California or Florida.

Miscalculating a bump in the road, they bounced off their seats. For the second time that morning, Rainey prayed for his safety and her driving. There was no telling what condition this rental car would be in once they returned.

"Dr. Reynolds," Josephine began—a pattern she developed when she was about to enlighten him. "We're an ocean apart. Internet and phone service are not always reliable."

"You can always return to the States." And once he got her there, Rainey would hijack her heart to where she wouldn't want to leave.

"I'm no longer an exchange student. Visas to your country are extremely difficult for non-diplomatic personnel. My father's employer, the ambassador, assisted in arranging a visa for me to study abroad. I experienced Western culture and obtained my master's degree and I have returned to stay."

"What are you saying?" Rainey gave her a pointed expres-sion, unsure if he wanted to hear her answer. "There is no way you can come back to the United States?"

Tilting her head, Josephine had a sudden interest in her driving as she checked her review mirror even though there were no cars nearby. She sighed before glancing his way. "Unless I marry an American—and I am not making a solicitation—only God knows when I can visit again. The process is long."

Marry...a word that would put dread into any man's heart, but at the moment Rainey was immune to that fear. He smirked. Only Josephine could utter the word with confidence.

He welcomed a status change if the right woman crossed his path. Josephine caused a roadblock. Attraction aside, there was so much they didn't know about each other. With three more days remaining in Ghana, Rainey would use them wisely.

"Okay, Miss Josephine Abena Yaa Amoah. You told me when we first met, but refresh my memory. Why so many names for one *wohofefe*—or something like that?" he butchered the translation for beautiful lady. Stretching his legs, Rainey relaxed to enjoy listening to Josephine's melodious tone and distinct dialect.

"*Woho yε fεw*," she corrected. "In Ghana, whatever day a child is born, he or she is given a certain name. Since I am a girl born on Tuesday, I'm Abena. On the eighth day, the father gives the child an official first name. It is at that time the baby is presented to the world to see. Amoah is from my father's last name. If you would like, you can even have a traditional naming ceremony while you're here."

It wasn't that serious. "I'll pass. Rainey Terence Reynolds is easy to remember."

"Come on." She glanced his way. "What day of the week were you born?"

"Monday."

"Rainey is a gender neutral name. If we add Kojo, then everyone would know you're a male born on Monday."

Somehow, Josephine had a flair for making everything make sense. "I wonder how that works with folks who say they are gay or a lesbian." Rainey said off handedly.

"The child is what God creates her or him to be. A person cannot decide later to change the course. Homosexuality is illegal in our country and against God's law."

"I'm not touching that one because I have colleagues and distant relatives who claim otherwise."

"Homosexuality and all sexual immorality are sins. Not manmade, but God-prohibited. It is important that we love everyone because the Bible says we were all born in sin and shaped in iniquity. Sin is in our nature and we all must be born again to overcome temptations. If we repent and get baptized in Jesus' name, then God will give us ammunition to fight sexual immorality and all other kinds of sins that try to overpower us. Amen."

"Amen," Rainey repeated to end the subject. No question, he was what God created him—one hundred and one percent male. Nothing could satisfy his lust, but a woman. He redirected his thoughts. What he felt for Josephine was more than that.

"Okay. You know I'm a twin, an orthodontist, have an older sister. Tell me about your family?"

"I have two sisters, Madeline and Abigail. I'm the second eldest. My father, Gyasi Yaw Amoah is Akan—the majority ethnic group. His name is translated to mean wonderful one. My mother, Fafa, is Ewe. Her name means peace." Josephine beamed. "Put their names together and I'm reminded of Isaiah 9 that describes God as the *Wonderful* Counselor, a Mighty God, Eternal Father and the Prince of *Peace*..."

"Unbelievable. You're good to sneak that in." Rainey chuckled and shook his head.

"The Lord put them together. Anyway, the Akans' ancestry dates back to ancient Kush in the Bible. My sister, Madeline, is recently married. I work at the university, and my sister, Abigail, studies there. I have one set of grandparents alive, numerous aunts, cousins, and a host of church friends."

What Rainey wouldn't give to have a bigger family. At least a few brothers—older or younger, he would take it. "So besides these slave castles, what else distinguishes Ghana from the rest of the continent?"

"Well, as a former British colony, once called the Gold Coast, Ghana was the first nation in Sub-Saharan Africa to win our independence. Ghana is also the second largest cocoa producer..."

Gold and cocoa? How could a country boast riches like these and need foreign aid? Rainey wanted to ask, but Josephine appeared to be on a roll.

"Here's something you might not know: the Ga tribe is world-renowned for its coffin business—the deceased can be buried in a shoe-shaped coffin, if that was his profession, or a brightly painted and exquisitely carved peacock-shaped coffin. Essentially, anything you can imagine, the craftsmen can make it."

Rainey gave her an incredulous look when suddenly out of nowhere, an imposing white complex came into view as their car climbed the road. "Whoa." He whistled.

"This is the Cape Coast," Josephine announced in an official tourism-guide manner. She joined a line of slow moving vehicles turning into a large gravel lot. Several tour buses were parked along with taxis and trotros. Once they were out the car, Rainey shielded his eyes against the warm sun as he looked beyond the ocean.

Satisfied with the view, Rainey then linked his hand through hers. In a silent reverence, others joined in the procession up the slight hill. The structure represented an Emerald City, a mecca, of sorts. It was an eerie quietness with each step on a wide bridge.

"How old is this place?" he whispered.

From a distance, an unknowing stranger would view the large white complex as picturesque with the ocean as a backdrop. Rainey couldn't imagine how something so majestic could be an open hell. The bustling sounds of a fishing village surrounded the monstrosity, carrying on business as usual. *How could they?* Rainey wondered and shivered, not from a cool breeze, but the complacency.

Leaning into him, Josephine rubbed his arm. "The Dutch built it in the 1400s as a fort."

"Amazing that anything manmade could last this long against the elements. So this is a tourist attraction? As disgusting as it is, why would anyone want to come here?"

"Our brothers and sisters throughout the African Diaspora say they come in search of their roots to be set free. They are drawn to Ghana's slave castles to find their beginning and understand their roots."

Rainey took the liberty to hug her closer and then rub her back. "I came for entirely different reasons. I still say tear it down."

Josephine seemed thoughtful. "I don't know. If it were to be demolished would that erase the sins of history? It's a reminder of the evil that has corrupted this world. Here on the shores of Africa's Gold Coast, we have the castles. In the United States, New York has Ground Zero. In Germany, Berlin has the Holocaust Memorial. This is our African Holocaust. An estimated fifteen million Africans were stolen from their families and enslaved in an institution unimaginable, not to mention the millions who lost their lives...our Ground Zero."

Rainey frowned and stopped her. "I left one place to escape the drama."

"We can't flee our past or troubles, but Christ has promised us peace in the middle of our drama." Josephine looked at him with such tenderness, Rainey wanted to kiss her.

He wished he could tap into Josephine's spiritual confidence. Humans who enslaved other humans called themselves Christians. *Who wants to be affiliated with that hypocrisy?*

I came as a Jew to save the Jewish people, they rejected me so I extended My invitation to anyone who will come, God spoke forcefully in his mind from Romans 11. *Will you come?*

Shaking off the question, Rainey wrapped his arm around her shoulder as they neared the castle.

"This is the most well-known castle, but there are more. At least twenty more of them."

When they actually set foot on the property, Josephine steered him toward a massive courtyard where others were gathered, listening to a tour guide. The four-story plus structure was intimidating and mocking, even for Rainey who was beginning to learn he wasn't as fearless as he thought. It resembled a world-class resort in its heyday.

He and Josephine climbed the steep chipped stone stairs to a landing that overlooked the North Atlantic Ocean. The crashing sounds of the waves fell short of a calming effect. Rainey spied the cannons that lined half stone walls, poised to fire at any possible threat of slave raiders.

Rainey surveyed the surface. It wasn't long before they retraced their steps to explore other areas within the castle. They trailed a group through a tunnel where artifacts of human chains and branding instruments served as evidence of the African holocaust. The passageway was narrow, the air damp, and the only lighting was what the sunlight could sneak in.

A guide advised visitors to experience the isolation their ancestors must have felt inside a cramped space not big enough for a closet. Rainey declined the offer; Josephine rubbed his arm. He seethed with anger, viewing the holding cells for female slaves and male slaves. The tour guide pointed to a worn stone circle used as a makeshift bathroom for captives to relieve themselves.

"The odor still lingers today. Hundreds of years later," the guide explained.

"I've seen enough," Rainey whispered, squeezing Josephine's hand. She nodded. "This was purgatory." The emotional and physical toll left him drained. "I wonder how many of my ancestors passed through here."

"Does it matter? One life changed the lives of many. What matters is Christ's death reversed the curse." Instead of going back to the car, Josephine tugged him toward the beach. She slipped out of her scandals and wiggled her manicured toes until they were buried under the sand.

"Come on, remove your shoes. Let's walk. I promise I won't look at your ugly feet."

Rainey mustered a snicker, despite his residual resentment about the evidence of what happened. It was hard denying her simple requests, so he kicked off his shoes and carried them in one hand while snaking his other arm around Josephine's waist.

Leaning into him, she mirrored his gesture with her arm. "We all lost loved ones. We lost our tribesmen, our children, sisters, fathers—"

"But your people helped." He wanted to blame somebody.

"True, Africans acted as middlemen, but you have to remember, no race is immune to slavery. God's chosen, the Israelites, served the Egyptians. Fast forward to today and slavery still exists—sex slaves, human trafficking is thriving in my country, on my continent, your country and all over the world."

Rainey wasn't buying her passive attitude. "Are Africans so detached that they can never experience what barbaric British and Europeans did to our shared ancestors in the Americas?"

"You are uninformed, Dr. Reynolds..."

Here we go with the title. Rainey wanted to roll his eyes.

"We have tasted both slavery and re-programming. The Danish enslaved Africans and built fifteen plantations on our soil. Frederiksgave Plantation is among half that were in the Akwapim Hills. Later, came the brainwashing through colonization."

Rainey baked in the beaming sun for the sake of Josephine wanting to walk on the beach. It was a toss-up as to whether what he was hearing was enlightening or disturbing.

"We were reprogrammed or de-cultured for England's purposes. Although Ghana was the first African country to win independence from Britain, we lost some of ourselves in the battle, because we speak, act, and are a reflection of them. Also, our African kings and other royalty were shamefully driven from their property and forced to live in concentrated ghettos with curfews and on and on. So the argument continues today, who had it worse?" Rainey hated to admit it wasn't so cut and dry as he was led to believe for years. "That's a tough call now knowing this."

"It doesn't have to be. These are remnants of the kingdom of men, but the Lord said to seek ye first the kingdom of God and all His righteousness." She paused. "I wish everyone who leaves this place would memorize one scripture.'

"And it is?" Rainey knew Josephine was going to tell him whether he asked or not.

"Romans 12:21: *'Be not overcome of evil, but overcome evil with good'.*"

It wasn't that simple. But Rainey didn't want to argue, so he held his tongue.

"There's one more place I want to show you. First let's eat at the Coconut Grove Bridge House." She pointed to a nearby two-level strip area.

"I'm famished, but no more slave castles." Rainey couldn't stomach another one. The imposing white castles' images would be with him forever.

"No. We're going from man's ugliness to God's beauty—Kokum National Park." She broke free and ran ahead of him, kicking up sand. Giving chase, they laughed when he caught up and scooped her in the air. He would have carried Josephine the rest of the way, but she protested, so he reluctantly let her go. Then hand-in-hand, she led him to a bank of shops and cafés.

Soon they were relaxing in a cool restaurant in direct view of the castle. They ordered bottled water—something Chad had insisted he do whenever he ate out—and chicken with Jollof rice. While waiting, Rainey reached across the table and grabbed Josephine's hands that were wet with sanitizer. Together, they played with the gel until it evaporated. He looked up into her face.

Josephine's eyes sparkled. The moment was surreal and time stopped. She was a dark beauty. He imagined she was a descendant from an African queen. He wanted her and it was to the point of by any means necessary. "You won't even try to see if you can return to the United States?"

She shook her head. "As I explained, getting another visa is extremely difficult. Besides, I'll miss home again."

"But I haven't stopped missing you."

Chapter 9

Why am I exposing myself to an unrealistic outcome with Rainey? Josephine's heart and mind definitely weren't in sync. With every glance, smile, and touch, she wondered what he was thinking. By the time they finished eating, Josephine and Rainey were debating their countries' politics. After leaving the restaurant, the two visited beachfront shops. Rainey haggling over cedis for family souvenirs amused her. It didn't take long until his few souvenirs filled a large shopping bag.

No doubt, Rainey was a man in control—or tried to be—even when things weren't going his way, such as luring her back to the States. That would never happen. Josephine wasn't budging from Accra.

Yet, he had a part of her heart that she couldn't get back. How did that happen? Despite the fact that Josephine had worked with professionals, mingled with church brothers, and even occasionally dated a few Ghanaian men, none of them stirred up the daydreams she captured with Rainey.

During the short drive to Kakum National Park, they had a lively discussion about nothing important—spicy foods, overpriced fashions, and work. Once they arrived, Josephine basked in Rainey's affections. A few times, he snuck in a soft embrace or brushed his lips in her hair. Now they sauntered hand-in-hand passed the Rainforest Lodge.

"Before we leave, I probably need to see if there is anything I can get for my nieces and nephews."

"More?" She teased.

"It's my prerogative as an uncle." He winked. "I've never been in a tropical rainforest, but I have to admit it's not what I imagined."

Josephine chuckled. "You expected a constant downpour."

"Maybe."

"The rainforest gets about sixty-three inches a year. Americans and tourists all say the same thing, not knowing the significance."

"Okay, Miss Josephine Yaa Amoah, tour guide, what's so special about this park?"

"You'll see and feel how breathtaking it becomes. The ground seems to drop from underneath your feet and you won't even know it. Kakum National Park contains rare animals, such as endangered Mona-meerkat, pygmy elephants, forest buffalo, civet cats, birds of course, and more than 500 species of butterflies."

His nostrils flared as he stared into her eyes. "I'm impressed."

"You will be," Josephine assured him. They bypassed tourists resting and eating under small pavilions in a picnic area. Campsites were nearby.

"Africa has so many treasures, including you. This is beautiful—*woho yε few*."

His pronunciation was almost perfect. Judging from his confident smirk, Rainey knew it, too. To keep from further feeding his ego, Josephine didn't respond, but continued walking.

"What you won't tell me, your eyes do." Rainey looked ahead. "When I first told my mother about this mission—which I'm sad to say, I haven't thought of once since I've been with you—she mentioned taking a safari trip when my father..." He stopped and cleared his throat, "comes home."

Josephine brought his hand to her lips and kissed it. The small gesture was meant to provide some comfort, albeit, it was she who initiated the public display of affection. "How is Dr. Reynolds?"

Rainey shrugged. "Prison can't keep him from being my father. We take turns visiting him, then we exchange letters and occasionally speak on the phone ... " Rainey paused as a colorful bird distracted him. He refocused. "We're in this together—all of us. We won't abandon him."

Family loyalty, even in the time of distress, warmed Josephine's heart.

"Most of the time, dad uses his brief phone privileges to speak with my mother..." When realization dawned, Rainey's look of confusion was priceless. "Whoa. When did this happen? I don't remember climbing up a steep hill or anything. How high are we?"

"High, about one hundred feet in the sky from the forest floor, but we're safe." Josephine moved forward first to prove it. As she gripped the steel cable, holding the walls of netting on each side, Josephine felt Rainey's presence close behind her.

In order to cross to the other side, they had to walk a narrow wooden plank that swayed with each step. There were at least seven manmade canopy walkways within the rainforest, totaling more than a thousand feet.

"This is like walking a tight-rope in a circus or one of those collapsible bridges I've seen in a movie. Hmm." Rainey's strong arm pulled her closer. Josephine smiled at his endearing gesture meant to protect her.

"I gotcha, babe."

Glancing over her shoulder, Josephine whispered, "God's got us—babe."

With no one near them, he rewarded her with a brush against her lips. She had to keep reminding herself that these brief touches might very well be the only intimacy they shared. They were from two different continents and mindsets.

"Thank you." Josephine loosened his hold to keep them from further temptation and concentrated on making it to a connection that served as an observation deck. Once on the deck, Josephine looked back, soaking in the beauty of nature. "Have you ever asked yourself, if you died this moment, where would you go?"

Twisting his lips, Rainey frowned. "I try not to think about it or ask myself."

"You should. When I bring friends to this place and we're suspended over the trees like this, I always think about what-ifs and say, "Jesus, You've got me."

Urging her onto another canopy, Rainey stated, "I'm not there yet."

"Maybe not today, but Jesus will come knocking at your door. Will you open it?"

"I promise." He paused and squinted. "I make very few promises, and any to you I plan to keep."

Josephine's heart pounded at his declaration and then plummeted in concern at the magnitude of what he was professing. *Jesus, let me lead him to You,* she prayed. Trusting God for all things, she continued to lead the way to the other canopy walkways.

Chapter 10

As the sun began to set, Josephine grew concerned about Rainey's uneasiness. "Are you all right?"

"You don't mind if we get out of here, do you?" He retraced their steps to leave the park. "Not much scares me, but the bite of a female mosquito is enough to make me run and hide like a chump."

"Of course." It wasn't a sprint, but they hurried toward their rental. "We can stop by the chemist—I mean pharmacist—for bug repellant."

Only after they were secured in the car did Rainey seem to relax. It would have been a comical sight to see such a powerful, fearless, six-foot-two or -three muscular man scared of such a tiny creature, but malaria was a threat, not only in her country, but in many parts of Africa.

"That's preferable to taking Lariam. I'm not prone to nightmares, but I dreamt the earth was on fire and I was the sole inhabitant. Chad said that an anti-malaria drug was the culprit."

Josephine glanced at Rainey. Sometimes dreams were whimsical, sometimes foretelling. Was the Lord stepping up His calling and beginning to pound on Rainey's door? "Are you okay?"

He nodded and rubbed his mustache. "The images were so real. The brightness of the flames almost blinded me. The stink from the odor made me nauseous and the pain..." He groaned.

"Being on fire has to be one of the most horrible ways to die." Rainey shook his head.

"Yes, I can't conceive the excruciating pain burn victims suffer, but I imagine it's horrible. Thank God for Jesus that He wants to save you from hell—all of us. To die without Him banishes us to hell and then in the end, to the Lake of fire and brimstone. Just like the Lord will give the saints an incorruptible body to live forever.

"Those diehard sinners will also receive a body that will never die, but will burn for eternity. Think about eternity and live. Read Revelation 20. Verse fifteen will determine your fate: *'And whosoever was not found written in the book of life was cast into the lake of fire.'*"

Josephine didn't mean for their conversation to be so dark on their drive back into the city, but God had begun to call Rainey. Although he said he would open the door if Jesus knocked, did he realize that God had begun knocking?

When it became quiet between them, Josephine assumed he had dozed off, so she refrained from turning on the radio to keep her company. Surprisingly, it didn't take long before she reached their destination.

After returning the rental, they went inside Jinlet Pharmacy. Before leaving the store, Rainey applied his newly purchased pesticide to her arms first before rubbing it into his skin. The loving gesture caused Josephine's vision to blur. It was at that instant, she knew that he loved her and cared about her. . .and that she loved him, too. *Oh boy*, she thought, *I'm in trouble.*

"Thank you for sharing your day with me," he lowered his voice to almost a whisper. "But it wasn't enough. I need more time. We need more time."

"I know."

If Rainey was waiting for her to say more, Josephine couldn't as she sniffed. God was stirring in his life. So as not to get caught up in the whirlwind, she had to stay on the sidelines.

"Well, I guess I better get you home." Rainey waved for a taxi for Josephine. At first, the driver attempted to quote Rainey an outrageous fare. Josephine intervened. Rainey waved another cab for himself to Chad's house and she negotiated a fair price again.

"Goodnight." More than anything Josephine wanted Rainey to wrap her in his arms. "Call me if you can't sleep."

"It's a given you'll be hearing from me tonight."

Grinning, she got in and gave the driver her address in Kanda, then waved at Rainey. He didn't move into his waiting taxi until she couldn't see him anymore.

Resting her head, Josephine closed her eyes. How could she love him when she didn't like him long ago and didn't know him? Yet, the longing in her heart was there. Was this the unexplainable feeling her sister felt when she agreed to marry her British boyfriend?

Yet, their situations were not the same. Madeline was unsaved at the time and enjoyed the experience of being a world traveler. Josephine was a homebody. She viewed travel as on an "as-needed basis", maybe because her father was gone for so long at times on official business. Then there was Rainey's salvation. At this point, it really wasn't an issue. The Lord was drawing him and it was just a matter of time before Dr. Rainey Reynolds surrendered.

With a sigh, Josephine recalled the night of Madeline's traditional Ghana ceremony where the father of the bride asks his daughter three times if she wants to marry the groom. Madeline had been so passionate in her answer.

"Father, I have lived a happy life without Dennis these many years. Now, I cannot continue in my happiness without him. Saying 'I love him' is not enough to express what my heart feels...."

"We are at the address," an unfamiliar voice invaded her thoughts.

She snapped out of it as the driver stopped the car. After paying the agreed fare, she stepped out and stood in the driveway facing her home. By American standards, she stayed in an upper middle class neighborhood. In Accra, there was no middle, either poverty or the rich—or so the locals argued. Still this was where her heart had lived for so many years. Since Rainey was taking possession, where would her heart reside after he left?

Walking through the wrought-iron gate, Josephine opened it and took the short walkway to her front door. Once inside, she was surprised to see her grandparents and other cousins.

With her mind elsewhere, she hadn't noticed their vehicles in the parking area off the side of the house. She greeted the elders first, then her parents before kissing her cousins' babies.

"Where is this young man you spent the day with? I expected to meet your friend," Gyasi said disappointedly in lieu of a scolding.

She eyed Abigail as the source of relaying this information. "I'm sorry, Papa. Today, he wanted to be a tourist," Josephine replied, knowing her answer would not pacify their customs of entertaining foreigners as a group event, not singular.

"Tomorrow?"

"Well, *Impaa,*" she addressed her paternal grandfather. "There is so little time. Rainey's mission has worked in the village for days and after he's finished at the orphanage tomorrow, I had wanted him to experience nightlife in Osu." Since respect was everything in her country, she hoped they would not oppose her plans.

There was a long pause before her grandfather consented. "Very well. We will gather for dinner on Saturday. Your young doctor is invited."

Josephine exhaled. Rainey had just been summoned.

Although it was late evening, her family congregated in the dining room. Her mother carried a bowl of warm water to the table for hand washing. An impromptu celebration followed prayer before eating.

She loved get togethers. God always gave them a reason to celebrate anything: a birth, a wedding, and even a funeral. Whenever some died, whether Ghanaians knew them or not, the community celebrated life and mourned the death with the family. As cousins drew her into discussions, Josephine pushed aside her growing feelings for Rainey to enjoy family.

Later that night, Abigail sat Indian-style on Josephine's bed.

"I did not realize that you would tell papa that I was with Rainey all day, Abigail Efia." Josephine added her Ghanaian given name, meaning a girl born on Friday. She wanted to be upset with her younger sister, but wasn't. Family secrets were not the norm for the Amoahs, but they had them.

"Are we going to talk now about the doctor, or do I have to wait with the rest of the family to get my questions answered? You do not disguise your feelings. Are you going to share your thoughts with me?"

Josephine sighed. She scanned every item in her bedroom, stalling to gather her wits. "I'm still processing my feelings. What happens if I am in love with him?"

"Simple. You tell him." Abigail shrugged as if it was no big deal. "The only thing I ask is that you have a long engagement because that will take the pressure off of me."

"An engagement?" Josephine didn't want to hear that. Bouncing off Josephine's bed, Abigail stood. "Then comes marriage, if he is worthy. I'm going to my room and my class notes. Goodnight." Abigail dismissed herself and left Josephine in more mental anguish than before she came home.

Had Josephine missed something? The Scripture said in 2 Peter 3:8: *one day is with the Lord as a thousand years, and a thousand years as one day.* How could so much emotion develop in such an accelerated pace? Although she couldn't stop her growing feelings for Rainey, she did have a lot of say so in regards to marrying an American.

There was nothing left for her to do, but prepare herself for bed. Sliding to her knees, she started, "Jesus, I'm not sure what to pray here. Cannot my feelings be duplicated for another man on this continent? I can't leave my family. If this is Your will, as You continue to draw Rainey into Your salvation, please consider moving him to my beautiful homeland."

Instantly, conviction filled Josephine's heart for her selfish request. She repented for praying amiss that had the potential to block God's blessings for her. Then Josephine began to petition God earnestly for the homeless, the sickly, the poor, world peace and an endless list, ending with, "Thank You Lord for Your abundant blessings. In Jesus' name, Amen."

Do not worry for tomorrow. For tomorrow will take care of itself, the Lord spoke Matthew 6:34.

She nodded as she tried to increase her faith to trust and believe God. Climbing under the covers, Josephine closed her eyes and waited for her dreams to descend upon her. Not long after she began to drift, her cell phone beeped.

"I was thinking about you," Rainey said after she said hello.

"I miss you," Josephine whispered.

"I've been waiting to hear that."

Josephine smiled. She had been waiting to say it, but she wouldn't reveal everything to him. "Would you be willing to relocate?"

"And do what, babe? I'm an orthodontist, not a dentist, which provides essential services. In my profession, no one has ever died of crooked teeth."

And that was their problem—not the crooked teeth, but his unwillingness to move, so Josephine changed the subject. "You are invited to the family dinner on Saturday. Feel free to bring guests. Your mission partners or host family."

"I'll see. Chad wanted to invite you to his house for dinner, but I told him I would get back to him."

"No. No." Josephine shook her head. "Ghanaians invite friends to eat with us. It is our custom. You do not turn down an invitation without causing hurt feelings. It's considered a rude gesture."

"I'm sorry," he apologized.

"Consider our dinner invitation as a summons." She waited for his response, but nothing.

"What in the world is going on?" Rainey sounded alarmed.

She sat up in bed, concerned. "What's the matter?"

"It's pitch back. I think the lights went out," he said as Josephine heard a faint voice in the background.

Rainey's host was probably telling him it's a way of life on the outlying areas of Accra where Lapaz was located. It was one of the many nice neighborhoods considered unplanned because of unmaintained roads, poor drainage systems, and insufficient water and electricity services.

Other areas faced the same inconveniencies, but those that could afford backup generators had them, including some of the best hotels. "*Akwaaba* to Ghana, where nothing is taken for granted."

"Get me back to America."

Josephine tried not to take insult, but the statement offended her anyway. "People in your country also struggle. It is the land of the haves and have-nots."

"Sweetheart, I'm sorry," he said so softly. "I will watch my words, so I don't mistakenly hurt you."

He knew how to take the fight out of her as the endearment spiraled throughout her. Smiling, she tried to recapture the happiness she felt when he first called. Unfortunately, their time was brief so as not to deplete his minutes on the international calling card.

"Are you going to sing to me before we hang up?"

"How about an Akan proverb? *Woto wo bo ase gua ntetea a, wohu ne nsono*, which translates to, 'If you patiently dissect an ant, you see its intestines.'"

"So besides being attacked by mosquitoes, I have to worry about an ant dissecting me?" Rainey grunted.

He had so much to learn about Ghana culture. "The lesson of the proverb says, a person who possesses great patience can overcome difficulties." *Maybe that proverb was meant for me*, she thought.

"Hmm. Next time, let me guess at the translation."

His lack of understanding was become endearing. "*Dayie.*"

"*Dayie,*" he repeated in Twi for goodnight.

Although she should have plugged in her phone to keep it charged, Josephine couldn't part with the last point of contact with Rainey. Soon, she drifted back to sleep.

Chapter 11

Rainey woke the next morning smiling. It was the first time he had slept so well in that netted contraption since coming to Accra. His father was right about having someone in his life who understood his past hurts and current struggles, but was still drawn to his strength. Josephine was the only one.

The distance wasn't his worry short-term. That's what planes were for. However, could they tackle their cultural differences so easily?

Sometime during the early morning, the power was restored, and the water was plentiful for a shower, Rainey dressed in record time. After breakfast, Chad drove him to rejoin his team at the Handi Children Outreach Home north of Accra. En route, Rainey shared his experience at the slave castle and the park.

Although he considered himself a passionate person, after visiting the slave castle, he felt more connected with the Ghanaians and their shared suffering at the hands of the oppressor, whether it was colonization or slavery. It wasn't long before the conversation turned to Josephine.

"My family would like to meet her," Chad stated.

Rainey recalled Josephine's reprimand about not accepting invitations. "Her family has invited us to their home tomorrow for dinner."

"Excellent! My wife will bring a dish." Chad grinned and gassed the engine in delight.

Rainey snickered and looked out the window. He had become accustomed to the vast wide-open land and the native trees that sprouted up every now and then. Soon, Chad turned onto a bumpy dirt road leading to what looked like a ranch with a pair of single story row houses nearby. They were in the middle of nowhere. Some of his fellow Dentist Without Borders team workers stood outside with the children. Thomas had instigated a game of kickball.

Mission work ministers to more than the body. A merry heart makes a cheerful countenance: but a sorrowful heart breaks the spirit, God spoke Proverbs 15:13.

What was happening to him in Ghana that he had become so in tune with God? Rainey didn't have time to delve for answers. As he got out of Chad's car, Thomas approached him with a group of boys trailing behind.

Handi Children Outreach was home to about fifty children. It broke Rainey's heart to hear the stories of how each came to live there; many were as young as three years old. Others were teenagers. Some were orphaned after the deaths of their parents. A number of them were abandoned and classified as street children. So Rainey whole heartedly agreed with the Lord on this. Laughing and smiling might help to mend their broken world.

These children—possibly his ancestors—needed more than dental health aid and education, they needed a bright future. As soon as Rainey returned home, he would gather support from his colleagues to make donations of toys and other supplies on a regular basis.

"So did you enjoy your sightseeing adventure yesterday, Dr. Reynolds?" Thomas asked with mischief dancing in his eyes. The boys around him seemed shy, but curious.

"As a matter of fact I did." He offered nothing more. A few of the boys ventured closer. A small one latched on to his leg. Rainey playfully rubbed the top of his head. "So why are you out here? I assumed there would be a long line."

Thomas chuckled. "Oh, there is inside. Most are children, but the prize after their checkups is a game of soccer."

Rainey nodded as he went to report for duty. He reflected on what God whispered to him minutes earlier. The children inside were excited to see him. Girls were among the group. Again, most sported short hair.

The team leaders outlined his assignment of disposing of some and sanitizing the other dental instruments. By the end of the day, Rainey was dispatched outside for a soccer game. Of course, he reapplied his bug repellent.

☙ ❧

Early evening back at Chad's home, Rainey heard the doorbell ring just as he slipped his sock-covered feet into his strapped scandals and then applied bug repellent. It definitely wasn't his choice of a fashion statement. Sandals were meant to let a man's feet breathe.

He listened as Josephine exchanged greetings with Chad and his family in their native Twi. It seemed so strange for a woman to chauffeur him. Rainey preferred being in control, behind the wheel and in his personal life.

He chanced a drop of cologne and checked his appearance before heading to the front room. Josephine's eyes sparkled as soon as she saw him.

"Ana wula," Rainey practiced good evening in Twi, which made her smile brighter and Chad beam. "You look *who ye few* tonight," Rainey added, getting cocky.

Everyone, including him, cringed as he massacred the word beautiful. Even Josephine struggled to keep a straight face. That blunder put an end to him trying to impress her.

"Ready?" he asked.

As they said their goodbyes, Chad added. "We look forward to accepting your family's dinner invitation tomorrow."

Nana agreed as Rainey guided Josephine out the door and to a Sonata.

"Is this another car for hire?" he asked.

"No, it's mine."

"Nice." Rainey whistled, then rounded the car and got in after tending to her first.

"Since we're only going downtown and the roads are good, it's safe to drive my own vehicle. Plus, I wanted to show you some other neighborhoods before we go to Osu."

Clicking his seatbelt, Rainey faced her. "I'm all yours for tonight." *And probably longer if we could work out some logistics.*

"I'm so glad you came." She reached for his hand.

Rainey linked his fingers between her soft ones and brought them to his lips. "I'm sorry it took me this long."

For the next fifteen minutes or so, they chatted about his assessment of his mission trip. Rainey's jaw dropped as the landscape of surrounding neighborhoods changed drastically.

The gated, luscious communities would shame golf resorts and country clubs back home. "Whoa. I don't have to ask the price range, but from the looks of it, a person would have to be at the top of *Forbes Magazine's* richest person list to have one of these."

"This is Buena Vista. The homebuilders just won an international award for excellence. Impressive, *yo?*"

Yo, impressive." Rainey mimicked. He enjoyed hearing Josephine's native words surface between her English.

Rainey rode speechless, cataloguing the details pumped into the estates at Trasacco Valley, Tema and some other neighborhoods Rainey couldn't remember or pronounce. It was definitely not the Ghana or Africa he had ever read about or seen on satellite TV.

From the pristine neighborhoods, Josephine took him to Oxford Street in Osu. The area was abuzz with a peppy, young professional crowd. The sidewalks were lined with palm and coconut trees, tropical plants and flowers—yet another look of Ghana. Of course, it wouldn't be Ghana without the hawkers. Even they appeared a bit upscale.

"Their restaurant has the best hamburgers." Josephine pointed and parked in front of a place called Frankie's Hotel. "Come on. After we eat, you might want to go shopping for more souvenirs for your nieces and nephews," she teased.

Rainey winked. "How perceptive."

He had forgotten about them. Once they were seated inside the restaurant with little wait, Rainey perused the menu and debated. "Besides the hamburger, what else do you suggest?"

"Try *red-red*. It's a popular local cuisine. It's fried sweet plantains with red beans, in palm oil, or *palava* sauce, which is egg & spinach and yam chips."

He squinted at the menu and then Josephine. Rainey enjoyed eggs and spinach, just not together. But this was her world and he wanted in; Rainey would try anything once. "Okay, for the sake of being a tourist, I'll brave the *palava*."

"Excellent." When the waiter approached, Josephine gave him their order.

Rainey glanced at each table, looking for salt and pepper shakers—none. He asked for that and a bottle of ketchup.

"We don't serve that here, sir," the waiter advised. "With our rich spices, there is no need." He shrugged and disappeared.

While they waited, Rainey reached for Josephine's hands. They were soft and perfectly created. From there, he rested his eyes on her face. Josephine's nose, eyes, mouth, cheeks, even her ears seemed to be artistically placed. She wore her braided hair down and curled. He fingered one. The style enhanced her appearance, which reminded him of the little girls that came to the clinic.

"Beautiful," he said in plain English. "Your hair is long, but I noticed a lot of girls we saw in the clinic have short hair. Pardon my ignorance up front, but doesn't it grow."

Jutting her chin, Josephine squinted. "Whether African or I'm sure, African-American, no little girl likes to get her thick coarse hair combed every day. Either we go every weekend to get it braided, which is not much better, or wear it short. Hands down, a young girl is going to say shave it off."

Rainey didn't comment. He liked hair. Most men did. His mother would gasp at the thought of cutting Janae or Cheney's mane when they were younger. He took a deep breath.

"I don't want to argue or insult you—"

"What questions are you pondering, Dr. Reynolds?" She flashed him a smile as a go-ahead, then lifted a naturally arched brow.

"I think I've seen all sides of your city. It amazes me the wealth of some areas in contrast to the severe poverty that plagues the same city. How is that possible? They don't call Ghana the

Gold Coast for nothing. I heard the Chinese are mining for gold in some Ashanti region...your backyard. Where is the accountability of your government?"

When Josephine sat straighter and her nostrils flared, Rainey knew he had over stepped his boundaries as a tourist and prepared for a tongue-lashing.

"You live in one of the top ten richest countries in the world, yet you have people whose homes are nothing more than cardboard boxes—sometimes entire families. Others live in homes with no heat or electricity...your people would rather throw out food because it won't taste fresh on a certain day rather than give it to a shelter for the hungry. That's the America I saw. When you return to America, look in your own back yard."

"I didn't want to argue, remember?" Rainey softened his tone. He wished she would possess that same passion and love him.

"I'm sorry." She bowed her head in embarrassment. "I love my country. We have good and not so good, but it's my home."

"In our high tech world of communication and speedy transportation, your home could be in your heart while you're physically somewhere else."

"It's good to hear you're a proponent of adaptability," she threw his logic back at him.

He smirked at his worthy opponent, but he was not deterred from getting Josephine back into the States. If paperwork could be shuffled to get her to North America once, he may have to use his connections to see that it would be done again.

Their hamburgers arrived, causing a cease-fire in their conversation, but Rainey's mind was building an arsenal of enticements to lure her back to St. Louis and in his arms. The rest of the night, they were carefree, visiting shops, and talking about anything besides the differences that separated them.

Chapter 12

How could a handshake be interpreted any other way than how it was meant—as a cordial greeting?

"Let me go over this again," Rainey quizzed as Chad drove to Josephine's parents' home the next evening. "Allow Josephine's father to extend his hand first, since he's the elder."

Chad nodded. "If he chooses, but you'll do fine. We're friendly people and are accustomed to guests in our country. And when speaking to an elder, it's best to avoid eye contact, so don't linger."

Really? You've got to be kidding me? He had been taught to always look a man in the eye as a sign of strength and respect.

How much would it matter if Rainey didn't get it right? He didn't want to take that chance as he squeezed the bouquets in his hand—one for Josephine, the other for her mother. As he noted the passing scenery, he concluded Africa could not be described in one word. It mirrored the U.S. in many ways. However, from the looks of some structures, Rainey couldn't determine if they were in the process of being gutted or constructed, so he asked.

"When city dwellers have the money, they build. When funds are gone, they stop," Chad explained.

"Like that?" Rainey snapped his fingers. Mind boggling. "In America, a project wouldn't start unless the money was already in the bank." He imagined Josephine would have a comeback about foreclosures.

The scenic route suddenly became stone walls, shutting off the outside world. A few minutes later, Chad parked in front of one of those stone fortresses. Rainey's first impression—he wasn't impressed. Chad had said Kanda bordered some of the wealthiest neighborhoods in North Accra. He couldn't see a thing except the palm trees that were trapped inside. Once they reached the front entrance, they must have triggered a sensor that opened a wrought-iron gate.

It was like he stepped into a small scale estate. Luscious greenery complemented the palm trees. The home's architecture and beauty were impressive, but hidden from view.

Not as if that was unusual. Back home, some affluent homeowners taunted passersby with look, but don't touch. Evidently, some of Ghana's nicer neighborhoods' message was 'if you don't see them, then you can't touch them.'

Colorful rocks lined the pathway to the front door, and Rainey noted the landscaping detail. With his entourage behind him, Rainey rang the doorbell. In his most confident stance, he cleared his throat and waited.

The door opened. He wasn't expecting Josephine's entourage to trump his by at least ten to fifteen folks. Rainey introduced himself and his host family.

"*Akwaaba,* I'm Gyasi Yaw Amoah, Josephine's father."

Rainey eyed the man's hand. It seemed to move in slow motion before he extended for a handshake.

Rainey exhaled and smiled. "Dr. Reynolds, it's nice to finally meet you. Please come in."

Stepping inside the foyer, Gyasi welcomed his guests. Despite being the center of attention, Rainey searched the faces until his eyes landed on Josephine, who stood between a younger and older version of herself. Commanding his eyes off of Josephine, he spoke to the others as Thomas had instructed him in the Ghana 101 lesson or whatever his fellow mission volunteer called it.

"*Ah-kwah-bah*," Rainey said hello repeatedly until he made his way to the woman of his affection.

Standing face to face, Rainey was pleased his presence caused Josephine to suck in her breath. Her younger version nudged her until she made the introductions. "This is my mum, Fafa."

Her mother's eyes twinkled. Rainey returned her sentiments. Next was Abigail who was equally as beautiful as Josephine with shorter hair, the same intoxicating eyes and the smile—a slight gap. It didn't take away from her beauty, but by trade, Rainey noticed the imperfection.

He handed one bouquet to Fafa and the other to Josephine.

"*Medase*," she and her mother thanked him in unison, then proceeded to give them away to two elderly women.

Frowning, she introduced them as her paternal grandmother and great aunt. Rainey might have passed the handshake test, but he definitely failed the flowers rule—if only he had known a tribe would be there. Other introductions were made, but he couldn't name anyone except for her immediate family.

"Come," Gyasi said. "We have prepared a celebration." Her father led the way to a large room where dishes of food were spread across a long table. To Rainey's relief, there wasn't a bowl with water for hand washing. That was one custom he could never get used to.

The elders sat and then the women. The teenaged cousins and small children would eat in the kitchen. Gyasi took the head of the table. His wife sat on one side and Josephine sat next to her mother. Rainey guessed he had the hot seat next to Gyasi.

"In your honor, we have prepared *ampesie*, which is boiled yam and unripe plantain. I'm sure you will enjoy roasted cassava, sugar, groundnut peanut and milk in *Gari*, and our delicacy in Ghana," he pointed, "is whitebait fish."

Rainey appreciated how insightful Gyasi was to take the time to explain the dishes served. He squinted at the tiny fish on the platter, no bigger than his pinkie. *Wait a minute. Were those...fish eyes? Had they not dissected their catch? Oh no.* He loved fish—smoked, grilled, fried, all without the eyeballs. He would graciously pass.

After Gyasi offered the prayer and everyone filled their plates, the inquisition began. "My Josephine has not mentioned your name until recently and you are here with the missions. How has your experience been so far?"

"A learning one..." Rainey was learning to hold his tongue in Ghana. He hoped he picked a safe topic. "What amazes me is the skill of the hawkers. They are so fluid in their movements with things on their heads. Fascinating. A couple of times, I purchased fruit that towered at least a foot on the top of one woman's head just to see how she would remove it to sell it."

Laughs and chuckles echoed around the table. Josephine's eyes spoke volumes, assuring him he was making a good impression with her family.

"And just think, my mother used dance lessons to help my sisters' poise and posture." Rainey said good naturedly.

"No brothers?" Gyasi asked, dabbing his mouth. Clearly, Josephine had mentioned very little about him.

"No, just two sisters. One is my twin, Josephine's friend."

She scrunched her nose at him in a tease. Without saying a word, Josephine had the skill to flirt and the power to make his heart beat faster.

"And what does your father do?"

Rainey's stomach dropped at Gyasi's question. Does one ever become comfortable answering the inquiry? "I come from a family of doctors." He paused, hoping the answer would suffice. It didn't.

"Is the elder Dr. Reynolds still practicing or retired?"

"Neither." Rainey took a deep breath, real deep. "He's incarcerated."

ʠ★ʠ

Josephine's heart ached for Rainey. She was not about to let him go through the pain alone. She knew first-hand how he struggled with Dr. Reynolds' fall from grace.

Mindful of her audience, she took a chance and reached across the table. Josephine clasped his hand, hoping her seemingly familiar touch would not be offensive to her elders as all eyes noted her gesture.

"This is most disturbing, Dr. Reynolds." Her father frowned with concern.

Josephine saw the questions forming in his mind. Glancing at Rainey, she squeezed his hand, not knowing what would come next.

The room was quiet as if the two men were strategizing their moves in Oware, a popular West African game where each opponent had forty-eight seeds to represent game pieces. The player who gathered at least twenty-five seeds from the other wins. So who would collect the most points? Would her father dare ask the circumstances, and would Rainey feel obliged to answer?

Gyasi faced her, seeking an explanation. She swallowed. *Uh-oh.*

"Were you aware of this Josephine Abena?"

"Yes, Papa."

He turned back to Rainey. The battle of the wills continued. When her father nodded, Josephine knew he had come to a decision. "What's your favorite sport?"

More than one sigh was audible. She admired Rainey for his desire to make a good impression, but she also knew he wasn't easily intimidated. Good for him—bad for her because she knew once he left, her family would grill her for the information.

For the next couple of hours, the topic shifted from sports, to food, then to international politics. Soon, the children became weary. Chad and Rainey jointly thanked the Amoah family for their hospitality.

Mindful of her actions, Josephine pulled Rainy aside. Holding her hand, he whispered, "I hope I didn't embarrass you, but it is what it is."

Interrupting them, her father extended his hand. Rainey accepted it. "Dr. Reynolds, it was nice meeting you. I hope we will see you again before you leave. Our church service begins at ten in the morning."

Josephine mumbled as her father walked away, "Again, that wasn't an invitation."

Rainey smirked. "There could be worse things, like he didn't want me to see you again. Goodnight." This time when he squeezed her hands, he held on a little longer.

"M'adwe."

Sooner than she wanted, Josephine was alone with her parents and Abigail. She braced herself for possible censure.

"Josephine, you care for him and he for you? I was praying for my daughters to marry good Ghanaian men, but I am comforted that Madeline has made a wise choice. Will you?" Her father phrased it to sound like a question. She knew it wasn't.

"Yes."

"Our daughter will follow her heart." Fafa patted her husband's hand. "If her heart is pure, God will give her the desires of her heart."

"Thank you, mum." Josephine thought that was the final word, but her father wasn't finished.

"What serious crime did his father commit to be sentenced to prison?" Gyasi demanded with a scowl.

How could she defend Rainey's honor? She waited a few minutes before she answered. "Murder."

"Murder?" her father asked, expressionless.

Her mother gasped. "I hope not with one of his patients."

"No, he confessed to being a drunk driver who hit my host family, Grandmother B's husband and left the scene of the crime." Suddenly, Josephine was angry that Rainey left her to clear up the confusion.

"Barbaric," her father murmured, then dismissed her.

Chapter 13

I was hoping you would call," Rainey said, fumbling with his cell phone. "Is everything okay?"

"Yes," Josephine said softly.

"I need more than that. What happened after I left?"

Emotionally drained, Josephine stretched out on her bed, then closed her eyes. Unfortunately with Rainey's calling card, they did not have the luxury of long meaningless conversation. Granted he'd purchased another one at the pharmacy the previous night, but there were never enough minutes for them. She sighed. "My father asked about Dr. Reynolds' charge and I told him. How serious do you want things to become between us?"

"Very serious, babe."

Babe. Josephine liked the sound of his endearments. "I'm not trying to lead you on—"

"Baby, neither one of us is playing a game, but the winner takes all."

She respected a man with confidence. He had plenty of that mixed with vulnerability. That's what attracted her, but she was also a realist. "Your home is in St. Louis. My home is in Accra."

"A minor inconvenience—for now. When I return home, I'm taking your heart with me because I'm leaving you mine."

His declarations continued until they both had to say goodnight.

❧❦

Rainey had not seen his Dentist Without Borders team since the Handi Children Outreach Home on Friday, but everyone eagerly accepted the invitation to attend Sunday morning worship at Jesus Church of Ghana on Mantse Nii Boi Street in Kaneshie.

Riding the trotro, the missionaries chatted about the children and their experiences.

As Badu advised they were minutes away, Rainey noted they had passed a mosque, and Catholic, Presbyterian and Apostolic churches.

Sitting next to Rainey, Thomas nudged him. "It looks like any street corner in America, huh?"

There is one Lord, one faith, and one baptism, Jesus spoke Ephesians 4:5, keeping Rainey from responding.

How? When the evidence of division was all around him.

God didn't answer, which made Rainey more curious.

Soon, the driver stopped in front of a large two story brown building. Absent was a steeple and stained glass windows. One by one, the team disembarked and followed the sound of music, leaving no doubt they were in the right place.

As they were about to clear the doorway, Thomas tried to get into the rhythm as he moved his body to the beat. He was unsuccessful. Rainey reined in his amusement. Inside, the open space could only be described as part auditorium and part banquet center.

Decorations were at a minimum. The cushioned chairs were stackable instead of immovable and the floor was concrete, definitely nothing fancy. Rainey spied out Josephine among the women dressed in colorful attractive attire. Although her clothing wasn't tight or revealing, it was wrapped around her body like a Greek goddess, an African princess...his temptress.

Unfortunately, he and Josephine had run out of face time. Early the next day, he and the volunteers would return to the States.

A whistle pierced the air, breaking Rainey's concentration. The offender was a woman who led others in an unconnected conga-style dance line. It was a sight he had never seen inside a church.

Josephine finally saw him. Her body swayed, not missing a beat as she made her way to him and his team. She mesmerized him as her arms danced in the air.

"*Akwaaba!*" she greeted him and the others. Then two women, acting as ushers directed them to seats near the back. Josephine had other ideas as she urged him toward the front where her family was standing and singing. They acknowledged him with a nod.

"You look so beautiful," Rainey said, a defeated man. This whole trip had been about him surrendering to his feelings. He succeeded. Each time she was near, their differences didn't seem to matter because he wanted her.

Trying to discard his inappropriate thoughts, Rainey began to clap his hands. He was clueless to the meaning of the words of the song.

"Close your eyes and you'll succumb to the rhythm," Josephine whispered.

Rainey complied.

"The words are simple," she continued in a hushed tone. "There is No One like Jesus...*Takwaba Uwaba Nga Yesu.*"

She was right as he relaxed. Soon, his body swayed to the beat, then he captured the words to repeat.

Too soon, the praise and worship segment ended to Rainey's surprised disappointment. Opening his eyes, he watched as a man stepped on the raised wooden platform and took the microphone. With a thick accent, he welcomed the congregation in English.

"I am Pastor Ted Yankson. Let's take a few minutes to give Jesus hand praise." The audience carried out his instructions in a thunderous applause. The pastor seemed fired up as he jogged in place. "I need people who will lift their voices in a shout to God in praise!" He cupped his ear.

Rainey wanted to cover his ears at the rowdy reply, akin to a sports event. He silently concentrated on his response. Merely saying, "Thank You, Jesus," didn't seem like it was enough. Yet, that's all he had within him.

"That's right, let's celebrate Jesus today because of Him and in Him we have salvation," Pastor Ted said with a grin. He bobbed his head as he waited for his congregation to quiet, then lifted his Bible. "Visitors, we welcome you today to our church for heart ministries. Did you know your salvation is near? It is present at this time, but you have to know the Word to receive it. Turn to Romans 10:8."

When Josephine scooted closer to share her Bible with him, she created a comfort zone, relaxing him. "Thanks."

"You are most welcome." Her lips curled in a smile.

"The eighth verse says, *'But what saith it? The word is nigh thee, even in thy mouth, and in thy heart: that is, the word of faith, which we preach.'* I'm preaching Jesus today..."

Despite the accent, Rainey listened with intensity.

"Faith begins in your heart that Jesus is God in the flesh and His sole purpose is to save you from yourself. You have to believe in His mission first. Once you accept that Jesus came to rescue you, then by any means necessary, you need to cross enemy lines."

Was there a war going on? Rainey wondered. Was there a battlefield he couldn't see? Had he been drafted and not known it? He held the questions at bay as he followed where the preacher was going with this.

Pastor Ted pounded the skeleton-thin podium. "That's right, if you call on the name of the Lord, which is Jesus, you shall be saved from the hands of the enemy. Paul reminded the Roman saints who were baptized in Jesus' name and filled with His Holy Ghost of that. During the Apostles' revival in the Book of Acts, they reminded them to continue to call on Jesus, walk with Him to maintain their salvation membership..."

Lifting his arms, Pastor Ted soon transitioned from preaching to closing. "Membership is free to join Team Jesus. I invite you to be on the Lord's side today. Take the first step toward salvation, confess with your mouth and heart your sins, then it's time to change uniforms. Remove your sin-stained garment for a white robe. Start with the baptism in Jesus' name..."

Something began to stir in Rainey's midst. He couldn't see it, but the intensity of a higher power was tangible. One by one, people around him started to submit to "it." On heighten alert, Rainey watched to see if anything out of the ordinary was about to take place. He didn't realize he had lifted his arms until soft whispers from Josephine encouraged him to praise God.

"Worship Him, Rainey."

The only problem was with all his education, degrees and status, Rainey didn't know how to do something so simplistic besides a hand clap. The only thing he could say was "God help me."

The praise around him took him to a secret place where his soul was at peace. When he later came to full awareness, Josephine's family and others had their hands stretched toward him, praying. Somewhat embarrassed, he composed himself and looked around for his teammates. Their eyes were closed, praying; others were sitting quietly in a manner of reflection.

When the service concluded, many bombarded the pastor for prayer. A few were led out and re-entered dressed in white garments. Rainey witnessed the baptism. He couldn't keep from wondering how that act was going to really change a person's life. It was too simplistic.

I died on the cross to make salvation simple, God whispered.

As Rainey tried to digest that, Gyasi appeared at his side and extended his hand. He accepted it, but his mind was still distracted by what God told him. "Please be our guest at dinner."

That request put Rainey on full alert. *Oh no, not again—round two.* Josephine shrugged. *Okay, no help from her.*

"*Medase.*" He didn't know which he would dread more, the food or the conversation. As everyone gathered their things to leave, Rainey knew he would soon find out.

Chapter 14

While feasting on fried yams and turkey tail, Rainey cautiously nibbled on hot spicy ground pepper seasoned kebabs. If the hot peppers hadn't burned a hole in his intestinal lining by the time he got home, he would pamper it with a week of bland dishes.

The atmosphere was once again festive and the conversations he could follow, engaging. Gyasi even insisted he sit next to Josephine this time. Relieved there was little discussion about his family, it appeared Rainey would survive dinner unscathed.

Gyasi chuckled at the exchange between his wife and Abigail. Sipping on his coconut juice, he faced Rainey. "I have visited your country several times and I have yet to understand the lack of unity among the brothers and sisters. The Black-on-Black violence in African American communities is inconceivable."

Was this a trick question, he wondered, *to draw him into a heated ethnicity debate?* As a family of socialites, the Reynolds always took a cautious approach when discussing racial and minority profiles. All eyes were on him for his opinion, including Josephine's.

How could Africans or any other ethnic group better understand the dynamics of African-Americans, than to acknowledge the atrocities of slavery, the humiliation of Jim Crow laws, the rejection of affirmative action, and the prejudices of other ethnic groups whose actions were racist, but vehemently deny they were? Rainey took his time.

"That's a fair question. Sociologists, politicians, and clergy-men have speculated probable causes and possible solutions to no avail. If I were to guess, maybe it boils down to hopelessness in a system of constant rejection until the victims begin to victimize themselves..."

Then he turned the tables so not to allow Gyasi to sugar-coat problems in his own backyard. "What about Africa's vio-lence, the genocide, the ethnic and religious wars. To African-Americans, those conflicts are primitive."

Gyasi snorted. He gave Josephine a pointed look before answering him. "Fascinating word 'primitive.' The United States is one of the richest, greatest and most powerful countries in the world, is it not? Yet the prevailing poverty rate in your inner cit-ies is primitive. An alarming thought."

The comparisons escalated until Josephine cleared her throat. "Dr. Reynolds and his team have an early flight in the morning and he probably needs to rest."

Good save. Rainey mouthed his thanks. Others agreed and began to stand. One by one, they wished him blessings. Gyasi extended his hand and so did Fafa.

Once Rainey had accepted Gyasi's dinner invitation, he called Chad and his host agreed to "retrieve" him at a certain time. That time was minutes away. At the door, he and Josephine had some private moments. "I will truly miss you," he told her, rubbing his hand against her cheek. She closed her eyes. "I will return soon if you don't come to me soon enough."

Fluttering her thick lashes, Josephine shook her head. Her lips formed an "o" to give some excuse Rainey probably didn't want to hear.

"Nothing is going to separate us—our love." He linked his fingers with hers.

Staring into his eyes, she whispered, *"Who shall separate us from the love of Christ? Shall tribulation, or distress, or persecution, or famine, or nakedness, or peril, or sword?"*

"What are you quoting?"

"Romans 8:35. Verses 38 and 39 say, *'for I am persuaded, that neither death, nor life, nor angels, nor principalities, nor powers, nor things present, nor things to come. Nor height, nor depth, nor any other creature, shall be able to separate us from the love of God, which is in Christ Jesus our Lord.'*"

The Book of Romans again. "Why did you think of that now?" Cheney did that. Sometimes his sister would interject scriptures when they conversed about subjects with no connection to the Bible.

"Nothing can separate me from God—nothing. It's not the ocean that separates us, but your heart. You're a good man, Dr. Rainey Reynolds, but…" She glanced away.

Touching her chin, Rainey made her meet his eyes. "But what?"

"You need Jesus. You have allowed situations and problems to separate yourself from Him. Cross enemy lines. That's important because if you want to pursue a relationship with me, then you're going to have to listen to God concerning me."

Verifying they did not have an audience, Rainey brushed his lips against hers "I agree." His answer had pleased her, which made him chuckle. When the doorbell rang, Rainey knew his time was up.

"Safe travels, Dr. Reynolds." Her eyes glazed as she turned from him. She nervously fumbled with the lock before the door opened.

"Sweet dreams, Josephine Abena Yaa Amoah." Rainey winked and then squeezed her hand. Once outside, he glanced back for his mind to flash one last image of Josephine to store in his memory. He would be recalling that memory in the days and weeks to come.

The ride to Chad's was sober. His host gave him space for his own thoughts and Rainey appreciated that. Back at the house, Rainey received gifts, hugs and blessings before his host family retired to bed.

In his brief stay, he hadn't expected to become attached to the people, the place or the food—well, some of it. His desire to get away and longing for Josephine brought him to the shores of Africa—slave castles and all. Now, he didn't want to leave.

Packing his things, Rainey eyed the mosquito net. Besides leaving his heart behind with Josephine, that thing was staying there.

When his cell phone rang, Rainey welcomed the distraction. "Hey, babe." It was good to know she was thinking about him, too.

"I know we said our goodbyes after dinner, but I'll be there when you depart in the morning," her voice was soft as if not to disturb a quiet night, but her declaration was strong.

"It's too early, baby. Get some rest."

"I will, but not tomorrow," she said in a clipped voice of finality. He loved when her sass overruled him in his favor. And he loved her.

"Then I look forward to seeing you soon."

"Yes. *Dayie.*"

"*Dayie,* baby." He would get one last chance to see and touch Josephine. The anticipation made his last night in the mosquito net tent worth it.

However, once he was secure within, Rainey was restless, he couldn't sleep. His mission of making his feelings known was accomplished. This was just the beginning. How will the ending play out? Then he thought about the scriptures Josephine quoted.

It wasn't a matter of Rainey surrendering to the Lord; it was Jesus acquitting him of some serious anger issues that had caused him to hate his ex, lash out at his sister and other acts that were so much unlike him that he was too ashamed to admit. He drifted off deep in thought.

Too soon Chad was nudging him awake, yawning. "Your transportation to the airport will be here shortly."

Drowsy, Rainey got his bearings before it registered that he had a flight to catch and his woman to kiss. With urgency, Rainey cleaned and dressed. Quietly, he placed his luggage by the door minutes before the minivan that contained his fellow mission workers parked at the curb.

"Please come back and visit when you return to Accra. You have been a most enjoyable guest," Chad said in a hushed manner so as not to wake his family. The two shook hands, then Rainey left.

Boarding the van, Rainey mumbled his good morning, claimed a spot, and allowed the bumpy ride to rock him back to sleep en route to Kotoka airport.

When the van stopped, Rainey scrambled out before the others, looking for Josephine. Since he was the last one on board, Rainey was the first to heave his luggage and walked hurriedly toward the terminal.

His Ghanaian beauty stood regally inside. Her bright smile and alert eyes mocked the sluggish passengers around them.

"*M'akye oo,*" he said for the final time in Twi, for who knew how long.

"Good morning," Josephine greeted in her signature English with an accent.

Rainey knew he didn't have much time. He took her hand. "You once said, 'Come to Africa.'"

She blinked. "When did I say that?"

"The day you enchanted me with tales about your country." He grinned, wondering if she remembered.

"At the library, during story hour?" she asked with a slight frown.

Rainey smoothed away the wrinkles with his finger. "Yes, but I took it personally. I came here for a purpose, and one of these trips I don't plan to leave without her."

Water blurred Josephine's eyes. "What if 'she' doesn't want to leave?"

"Besides the love of God, I believe there are other things that Jesus won't separate." Rainey glanced at his team. Thomas was waving, trying to get his attention. He sighed in frustration. "I have come to Africa. All I ask is that you try to come back to America."

"Rainey. Visas are not like going to your post office and buying a stamp. The process is tedious—"

"What can separate my love for you? I've been thinking about that scripture you quoted. I will be spending more time reading my Bible."

Lifting her hand to his lips, he kissed it, staring into her eyes, Rainey delivered his departing words, "And I'm a determined man, Josephine, very determined." He chanced a quick kiss and then backed away. "I love you."

Her eyes revealed she expected it, but it wasn't enough for either of them. Nodding his understanding, he picked up his luggage and walked away. He told himself not to look back, but he couldn't help it.

When he did, Josephine remained rooted in place. "I love you, too," she mouthed.

God, I don't know entirely what I have to do, but I don't want to be separated from her. After going through Customs and the security checkpoint, the team boarded the shuttle bus and sped toward the plane on the tarmac.

Rainey wasn't looking forward to going home. He could wait to see his mother, sisters, nieces, nephews, brothers-in-law, colleagues, patients and the list went on. His focus was on what—who—he was leaving behind that couldn't fit into a carryon.

Chapter 15

Josephine's vision blurred as Rainey's last expression held her captive. She couldn't move as she followed his retreating muscular figure. Although she was frozen in time, her heart shattered.

Trying to capture the remnants of Rainey's lingering cologne, Josephine inhaled quickly before the scent dissipated. With each breath came the realization that Rainey was gone. Wasn't this the part in some movies where the man rushes back and sweeps the American woman off her feet and into his arms, and they live happily ever after?

Although she didn't read romance novels, Abigail read plenty of them and regaled all her favorite scenes whether Josephine wanted to hear them or not. She would welcome a fairytale right now if Rainey was the prince and she was the damsel. She patted at her eyes and forced herself to turn around. Life went on even after love was found and possibly lost. Josephine failed to guard her heart.

A plane soared off in the distance. Josephine hastened her steps to a nearby window and checked the time—three-forty a.m. Rainey's flight would leave in twenty minutes. There was no reason to remain there, so she composed herself. Jutting her chin in the air, she left the premises. She would return home and crawl back into her bed. Josephine wanted to be asleep when the sun rose because it would mark day one of living without him.

৵৶

"Josephine...Josephine, wake up," Abigail's voice echoed above her. "Hurry. You're going to be late for your employer."

Pulling the covers tighter over her head, she groaned. "I will not work today. I'm sick."

"What is wrong?" Abigail sounded concerned.

"My heart is broken and it hurts."

"Oh sister..." she paused as Josephine recognized Abigail's approaching footsteps. "It is time to pray for a healing. Dr. Reynolds is gone?"

"*Yo.*"

They prayed and Josephine went back to bed. She stayed in her room most of the day, venturing out only to eat and then shower to return to bed for the night. Her family was kind enough to give her space.

Day two wasn't any better, but Josephine did not have the luxury of moping. She greeted her employer and coworkers with smiles. If only she could convince herself that she was happy.

Kim was not fooled. "It's not good for man to be alone. The Bible says so. Think about that if you think your doctor is replaceable," She almost pleaded before returning to her workstation.

Late that afternoon, Rainey emailed that he had arrived safely. "Thank You Jesus," she whispered. Although it was lengthy, one part gave her pause.

I mean it, Josephine. You can't expect a man in love to leave his precious jewel behind. Please check into a visa for traveling to the United States again. There is no turning back now—ever. Get ready, your doctor is in the house.

Rainey, a man on a mission.

Josephine sniffed then closed her eyes to memorize his words. She reflected on an African Proverb: *A fish and bird may fall in love but the two cannot build a home together.*

Ghana was home, and if—a big if—she should tempt fate and chance another visit to the States, she knew Rainey would do everything within his power to ensure that she never returned to Accra. She felt that in her heart, but without him it would be the torture of wanting something and knowing she couldn't have it.

One night before bed Josephine knelt. "Help me to pray, Jesus," she uttered.

Almost instantly, she felt the presence of the Lord fill her bedroom. Soon the power of the Holy Ghost began to stir from within her until an explosion of God's anointing filled her mouth and she began to speak in other tongues.

With tears streaming down her cheeks and her hands lifted high, Josephine listened to the godly language where the Holy Ghost was praying for her as in 1 Corinthian 14:2: *For he that speaks in an unknown tongue speaks not unto men, but unto God: for no man understands him; howbeit in the spirit he speaks mysteries.* Pumped every time she experienced the intimacy with the Lord, Josephine yielded the floor to Him.

I know the desires of your heart, God spoke to her spirit.

As the Tongues faded from her mouth, Josephine remained on her knees to absorb all the strength a good prayer left with her. At peace, she smiled and concluded with, "In Jesus' name. Amen."

When she opened her eyes, Abigail was sitting quietly in a chair with her head bowed. "In Jesus' name. Amen," her sister whispered.

Getting to her feet, Josephine stretched out her arms. "Where two or more are gathered in His Name, He shall be in the midst."

Abigail bobbed her head and hugged her. "Indeed. I would say Jesus showed up and showed out." They exchanged a hand clap. "Have you heard from the doctor?"

"Yes, every day. Sometimes, he sends more than one email. He loves me."

"And you love him." Abigail reminded her.

"*Yo*, of course. I just can't see how this will work."

"So what is the holdout—your stubborn mind? Doesn't your heart want it to work?" She kissed Josephine's cheek, and then left without waiting for an answer.

Although Josephine was confident and held firm to her convictions, one glimpse into Rainey's eyes, and she saw something stronger, fiercer than any African warrior that she had ever read about. So the question remained, "Should I or shouldn't I try to renew my visa?"

Sliding under the covers, Josephine decided to sleep on it.

Chapter 16

For almost a week after returning from Africa, Rainey fought jetlag. He had barely enough energy to go into his office every day to see back-to-back patients. When Rainey got home, he oftentimes crashed before eating dinner only to wake in the middle of the night famished.

The only constants in his life at the moment were emailing Josephine throughout the day and reading his Bible. Maybe his approach was too philosophical. Plus, God hadn't reached out to him again.

Of course his reclusive behavior didn't go unnoticed. "I'm glad I caught you before you left," Janae called his office minutes before the phone system switched to night service.

"Hey, sis. What's up?" Rainey waved goodnight to his staff as he pinched his phone between his ear and shoulder to grab his coat.

"Well, we haven't seen you since you've been back and mother is a little concerned because it's so unlike you—" Janae rambled on while Rainey locked his office and headed to the parking garage.

Too tired to be cordial or patient, Rainey interrupted her as he got behind the wheel of his Benz. "Janae, I'm still adjusting from my trip."

"Which brings me to my point…"

"Finally," Rainey mumbled.

"About your trip. Could your tiredness be connected in any way to early symptoms of malaria? You did mention to Mother about having chills a few days ago."

Malaria? That had been the farthest thing from his mind. It had been his major concern while in Africa. After his nightmare, Chad had suggested he switch to Malarone because the side effects were minimal. Since that prescribed dose was only for seven days after returning from Africa versus a month on the other, Rainey was almost finished.

Assuring Janae that he was fine, Rainey thought that was the end of it until his mother called minutes before he entered his condo through the garage door into his kitchen. *Thanks, Janae, for successfully scaring our mother.*

"Sweetheart, I really advise that you contact your family doctor. A blood test should confirm or alleviate any concerns about malaria," his mother stated as if he wasn't aware of the procedure.

Since to Gayle Reynolds it sounded too clinical, she had to mention it to his father who gave his wife the dictation. *Great.* As a dutiful son, so as not to put more burdens on his family, he called his physician.

A few days later to everyone's relief, including himself, his blood work came back normal. "You are in good shape," Dr. Wilson stated over the phone.

"Take your vitamins, eat healthy and get plenty of rest. If you don't feel better in a week, then make another appointment. Otherwise, you should live another seventy years," he joked before disconnecting their call.

A few days later after following his doctor's order, Rainey woke with renewed energy. Whistling, he padded into his master shower and dressed before his housekeeper arrived for her weekly cleaning. If there was any hint that Miss Hazel's—a name to match the color of her eyes—employer was under the weather, she would whip him one of her old-fashioned Southern-style stews. Maybe, he could feign a few coughs, throat clearing or sneezes.

Twenty minutes later, Rainey was making a cup of Espresso when Miss Hazel rang the doorbell three times—her signature announcement—then proceeded through inside, using her key.

"Yoo who? Good morning, Dr. Reynolds?" The older thin-framed woman's voice echoed throughout the condo as she closed the front door.

"I'm in the kitchen."

Rainey turned around to greet her as she neared the marble countertop that served as a divider between his kitchen and family room.

"*Makyeoo*, Miss Hazel. That's good morning in Twi."

"Good morning to you, too, Doctor. I guess I don't need to ask how your trip was. You're tanned and you seem to be in good health. Thank God for bringing you back safely." She nodded. The woman always arrived in freshly pressed coordinated sweats, but always toted an oversized vintage designed shopping bag to carry her "work clothes." She began to pull out a dingy t-shirt and faded jeans.

"Yes, thank the Lord." His mind immediately thought of Josephine as he took a seat, then Miss Hazel joined him as if she needed a break before she worked.

From the kitchen design to every accessory in place, his mother and Janae insisted the décor be a reflection of their bourgeois class. As a busy bachelor, Rainey didn't protest. In earnest, all he needed was hot meals—home cooked or takeout. He thought about the Ghanaian cuisine he shared with Josephine.

"And God bless you for volunteering your time to help those less fortunate..." Miss Hazel said.

The mission work. "Yes, there is a need. I plan to return in a month or sooner. I have to rearrange some things," Rainey said and chanced a sip of the hot brew. "Besides providing dental services, we had down time to experience the culture. I had the prettiest Ghanaian woman as my tour guide." He winked and took another sip.

"You don't say." Miss Hazel's eyes sparkled with her knowing smile. Not one to pry into his personal affairs, she wouldn't ask. That didn't mean she didn't want to know and if he started talking, Miss Hazel would listen.

When Rainey wasn't forthcoming on more tidbits, she disappeared into his guest bathroom to change out of her "street" clothes. Torn between amusement and chastisement for teasing his longtime housekeeper, he was about to share details about his love interest when his home phone rang.

He checked the caller ID—Cheney. Rainey knew his twin had been holding her peace about what happened between him and Josephine. He had planned to call her sooner, but he would soon put her out of her nosey misery. He chuckled. "Hey, Twin."

"Hi, big brother," Cheney said cheerfully. "Ooh."

"What's the matter?" Rainey went on guard.

She giggled. "It's your next niece or nephew. I thought I felt the baby fluttering. Maybe she—I'm hoping for a girl—wants to say hi to Uncle Rainey."

Rainey snickered. "How far along are you again?"

"Almost twelve weeks. I know it's too soon, but these babies come here advanced." For the next few minutes, Cheney brought him up to speed on the Jamieson clan antics, then switched to talking about the new baby. Knowing his sister, she was probably glowing about being a mother again. "I wish Daddy was here." She sighed.

Setting his mug on the counter, Rainey stared out the window. "Me, too." His father would want Cheney to take care of herself, and expected the rest of the family to make sure that happened. "I know Parke is making sure you get your rest."

"That man acts like it's our first one," Cheney complained, she thrived on her doting husband's attention.

"If Dad were here, he would tell you every pregnancy is different."

"True, so," she paused, "tell me about Ghana...no tell me about Josephine first. Was she surprised to see you? Did you two settle your differences? Is she fat?"

"Fat? Are you kidding me? She's proportioned perfectly."

"Fat isn't obese in Ghanaian culture. It means healthy. I hope you didn't call her skinny. Anyway, did you visit the slave castle?"

Rainey growled. "Yes, I visit that dungeon. Once I recovered from my anger and disgust, I became curious about our ancestry. What has Parke discovered about the Reynolds?"

"Quite a bit. Finally, someone in the Reynolds family who wants to know about our heritage. You'll have to talk to my genealogy guru husband, though. No one can tell the stories like Parke with all his theatrics. You're planning on going to Mom's house Sunday for dinner, aren't you?"

"I wouldn't miss it. Plus, I have gifts for everyone."

"Stop evading the question. What happened between you and Josephine? Did you kiss and make up?"

"You've never known me to kiss and tell. See you later." He barked his amusement and disconnected. Then once Rainey thought about it, he became annoyed. The problem was, he didn't get enough kisses to tell about.

Miss Hazel's off key humming traveled from room to room as she dusted and vacuumed throughout his three-bedroom condo. Once she was in her zone—as she called it—she didn't like to be interrupted. They could talk later.

Making himself an omelet, Rainey added an extra dash of red pepper. Not that he had acquired the taste, but wanted to hold on to more memories of Ghana and Josephine for as long as possible.

Next, he paid bills online and returned calls. The upcoming weeks would be just as hectic as this one with double-booked appointments and attending an all-day seminar on orthodontics.

Before he signed off his laptop, he emailed Josephine. *I'll never get you out of my system. I miss you and I miss Ghana. I'm willing to try and make this work between us, are you? Love, Rainey.*

Sunday evening at his mother's house, Rainey received a hero's welcome. There was no place like home. When his brothers-in-law offered him a handshake, Rainey thought about Gyasi, which in turn evoked images of his lovely daughter. He wished Josephine was there.

The children screamed when Rainey held up his bags. He made a ceremony out of passing out the presents, telling them what he saw, where he visited, and why each person got what gifts.

After the impromptu presentation, his mother instructed everyone to wash up to eat. Washing his hands in the sink brought back more memories: Chad and his family's community cleansing. Janae would have fainted.

His brothers-in-law, Bryce and Parke, had prepared a feast. The men placed the platters of chicken, pasta, green beans with potatoes and rolls on the table. It was too much food even with the children.

Bryce planted a kiss on Janae's cheek and she blushed, which had become a rarity as if she pushed happiness away. She didn't hide her irritability as one by one, family members strengthened their ties with God. To her, a conversion couldn't hide the shame of the slur campaign against her family's pristine image.

Not to be outdone, Parke lingered on Cheney's lips and patted her protruding stomach until his mother cleared her throat. "Children, there are children present." The adults laughed at the play on words.

In honor of his return, his mother asked him to bless the food. Bowing his head, Rainey reflected on how Gyasi said grace. Rainey felt the urge to duplicate those heartfelt words. "Father in the name of Jesus, thank You for this food, the chefs who prepared it and my family gathered today as well as Dad who is here in spirit..."

"Seven months, three weeks," Gayle added.

"Yes, bless our father, protect him and accelerate his time spent so he can return to us and say grace again. Please sanctify our food and bless it in Jesus' name. Amen," Rainey finished.

"Amen," murmurs circulated around the table.

Janae lifted a brow. "You really got into it. For a moment, I thought it was Daddy. Great job mimicking."

Not sure if it was a genuine compliment or snide remark, Rainey accepted it at face value.

"Ooh." Cheney moaned between nibbles. "I'm telling you, either I'm farther along or your child will be a natural born swimmer." She teasingly said to Parke.

As was customary, everyone shared what was going on in their lives, whether it was business or a new toy; everybody had a few minutes of fame as far as his mother was concerned. Once dinner was finished, the adults moved to the living room where the gas log in the fireplace radiated its warm.

The children cleared the table. His bossy nieces, Kami and Natalie were the supervisors over the boys. There was definitely something wrong with that picture.

"I envy you, Rainey," Parke said as he stretched his arm around Cheney's back. "You were so close to my ancestral land of Cote d'Ivoire. I can't wait to take my family there."

"Ghana is scenic. It's as metropolitan as New York City and as colonial as the first pilgrims to America." Resting an ankle on his knee, Rainey relaxed against the back of the sofa next to his mother. "So you're what, ten generations removed from a King?"

Parke nodded.

"Hold up." Cheney leaned forward. "Before you get my husband started, what's going to happen between you and Josephine? All I got out of you is that you two made up." Lifting a brow, Cheney slowly snuggled deeper into the protective custody of Parke's arm.

"Considering we're living on two separate continents, it's not like we can go to the movies on Friday, but I'm working on it."

"Maybe my husband can give you needed lessons. I didn't even want to be wooed, yet here I am," Cheney advised.

"She played hard to get," Parke teased as Cheney elbowed him.

"Hey, they say every woman needs a fairytale, and in my novel, she chased me," Parke defended.

Shaking his head, Rainey watched the two lovebirds with at least ten years of marriage act like they hadn't left their honeymoon. Janae and Bryce had been married a few years longer. Bryce was a good guy, but Janae was letting their father's imprisonment take a toll on their marriage needlessly. Humility was never fashionable for any of them, but Janae was taking it to the extreme.

That was too bad. Rainey refused to let the past haunt him. He was moving on and for good. Ignoring his twin's question, he redirected the conversation back to his ancestry. "Parke, what have you found out about our family history?"

"On your mother's side, it was tricky. She's from four generations of twins, and they altered some parts of their names on every census. That's not usual, but amusing. Such as Rhoda also went by Lena, her twin Paul once was listed as Burly. Get this, Genevieve and Floyd were called Snake and Rattle," Parke stated from memory.

The room erupted in laughter. Gayle wiped at her tears.

"Of course there was Ellis and Louis, who happened to be the only male set and finally, Major and Solomon. There was no guessing the inspiration behind those names." Releasing his hold on Cheney, Parke got comfortable. "Now, your father's side was more interesting."

Cheney feigned boredom as she yawned. Janae rolled her eyes. "What's the point?"

Rainey cast Janae a stern look. "Sis, do you always have to be so disagreeable?" He raised his hand. "Don't answer that." Then he cut Janae some slack. Until recently, he wasn't too interested either. It was yet another remnant of his visit to Ghana. "I became interested after I visited the Elmira slave castle. Now I want to know about our ancestors."

Parke reached for his tablet and began to touch icons to open files. "I was able to trace your eighth great grandfather, Hyden—possibly Hayden—Williams, to a prison in Prince William County in Virginia in 1834."

This was not what Rainey wanted to hear. He was a descendant of outlaws.

"What did he do?" Bryce asked.

"What other folks did when they refused to be enslaved. He was jailed for being a runaway." Parke shrugged.

"Good for great grandfather." Rainey exchanged a high five with Bryce.

"But it's what happens next that I find amusing," Parke continued. "Sheriff Deputy Basil Brawner sold him to a man, acting as an agent for an unnamed slave trader. When the trader showed up to collect his new slave, he took one look at Hyden and refused to pay.

"Then the sheriff deputy paid another slave trader, who was on his way to Fredericksburg and Richmond, to sell Hyden. No one wanted him either."

"What was wrong with our great-grandfather?" Janae asked, suddenly interested.

"Are you ready for this?" Parke paused and imitated a drum roll. "It appears Mr. Williams was too White."

The room busted into cackling. Cheney held her stomach. Rainey smirked. He had to give Parke his props; he was the master storyteller.

"There's more." Parke waited for everyone to quiet down. "The second slave trader got frustrated and returned him back to the deputy sheriff who took him to Brentsville and tried to sell him on a court day. The sheriff struck out, too. It was a blessing for Hyden because no one wanted to make an offer, because his color was too light and that would make it too easy to escape from slavery and pass himself off as a free man."

"Can you imagine he would want to do that?" Cheney smirked.

"And as expected, your eighth-great grandfather did escape." Parke hooted with the others. "As it happened, Hyden did escape, and the deputy sheriff went to court to seek compensation for apprehending him, confining him and advertising his sale. Hyden ended up in New York and changed his last name to Reynolds. And there you have it. Truth is stranger than fiction. I couldn't make this stuff up." Parke stood and bowed to a thunderous applause for his theatrics.

"Serves them right," Cheney said. High fives went around the room as Parke shared more information about generations that followed Hyden Reynolds.

The family wanted more tales and Parke pulled up one document after the other to verify everything he told them. Too soon, it was time for everyone to say their goodbyes and get their families home and children ready for school the next day. Rainey hugged his twin. "I appreciate your husband looking that up and I know there is more information to uncover, but something else changed for me while I was in Ghana."

"Besides Josephine?" Cheney teased.

Rainey nodded. "You won't have to invite me to church anymore. Isn't there always an open invitation?"

She burst out in tears as she wrapped her arms around his neck. "Praise God. Praise God. Thank You, Jesus," Cheney whispered. Overhearing, Parke gave him a pat on his back.

"Okay, I'll see you next Sunday." Rainey walked out the front door and got into his car. As his engine purred to life, Rainey thought about that nightmare. There was no way he was going to get caught off guard and burn in hell. He was about to cross enemy lines. It was time to surrender.

Chapter 17

Exactly who was in control? Josephine pondered as her head-strong mind matched wits against her yearning heart. For the past couple of weeks, all she could think about was Rainey—his smile, the way he listened to her every word and his possessive touches.

Out of sight, out of her mind didn't work. Rainey's endearing emails made sure of that. Thank God she had a distraction.

"I am so excited for Rose," Fafa drew Josephine's mind back to the dinner conversation. "We weren't sure if God was going to bless her womb after almost a year of marriage."

"*Yo*," Josephine and Abigail said in unison.

Rose was Josephine's second cousin. Growing up they were close like sisters until Rose married, then her focus turned to her husband, Frank.

"I hope Madeline will not have delays in making me an *impaa*," her father stated.

"And me a *nana baa*," her mother added, beaming. Her mother had wished for more children, especially sons. The Lord didn't grant that.

But babies were babies and Josephine's family loved them. Rose had delivered a baby girl seven days earlier on Sunday. Any girl born on a Sunday was named Akosua in Twi. On the eighth day, before sunrise under the West African tradition, Akosua's official naming celebration would take place. Unless the Lord gathered the baby's soul back to Him.

So for seven days, no one planned baby showers or baby shopping sprees. If Akosua survived, then family, friends, villagers, those nearby and afar would come to celebrate the new life with drummers, food, and dancing. One by one, the elders would cuddle the infant until the eldest took possession and stood by the parents.

Josephine could hardly wait. It was all her family talked about. After dinner, they all retired early to rest for the morning ceremony. "Are you going to check your email before you go to bed?" Abigail asked, coming into Josephine's bedroom.

"No, not tonight, then I would not get sleep. If Rainey is online, then he would engage me in back and forth emails. I'm already excited about seeing the baby."

Abigail sat next to Josephine, then rested her head on Josephine's shoulder.

It was torture not to check for a message from him, but she gave herself an excuse. "I love him so much."

"Hmm. Soon daily emails and weekly phone chats will not be enough."

Josephine sighed. "I know. Enough about my emotions. Let us rest tonight so we can celebrate with Rose tomorrow."

Abigail agreed and went into her own room. Josephine said her prayers and got in bed. Too soon mother's voice urged her awake. "Let us hurry. The water pressure is low. We should use it before it runs out."

In no time, the Amoahs were dressed in their best garb and made it out the house before they ran out of water. The last time she was up this early was to see Rainey off at the airport. She was fighting a losing battle. Rainey might be thousands of miles away, but almost every thought would eventually find its way to a memory.

The drive to the Maamobi was a short distance away in an area considered an unplanned neighborhood because of its rapid growth, but it was maintained.

Several cars were already parked inside the gated yard. Inside the home, Josephine greeted her elders and others. She hugged and congratulated Rose. Peeping over a couple of shoulders, she was able to see her newest *sewaa,* the youngest cousin in the family.

Akosua was breathtakingly beautiful with rich brown skin. When she opened her eyes, they were alert with a blue hue emitting from the iris before closing again. Josephine's heart swelled with pride as a hand slapping the drum began the ceremony. Soon the festivities would kick into high gear.

Her eldest great uncle lifted Akosua up in his arms and began to pray.

Unfortunately, some elders in her family still believed in the deities, but Josephine and others who had been converted in Jesus' name, called on the Lord Jesus. "What will be Akosua's given name?" he asked Frank, once he finished the prayer.

The climax of the celebration was learning the given name. The father always named the child after an ancestor, honorable leader, Biblical name, or anyone the parents deemed a role model.

Rose glanced as her husband who barely took his eyes off of his daughter. "She is to be called Beatrice."

Beatrice. Josephine smiled. Beatrice Tilley Beacon aka Grandma BB would be proud. Although she questioned Grandma BB's honorable and leadership qualities, it was the infamous stunts she was known for. Of course, Beatrice also reminded her of Rainey, another memory that found its way back to the man who held her heart.

✂∽

Tuesday morning, Josephine struggled to get out the bed for work. There was nothing like celebrating life, but the hangover would be felt for days—no strong drink needed. It would be a short week anyway.

In two days, her family would be en route to Calvary Temple Church in London. If Madeline's African ceremony was any indication, Josephine expected the British affair to be lavish, judging from the eye-stopping photos of her white wedding dress and the elegant bridesmaid dresses Madeline emailed. Her sister acted as if she hadn't already been married for three months.

Josephine knelt to pray. She asked for nothing. Her heart was too full over the life of her new little cousin, so she just praised God. Next, she gathered her clothes to shower. *Beatrice.* She shook her head.

Afterward, Josephine logged onto her computer, hoping for a quick one liner from Rainey—nothing, but three messages from Madeline. Scanning the others, an email from Cheney with *What have you done to my brother?* The subject line put Josephine on alert. She opened it immediately.

Praise the Lord my sister and friend.

Good news from the family. When you get a chance, clink on the link. FYI warning, Grandma BB and Imani are making plans to visit soon. The whole continent of Africa isn't ready for those two. I am soooo jealous! Anyway, click on the link.

Love,

Cheney

Josephine stared. What about Rainey? Odd. She followed the instructions and opened the link.

It was a video of a church service—Parke and Cheney's pastor, Baylor Scott, was conducting the altar call. Although the audio was muffled at times, Josephine heard most of the words.

"Don't let your pride, family, job, or the devil himself, separate you from the love of God. Come today. Repent of your sins—the ones you remember and those you want to forget. The good news is despite God's perfect record keeping, He's waiting to acquit you. Don't take a chance that your name won't be listed in the Book of Life, according to Revelation 20. Be baptized in the name of Jesus and He will arm you with the Holy Ghost, with power to withstand the devil's trickery. Come on." Pastor Scott waved his arm. "You don't need an appointment. Jesus is standing by."

Experiencing the presence of the Lord, Josephine was momentarily transformed to the sanctuary. The anointing never expired. It was actually amazing that God ordained the foolishness of preaching to save people, even if only one soul repented. It still was evidence that the Blood of Jesus never lost Its power.

She gnawed on her lips as she watched the clock. Although she was dressed, she had yet to eat. She would definitely bless a hawker this morning. Several people hurried down the aisle for salvation. Josephine pumped her fist in the air. "Yes!"

"Hallelujah, Jesus!" She recognized Cheney's voice in the background. She gasped when she identified the arrogant swag as belonging to Rainey. He was actually making his way to a minister waiting at the altar.

Grabbing her cell phone, she alternated between texting her employer and watching her computer screen. Unfortunately, I will be an hour or so tardy, but I will make up my time before going home this evening.

She hit send and refocused on the altar call. At least six baptismal candidates stood on the platform above the pool when Rainey joined them. Gone was his nice tailored suit, exchanged for a white t-shirt and pants.

As he descended into the water, her vision blurred. The minister instructed Rainey to cross his arms. Josephine heard a sniff. Was that from Cheney on tape, or her?

"My dear brother, upon the confession of your faith and the confidence we have in the blessed Word of God concerning His death, burial and grand resurrection, I indeed baptize you in the name of Jesus for the remission of your sins and God will fill you with His Spirit."

The minister tugged the back of Rainey's t-shirt until he was submerged and just as quickly, pulled him forward. A tear slid down Josephine's face. This time it was Rainey who pumped a fist in the air.

"He's free," Josephine whispered as she recalled the scripture in Isaiah 61 where the captives were released from the devil's clutches.

Her spirit rejoiced with Rainey. The Holy Ghost took swift control of Josephine's mouth in a private conversation between her and God. She was caught up in spontaneous worship as she thanked Him for Rainey's soul and the others that wanted a change in their life.

"What's wrong?" Abigail asked, poking her head inside the bedroom.

Tapping on the screen, Josephine tried to compose herself.

Coming closer, Abigail rewound the video until she could figure out what was going on, then her hand went up in the air as a praise wave to the Lord. A chime alerted Josephine to a new email. More in control now, she checked her inbox. It was from Cheney. Subject line: *Praise report.* She opened it.

God filled Rainey with the Holy Ghost late last night. Praise the Lord, one sibling down, one more to go and I'm sure Janae will be kicking and screaming before she repents.

Abigail was peering over Josephine's shoulder, reading it at the same time.

Turning around, Josephine gave her sister a high five. "I can't wait to hear about his Holy Ghost experience."

Her computer alerted her to another email. Josephine twirled around. It was from Madeline.

"Aren't you going to open it?" Abigail asked.

Shaking her head, Josephine signed off. "Not now. Later. I've had enough excitement for one day."

Her sister muffled a childish giggle. "We can talk on the way. I've got a late class and you need to get to your employer."

They hurried to get in line for the trotro. The vendors seemed to be in full force. Recently on the newscast, officials were debating if hawkers and peddlers were taking over the sidewalk and in front of businesses. Politicians threatened to crack down, citing safety concerns. Josephine disagreed. Life taught her that all opportunities weren't equal: neither an education nor steady good employment, so she and Abigail patronized two hawkers.

Once the sisters were crammed into a rear seat, Abigail pried, "Does Rainey's salvation mean you no longer have hesitations about commitment with him?"

Josephine wished it were that simple. "It was a matter of time before he surrendered. Too many people were praying and planting seeds for him not to grow in the Lord. Others came by and sprinkled water on that seed and finally, God caused the increase."

"Excellent."

"Yes, but there is no commuter rail between Africa and America. I happen to love my country with all its good, bad, and ugly—it's home. In America, I would be mistreated as if I were a

Black American, which I'm not. I want no part of that stigma—I'm African," Josephine boasted proudly.

"You do have a point. If someone is going to deny me access to housing or employment, I want it to be for legit reasons not because of pre-conceived notions based on my skin. God gave us this beauty." Abigail *tsk*ed and folded her arms. "That is so disappointing."

Josephine agreed as she bit into her mango. "I know. Who wants to live under those conditions?"

"I'm speaking of your refusal to fight for love," Abigail corrected her assumption.

Turning in the confined seat, she eyed her sister. "Did you not listen to how Blacks are ill-treated?"

"I heard you say that God has redeemed Rainey with the Blood and filled him with the Holy Ghost, and he loves you and—"

"What conversation have you been listening to?"

"Yours. Since the day you told me Dr. Reynolds was coming to Ghana for a mission trip, your world hasn't been the same. I believe in fairy tales." Abigail didn't say another word about Rainey during the remainder of the ride to the campus.

Chapter 18

Josephine and Rainey weren't in sync. They were on one accord spiritually, but suddenly their schedules conflicted, or a power outage struck the night they were supposed to Skype. The obstacles were becoming endless.

She still coveted Rainey's emails, but she wanted to hear the jubilation in his voice about his Holy Ghost experience. Unfortunately, this weekend she would be unavailable as she and her family traveled to London.

Settling in her window seat on the plane, Josephine clicked her seatbelt. She stared out the window to recall one of Rainey's emails.

I did it, Babe. It was so easy, so simple to be saved. As Cheney's pastor preached about being separated from God, I had a flashback to that nightmare I told you about. Then the choice was clear. Live with Jesus or live without Him, burning in my sins. I had to cross enemy lines.

I know my twin tried to explain her salvation to me, but it was as if the Lord sent me to you for your pastor to drive it home. God, I love you and I hope to see you soon and wrap my arms around you. I'm still trying to find the loophole in your culture about the kissing part. Did I say I miss you?

"I miss you, too," Josephine whispered, praising God for the increase in Rainey's faith.

Maybe it was a blessing that the United States had instituted greater restrictions on its visas than England. Otherwise, after she witnessed Rainey's Nicodemus moment, nothing would have held her back from going to America and being a part of his salvation celebration.

"What?" Abigail nudged her.

Eying her sister's grin, Josephine blushed from embarrassment. She didn't want to entertain those thoughts that could turn into lust when she saw him again.

"You are so going down, sister." Abigail lifted a brow. "It's part of the fairytale."

Jutting her chin, Josephine didn't think so. "God can keep me from falling and…

"Present us faultless before the all wise and knowing God," Abigail recited Jude 1:24 in unison with her.

Josephine played it safe and pulled out a magazine she had purchased in the terminal. She read it from cover to cover as a diversion, but it seemed as if every article and picture somehow found its way to Rainey until she finally drifted off.

Six and a half hours later, her family landed in London. Her new brother-in-law, Dennis Harper, had a limousine waiting for them. When the Amoahs arrived at their five bedroom palatial home, it was buzzing with activity for the reception following the nuptials that would take place in two days.

"*Akwaaba!*" Madeline beamed. Her African dark skin glowed in the soft pastel sleeveless sundress. She proceeded to kiss their grandparents, parents, sisters and the handful of cousins that accompanied them.

She and Dennis gave them a tour, dodging staffers along the way, before showing everyone their room. "Dennis will sleep on a makeshift bed in the study the night before our wedding. He's not supposed to see his bride." She teased while Dennis didn't look amused.

Although Josephine had never seen her sister so happy, the couple had already been married three months and had seen more than anybody else present. Shaking her head at the absurdity, she had told her sister as much.

"I agree with Madeline." Abigail added, "I think it is romantic….the anticipation of the kiss, the hug…" She sighed, caught up in the moment as if she was an actress.

Josephine rolled her eyes while Madeline laughed.

As fatigue began to claim them after their long flight began, one by one, the family retired to their appointed rooms. Most were still sleeping when the women were up bright and early the next morning for a day of shopping on Oxford Street.

They returned hours later after spending a ridiculous amount of time and money at Fenwick. Her mother and Abigail feigned exhaustion, and went for a nap. Josephine could have used one, too. Instead she pulled Madeline away from her husband for a private chat. Neither seemed happy about her interruption.

Dennis was an inch or two taller than Madeline's five-eight height. He sported a bald head, a contrast to his thick black mustache. His skin-tone reminded her of peanut butter. A polished and educated man, he was handsome enough, but not as handsome as Rainey. No matter what she did, saw or heard, everything always came back to the man she loved.

"Just a few minutes, Dennis, then I will return her." Josephine hadn't let go of Madeline's arm so she could make a quick escape.

"Take your time. I know she misses you and is glad you're here," Dennis said.

After planting one more kiss on her husband's lips, Madeline ushered Josephine through the kitchen to a closed-in garden.

Beauty surrounded them as they relaxed in adjacent recliners. The housekeeper appeared with a fruit platter and two glasses of iced tea. The sisters thanked her.

"How do you make this seem so easy and seamless." Josephine waved her arm in the air.

Madeline ceased sipping from her glass. The confusion was evident on her face. "What?"

"Your marriage," she whispered. "I know you miss home. Your husband stated as much." She was clueless how Madeline could be satisfied without family near.

Her sister didn't hesitate answering. "I do miss home at times, I suppose, but I am far from lonely. Dennis makes sure I am content by smothering me with his love. When I return to Accra soon, Dennis will be by my side."

Despite her intelligence, Josephine could not comprehend Madeline's stance. There was not one day when she lived in the States that she didn't think about home—her parents, grandparents, and cousins. While observing African-Americans in America, Josephine measured everything against her own Ghanaian culture.

Didn't her sister feel one ounce of allegiance to her homeland? Madeline cast an odd expression her way, as if she was reading Josephine's thoughts.

"You underestimate the power of our love. I've never been so happy. By the grace of God, I'm living a fairy tale..."

There's that word again. *Life is not a fairy tale!* she wanted to scream.

"...and it's not because of all the possessions you see around me, but Dennis' love that possesses me."

Her sister's words, smiles and animated gestures had her almost persuaded that love conquered all—well Christ's love, anyway. Madeline's love was tangible.

"Dennis loved Jesus first and when he found me, he matched my stubbornness with a spiritual strength that overpowered me. I was forced to concede."

"How can anybody forget your refusal to graduate from baby's milk to solid food in Christ?" Josephine laughed at the memories. Madeline's mantra was, 'God is enough and working in God's vineyard is optional'.

"I know. I know the Nicodemus moment was truly indescribable. Dennis wouldn't have a wife any other way. I'm glad he persisted in showing me God's love first." Madeline seemed reflective. "So from the nation that celebrates, I'm excited about celebrating my marriage as much as I can. Our love is consuming."

"What is the saying, 'You're still on your honeymoon'?"

"For a lifetime." Madeline boasted a magnificent smile.

Ignoring her drink, she touched Josephine's hand. "What is disturbing you? This isn't all about me, is it? I know you want my happiness. What has frightened you Abena?"

The future, she wanted to say. Seeing her sister's contentment stirred something within Josephine until she sniffed. "You gave up so much to be with Dennis."

"You should have seen how much he gave up for me, and I'm not talking moneywise. I'm—as the saying goes—a pure diva." Madeline winked.

The more her sister spoke, the more Josephine had to rebuke her insecurities. They stole a few more minutes, laughing at childhood memories, Madeline telling her about Ghanaian hot spots in London and food.

Josephine wasn't ready when her husband came to retrieve his wife. With the others awake and refreshed, they prepared for dinner. After they ate, Dennis announced he had opted for a night in a hotel suite instead of sleeping under the same roof without his wife.

No one gave him any pity for his discomfort as they waved him goodnight. On the wedding day, as a bridesmaid, Josephine was escorted down the church's center aisle to her post at the altar. Abigail followed, then one of Dennis' two sisters. When Madeline made her entrance with their father, Josephine glanced at Dennis. His loving smile couldn't compare with Rainey's alluring smirk.

She heard Abigail sigh behind her. As her brother-in-law reached for Madeline, Gyasi acted as if he wouldn't release his eldest daughter. Her father's stunt amused the guests. The stalemate only lasted seconds before her father kissed Madeline's cheek and securely placed her hand in her husband's.

The pastor's voice commanded everyone's attention as the music faded. "Since this is a rededication of the Harpers' vows, the couple has written expressions of love to share." He nodded at Dennis to begin, who was staring at Madeline with such awe.

"Madeline, thank you for agreeing to be my wife. What we have begun, I pray to God we finish until our last breath … " Josephine couldn't catch all of what Dennis confessed, because he choked a few times, but the words she heard were eloquent. More than once, Dennis wiped at Madeline's tears.

Josephine sighed as she scanned the sanctuary. Most couples scooted closer. The single women in attendance had a look of yearning that had to be reflected in her own eyes. Soon it was Madeline's turn. "Dennis, I love you. I thought I was satisfied with my life until you walked into … "

It was as if her sister's declaration was plucked out of Josephine's heart. She was satisfied with her life, but Josephine still longed for Rainey. *Would I trade it all for love? Would I?* The rest of the ceremony was a blur. One thing was for sure, as the saying of Missouri's "Show-me" state, Rainey would have to show her that he was worth leaving everything for.

Chapter 19

"You've been missing in action since your return from Africa." Dr. Shane Maxwell chided Rainey in a phone call early Saturday morning. He had just finished reading his Bible scripture for the day and was mulling over James 4:3: *Ye ask, and receive not, because ye ask amiss, that ye may consume it upon your lust.*

Rainey's only request lately was for Jesus to bring him and Josephine together. As far as lusts...he still worked on that one. Maybe that was throwing his prayer off.

"No defense?" Shane prompted.

Snapping out of his reverie, Rainey apologized. "I'm sorry, man. I've been exhausted from seeing patient after patient since I've come home. Plus, we spoke at the conference last week."

"If I recall correctly, which I always do, besides discussing streamlining office expenses, the newest trends in applications, and more, our colleagues were more impressed with a Black man getting an African tan in the middle of a St. Louis winter. Of course, you couldn't resist regaling them with your missions work in Africa … "

Unfazed by his friend's tirade, Rainey interjected, "You have to admit the attention allowed me to get donation commitments for Dentist Without Borders,"

"Right, you and I both know it was just a cover."

"Guilty at first, but things have changed. You're right to call me out on not communicating with you one on one since I've been back. Josephine's in London this weekend, so I'm free to bring you up to speed."

"How convenient that you have an opening in your schedule to see me."

Dismissing Shane's sarcasm, Rainey tried to placate him. "Tell you what. I had planned to hit the gym at the athletic club this morning and relax the rest of the day. What are your plans?" He stretched and rolled his shoulders.

"I just cancelled them. Suddenly, I feel the urge to work out."

Rainey grunted not at all surprised. It was Shane's character to set everything aside for the well-being of a friend—him. However this time, Shane didn't need to be concerned. Everything was fine in Rainey's life—well almost. "Okay, one hour." They disconnected and Rainey immediately turned his thoughts to Josephine.

London. His woman was unavailable when Rainey craved to hear her clipped British voice. He refused to feed the international card industry when he could take that money and book a flight. Skype didn't showcase the clarity of Josephine's beauty when her country's power outages didn't sabotage their connection.

He missed her. How could she be in England when he needed her in America? He dismissed his musings to prepare to do a battle of the minds with his friend.

An hour later, somehow Shane had beaten him to Wellbridge Athletic Club & Spa, considering Rainey lived closer to the elite Town & Country location than his friend. Shaking his head, Rainey pulled alongside Shane's Lexus SUV.

Grabbing his duffel bag, Rainey got out and went in search of his friend. Shane had been detained in the lobby. A very interested fitness instructor had him spellbound. He was a sucker for a woman with a good body—brains optional.

"Good morning, Liz," Rainey spoke and patted Shane on the shoulder without stopping.

When Shane was able to pull himself away, he joined him in the locker room. The two shook hands, then slapped each other on the back. "It's good for us to have some one-on-one time since you've come home."

Rainey bobbed his head. "You're right. It's good to recharge, but I'm making plans to go back to Ghana. I don't like being away from Josephine." As he waited for his words to sink in, Rainey yanked off his sweatshirt.

He ignored Shane's slack jaw as he processed what was said. Seemingly recovered, Shane set his bag on the bench. He began to undress as if Rainey hadn't said a word. But the questions were forming.

"What exactly happened in Africa that wasn't on the missions trail?" Shane asked while forcing his muscular arms through his t-shirt.

"Your trip was supposed to be a get-away to clear your mind and come to terms with your mixed emotions about Josephine. What insidious bug bit you in Africa that is sending telepathic messages for you to want to return? Do I need to seek power of attorney because you've lost all your common and educational sense?"

Rainey didn't reply as he stored his clothes in the locker and slipped the key into his pants. "Cardio or weights?"

"Answers." Shane snapped, then apologized. "Cardio. It's safer for you in case I feel the urge to knock some sense into you. I wouldn't want to have a weapon handy."

"Cardio it is." Helping themselves to a white towel and a complimentary bottle of water, they made their way to the bank of machines. The two smiled and waved at the regular female admirers. Once they selected their choice of equipment and adjusted their levels, Rainey was ready to talk. "Some things have changed."

"No bro, everything seems to have changed. We have an hour on the tread, start talking. Believe me, I'm listening."

"I guess the first thing I should have shared is I bit the bullet and took the plunge—

Shane punched pause on the dashboard. "What?" He roared, then looked around him before calming down. Giving a few concerned patrons an apologetic grin, Shane lowered his voice. "You got married? Have you lost it? I knew I should have done more to keep you from going—"

"Time out." Rainey was tickled by his friend's misconception. "I'm talking about literally in the baptismal pool. I repented."

"Are you dying? You can confide in me." Shane looked worried.

"To my old way of thinking—yes, I'm completely dead. Spiritually, I am alive and well. It was an amazing experience; I would definitely recommend it."

"We're not talking about you sampling a new product. Start from the beginning and I do not want to hear about the day you were born," Shane said, a bit irritated.

Rainey noted his heart rate and calories burned before explaining. "It's hard to describe, but I lost control of my mouth as I listened to the fluency of a language foreign to me, while at the same time my struggles and issues seeped out of my body. It was a spiritual awareness, I guess, similar to when Adam and Eve's eyes were opened after one bite of that fruit."

Shane cursed under his breath as he wasted valuable time watching him, versus exercising. "Man, I feel terrible I didn't realize how rough things were between you and your family since your dad's been gone that you had to resort to this—"

Increasing the incline, Rainey huffed. "Everything worked itself out. I was way overdue on a spiritual reconciliation with God. The money, the clout, and material possessions just weren't enough anymore. Cheney has been touting that Jesus completely saves for years. My parents embraced that, but Janae and I have been the holdouts. But somewhere along the line it had become old fighting against God, so I surrendered or switched sides. I repented of my own free will."

"Just like that, huh?" Shane questioned as he resumed his workout.

"Ever since the nightmare—"

"Okay. Hold it." Shane pushed pause again. "Why do I feel I'm new on this planet or my brain cells have been frozen for a thousand years? I'm missing something here. What nightmare?"

Rainey hid his humor. By the time Rainey clocked sixty minutes, Shane would be lucky to have gotten sixteen minutes in with his stop-and-go routine. "While I was in Africa, something happened to where I could feel God's presence. My senses were on heightened alert after I had this nightmare that I was the only person on earth and it was going up in flames. Come to find out, Chad—my host—said it was probably my anti-malaria medicine. By the way," he pointed, "did you come to work out or not?"

"Oh, I'm getting a workout all right. My mind is exhausted playing catch up. You've just killed my physical workout." He resumed the speed on his machine. "And I thought Josephine was behind all this." He shook his head.

"Oh, she had her hand in my spiritual cookie jar, too. When I told her the ocean can't separate me from her, she replied, 'Nothing can separate us from the love of God.' When I'm with her, I'm satisfied."

"Why am I not starting to like her every time she opens her mouth?"

Rainey took the offense out on the machine and he pumped his speed up to eight instead of his usual max of six and a half. He and Shane were the best of friends, but one way to get on his bad side would be to speak negatively of Josephine.

His father treated Shane as a son and asked about him from time to time. People thought they were siblings. However, if anyone stood in the way of getting something Rainey wanted—and he wanted Josephine—he wouldn't think twice about severing ties with family or friends.

Since Rainey was known for not issuing idle threats, he warned Shane. "Watch it, Dr. Maxwell. I happen to love Josephine and I'm one breath away from asking her to be my wife." He was about to say more, but couldn't. He held his tongue, or maybe it was God again, keeping him tongue-tied.

"Wife?" Shane almost choked on his own air, causing him to stumble on the treadmill. Ending his cardio twenty minutes in, Shane picked up his towel and wiped whatever sweat he managed to produce and threw it back on the machine.

He stormed away and came back pumping hand weighs. Rainey eyed him. "Should I be concerned that you're about to go ballistic?"

"Mission accomplished. I'm about as unstable as you. I'm going to do a few more weights, shower, and I'll meet you in the lounge. I think I need to be sitting down to hear the rest of this story."

As Shane disappeared, Rainey rewound the words he just uttered—wife. Every man eventually wanted one. They admitted they loved each other. Now, he and Josephine needed to grow together and work their way to that lifetime commitment in America.

Rainey wasn't about to relocate outside the states, especially to a third world country. Without Shane to talk to, he pointed the remote to the overhead television and clicked to ESPN for the remainder of his workout.

After completing his cool down, Rainey showered and dressed. Ready to do battle, he went in search of Shane upstairs in the lounge. Liz was keeping him entertained, but when Shane saw him, he put an end to their conversation.

"I've had one drink. Will I want another one?" Shane asked.

Rainey shook his head. "I don't drink anymore, remember? Neither should you." He had lost the taste for liquor after learning how drinking and driving impacted lives. Taking a seat, Rainey scanned the menu. They both ordered a sandwich and salad.

Shane folded his arms and leaned across the table as if he was about to have a father and son talk. "Rain, is it that serious, really? You barely know her—unless that's another thing you haven't told me.""She has my heart and I'm comfortable with that. I need to know you have my back on this."

It was an apparent struggle for Shane to concede voicing any further concerns. He did nothing to minimize his loud reluctant sigh. "You have it."

Rainey appreciated that as he wiped the imaginary sweat from his pores.

"As long as you're not applying for dual citizenship—wait. Oh no, please don't tell me you've already started the paperwork." Shane gritted his teeth.

Seeing his friend sweat, Rainey piled on the torture. "Blacks may have migrated back to the South without a backwards thought about the Old South's mistreatment of African-Americans, so why can't African-Americans move back to Africa?" He decided to come clean. "But to answer your question—no."

Shane physically collapsed back in his seat in relief. "You had me concerned."

Their food arrived and Rainey said grace for the both of them. After taking a bite of his sandwich, he picked back up the conversation. "You really have nothing to worry about. I have no plans to change my zip code."

Rainey didn't say another word on the subject as they devoured their meals.

⌘⌘

The call came in the middle of the night on Sunday. Rainey thought he was dreaming when he answered his cell phone.

"I know the hour is late, but I just wanted to hear your voice," Josephine said.

Smiling, he reached for his bedside lamp. Rainey wanted to be wide awake and have no doubt they were speaking. Scooting up in his bed, he confessed, "I missed you, babe."

"I as well. That is why I am calling so urgently. I am just returning from England and I wanted to hear your voice if only for a minute."

Glancing at his clock, Rainey noted it was one in the morning. Their phone calls never seemed to be in perfect timing.

With schools out for spring break, his waiting room would see a steady stream of patients beginning at eight in the morning. It would be so busy that he would have lunch catered for his staff. His body would punish him later, but Rainey would enjoy the moment.

His life seemed to be on hold in between his talks with Josephine. He could hear her longing. "I have more than a minute. I'll call you right back."

He grabbed his international card and credit card to load up another hour at fifteen cents a minute. Each month his credit card bill reached a new record on the money spent for adding minutes. After punching in his international access code, then the 2-3-3 Ghana's country code, he tapped in Josephine nine digit mobile number.

"I love you," spilled from Rainey's lips the moment Josephine came on the line.

"*Ete-sen,*" Josephine replied.

Rainey smiled. He loved hearing her say hello in Twi, but he needed something stronger than that. Finally, he coaxed 'I love you' from her and he was ready to move on.

His first mistake was to ask a woman about a wedding. Josephine told him more than Rainey wanted to know about her sister and brother-in-law's affair. She then asked about his walk with God.

"I'm getting steady on my feet with this new Bible foundation. The sermon this morning—or should I say yesterday morning—was 'Without Holiness, it's impossible to see God.' the eleventh chapter of Hebrews."

"It's impossible to *please* God—verse six," she corrected.

Rainey frowned. He was adamant about his interpretation. "I'm pretty sure Pastor Scott said see God. If a man doesn't please the Lord, then we won't see Him."

"I receive that Word."

Closing his eyes, Rainey could imagine her smile, but he was about to shatter their happiness. "Listen sweetheart, you have no clue how much I want to stop the clock and minutes on this card and stay connected to you...but I do have a busy schedule tomorrow, and I need to go. Thank you for thinking about me."

Her throaty laugh soothed his heart. "I always think about you, more than you know."

"That's your job to let me know. A surprise trip to America would make me the happiest. " He exhaled. Rainey was not about to let that thought frustrate him. "But since you say you can't come to me, I'm coming back to you sooner than you might expect. Be warned, I expect to be your sole focus."

"You have my word, Dr. Reynolds. Love you."

For the next month, Rainey faced one obstacle after another that kept him from booking a flight to Ghana. There was a conference Shane had to remind him about, then the peak of flu season caused cancellations that only triggered weeks of overbooking to make up the appointments.

When Rainey thought everything was back to normal and under control, Josephine mentioned the upcoming rainy season that would begin in April. Thanking her for the heads up, Rainey tackled his obstacles. He switched visitation dates with Cheney to see his father ahead of schedule, so by March 20th, he was en route to Ghana.

Chapter 20

Josephine stood in the outdoor pavilion-style waiting area at Kotoka Airport. Shading her eyes, she scanned the sky for Rainey's plane. She wanted a fairy tale, thanks to her sisters' constant harping that Josephine could have a happy ending.

For months, she and Rainey had made it work without being together, but for five days, the things they had professed and confessed to each other could be said face to face. Josephine had been praying God's will about the direction of their relationship. So far, Jesus hadn't given her a clue. With no choice, she had to let patience have her perfect work.

The roar of an engine overhead made her twirl in that direction. It was a false alarm. A plane had taken off. The scene was repeated a couple more times until one plane in the distance pierced through the clouds heading for the runway. She checked the time. Her heart pounded with excitement—Rainey.

She said a quick prayer of thanks for his safe arrival, then hurried inside the terminal to wait. Would she ever get used to the excitement of his arrival, only to bear the sadness when he departed?

After checking her light makeup, Josephine smoothed her clothing. She practiced a few breathing techniques to calm her nerves. She kept her focus as a man emerged, outshining the rest. The swagger was copy written by Dr. Rainey Reynolds. His eyes searched for her. Josephine lifted her hand with a slight wave. His look of love weakened her knees.

"Jesus, I love him," she whispered as Customs scrutinized his passport and luggage.

Once he was cleared, Rainey didn't look to the left or right, but stayed on course until he invaded her personal space and stared into her eyes. With his trench coat resting over his arm, a man never looked so photogenic in casual attire of a white polo shirt and tan khakis.

"You came to me," she whispered in awe at the realization that he was there for no other reason, but to see her. He had grown a thin beard. How could he look any better than before? Josephine wanted to snuggle in a hug, but she wouldn't.

"Yes," his voice was low. "I'm going to make this quick." Dropping his bag, Rainey swept her off of her feet with a possessive hold around her waist, then released her. "I could have snuck in a kiss, but I don't think I could have stopped." He grinned. "Babe, you look so good."

Josephine blinked, registering what just happened. She would never admit that despite her country's protocol on proper conduct, she needed that embrace.

"My eyes do not deceive my memory. You are more than handsome. Did you have a good flight?"

"I did, knowing I would see you." His nostrils flared.

She shook off the temptation to hug him. The only option was to intertwine her fingers through his.

"I missed you, lady."

Without words, she knew how he felt about her. "I missed you, too." she said, knowing Rainey was confident in the love she possessed for him. "Are you hungry?" Josephine lifted her bag of banana peanut cake, which resembled miniature cookies. "My mum made them just for you."

"Please tell Mrs. Amoah *meda wo ase*."

"I will," she promised and then steered him out the terminal to where she parked her vehicle. Rainey seemed to tempt oncoming traffic, only to pull her closer to him to avoid collision.

After a few near misses, she caught on. "Are you doing that on purpose?"

"Can you think of any other reason for me to hold my lady, but to protect her from harm's way?"

How could she protest? She became a willing participant in the game. Once they arrived at her car and Rainey stored his bag on her back seat, genuine contentment draped her as she started the engine.

Rainey reached across the seat and squeezed her hand. "Why are you smiling?"

"I'm happy."

"Me, too." He smiled and reclined against the headrest. Quickly he glanced out the window. What liberty they had to talk non-stop without concern about time restrictions or cost.

There was still mayhem on the roads late afternoon, but Josephine was able to maneuver through traffic with minimal delay to Asylum Down in Accra. She booked him a room at the Highgate Hotel. It was close to the National Theatre of Ghana, which Josephine wanted him to experience. Lost in her thoughts, it dawned on her that Rainey hadn't said a word.

Stopping at a streetlight, Josephine peeked at him. His breathing was steady and his expression peaceful. She tried to ease her hand out of his grasp. Almost immediately, he wrapped his strong hand around hers.

Forty-five minutes later, Josephine exited onto Mango Tree Avenue. She parked in front of the hotel and nudged Rainey until he stirred. "We're here, Dr. Reynolds," she liked to call him that from time to time. "I hope you like your accommodations."

His long lashes fluttered. His eyes were bloodshot when he finally looked at her.

She pouted, sympathizing with his jetlag. "Get some rest and phone me when you wake." She stated her discomfort of walking into a hotel with a man who was not her husband.

There would be no sufficient explanation that would void the scripture in Romans 14:16. Although she would be innocent of any wrongdoing, she would not give way for misunderstandings.

"Babe, I'm a man of God now. I understand." He caressed her cheek. She closed her eyes and enjoyed the feel of his hand.

"What if I'm knocked out until four o'clock in the morning?" Rainey asked as he reached in the back to grab his things, including the treat from her mother.

"Then I will anticipate your call at that time. Listen," she paused and faced him. "I know you don't want to play tourist, but there are a few places for us to enjoy together."

"And I'm sure that includes a dinner with your father?" He lifted a brow.

"Papa would not have it any other way." She hoped he didn't mind.

Rainey offered her a tired smile. "Okay, babe. I'll see you in my dreams."

Watching him retreat to the hotel entrance, Josephine inhaled the remnants of his cologne. When he disappeared inside, she headed home with fresh memories to keep her company during the ride home.

"Has Dr. Reynolds arrived safely?" Her father asked soon after she walked through the door.

"Yes, and he said to thank you for the treats, mum."

Her mother beamed. Josephine chatted with them briefly, then showered. Although it was too early for her to sleep, she reclined on her bed and closed her eyes.

"Jesus, You know all things. Lord, You know I don't believe in fairy tales, but I'm asking for a happy ending for Rainey and myself."

She hadn't realized she drifted off to sleep until her cell phone jolted her awake. She patted around her bed for it while glancing at the clock: 3:45 in the morning. "*Makyeoo.*"

Rainey chuckled in a husky voice. "I'm sorry, baby—"

"Don't apologize. You are a traveler crossing time zones." When Rainey stifled a yawn, Josephine stretched quietly. "I think we should rest," she suggested.

"You're right. I'll return to my dreams where you await me, but one day the time zones won't separate us and we'll be in perfect harmony," his voice faded.

"You sound so sure of that," she prompted, wanting to know his plan, instead she heard a light snore. She softly kissed the phone, disconnected, and got up to dress for bed before climbing under the covers.

Chapter 21

The next morning, Rainey woke well-rested and called Josephine. "Good morning, babe. If you don't mind, I'll eat breakfast downstairs in the hotel restaurant."

Since he had slept through dinner the previous night, he was too hungry to wait for her to take him out to breakfast. "I devoured the cookies your mother sent in the middle of the night."

They laughed together, then agreed on a time to pick him up.

While sipping on black coffee, Rainey stared out the large window. From the people to the landscape, Accra could be any city in America. How different were African and African-American cultures, really?

In America, Josephine appeared to enjoy herself in St. Louis. She fit right in with his sister and her friends. Yet, she stood out in a crowd as an exquisite beauty with her rich brown complexion and strong striking features.

There was nothing like a woman's walk to get a man's attention. Josephine's confident strut could freeze time so the casual observer could catalog each movement and drool. Rainey was drawn to her the moment he laid eyes on her. Their apparent dislike had been nothing more than a tug of war of their affections.

Unlike a few months ago, there was no pretense why Rainey was back in Accra this time. No undercover missions work.

He didn't even alert Chad that he was coming. Josephine was his sole motivation. He planned on wooing her back to the U.S.

Have you eaten? Josephine texted him as he tipped his server. Rainey texted back Yes. It was a good thing he kept the cell phone he purchased the first time in Ghana.

She called him. "I'm not far away. Are you ready for a day of sightseeing?"

"I'm a tourist. Show me your world. Where you work, what a day is like for you. Show me you, baby."

She didn't respond right away. "I had planned to take you to the monkey sanctuary, the National Theatre of Ghana, Tagho Falls..."

Rainey would not be deterred. "Not today. I just want to relax with you. Being a tourist is work when you try to cram in every sight and sound. I don't want that this time."

Evidently, she did not like his suggestion, but agreed. "If that is what you wish. All right."

"I wish that and more." He crossed the lobby and sunk into an overstuffed seat that faced the entrance. *"Meda wo ase.* I'll see you when you arrive. Drive safely. Love you."

"Me Dor wo more." They disconnected.

Her declaration was like a warm syrup coating his heart. *Jesus, I'm learning, it's not about what I want in life, but what You have for me in life. If I can have one thing—one someone—please let it be Josephine. In Jesus' name. Amen,* he prayed silently, then realized he had forgotten to read a Scripture for the day when Josephine pulled up to the curb.

Disappointed in himself, Rainey didn't want a one-sided relationship with God. He no longer wanted to take, take, take from Jesus. Cheney's pastor had preached that a moment of prayer, singing a song, or reading their Bibles was an expression of giving back to God. That's easy, he had remembered thinking.

Rainey stood and exited the lobby. Once sitting in Josephine's car, he was in awe of her beauty. Simply dressed in light colors, her brown skin glowed—gorgeous. "I could never get used to this."

"What?" She smiled.

"Admiring you and not even getting a good morning kiss. A right every man has who loves a woman. I could never adapt to that custom to live here."

"The only woman a man has the right to touch lovingly is his wife. When you start touching, things get out of control. Think of it as us having an invisible chaperone. I love it and embrace it because my heart is here in Ghana."

Rainey reached for her hand and brought it to his lips. "So is mine—you, and that's a problem."

"It is, isn't it?" She wore a defeated expression.

"Yes, baby, it is." Rainey's father taught him, before he ever had a girlfriend, to never pressure a woman and he never had, but he was so close to breaking that rule. The time was ripe to discuss her visit to the States.

When he opened his mouth, something totally different came out. "I forgot to read my Bible before I left my room. Will you share what you read with me?"

Her eyes twinkled. "I read Psalm 119:11 this morning. *Thy word have I hid in mine heart, that I might not sin against thee'.*"

"Interesting." Rainey nodded and took in his surroundings.

"People hide their treasures. I think that scripture and Jude 1:23 go hand in hand."

"Which is what? It's not that I don't know what's in the Bible—well, maybe I don't, but when I stumble upon those phrases

I've heard throughout the years, it makes a believer out of me, if that makes any sense."

"It does. We hear so much, that unbelievers—even church-goers—don't know what is fact or fiction Scriptures." She paused. "Jude 1:23 basically says by any means necessary, the saints need to save unbelievers from the fire. But the part I connect with as far as hiding the treasure of God's Word within me, is that I don't want to make myself dirty with a sinful lifestyle."

He was impressed how Josephine applied God's Word to everyday life. "Thank you for my morning Bible class. If I hadn't forgotten to read my Bible, then I never would have asked you to share that with me."

"It's so refreshing to talk about Jesus with someone of the same mind."

"I'm not there yet, but I've concluded that after the Lord saved me, my objections about turning my life over to God was a much-ado-about-nothing. I have no regrets." Rainey meant it. Cheney felt the same way. Now they would have to work on Janae.

"Oh how I wish I was there to witness your blessed event of the Water and Spirit baptism. We would have celebrated into the night for your redeemed soul."

"Yes, that's right. My woman comes from the land of celebrations," Rainey boasted.

"As a matter of fact, the Adae Festival is Wednesday." She slowed to avoid a hawker, then resumed speed. "It is an elaborate Ashanti region celebration held every six weeks or nine times at the palace. It's been a tradition since ancient times to recognize deities; as Christians we use the celebration to remember our ancestors."

"That seems like such a conflict..." Rainey frowned and adjusted his body to face her more directly. "...Christians celebrating a tradition meant for pagan worship."

Josephine didn't respond right away. "I never looked at it like that. But how is that different from Christians celebrating Christmas, sharing Christ's glory with Santa?"

It was Rainey's turn to think about it. "Checkmate. Good point."

Their conversation then turned to family. Josephine inquired about Cheney's pregnancy and his parents, especially his father. Outside the family, Rainey seldom welcomed any discussion about Dr. Roland Reynolds. There was no condemnation when she inquired about him.

"My father is in good spirits. Every time he writes us or we visit him, we are reminded of the countdown to his release."

What Rainey didn't say was her name was now part of his conversation—written or oral—with his father. He thought about his visit, days before leaving St. Louis. Separated by a glass partition, his father had smiled as Rainey's every other utterance was Josephine.

"I'm chasing after a dream to see Josephine again."

Roland nodded. "Dreams become realities."

"Shane is concerned about my mental health, but I'm concerned about my heart. I can't leave her there."

"I'll be praying with you son that Josephine gets to the point where she can't bear the separation..."

"Yes, my father is faring better than we all expected. The other prisoners respect him and come to him for medical advice when the prison infirmary ignores complaints from inmates seeking treatment. God is protecting and blessing him. The day can't come fast enough until he is freed."

"That is worthy of a celebration!" Josephine glanced his way.

"Ah, Babe, I don't think so." Rainey mumbled under his breath. "It would definitely be a private party." He didn't want to talk about his father anymore. His mission was to convince Josephine to get on a plane—at his expense—and come back to America for an extended visit.

Changing the subject, he had a relaxed conversation with Josephine about nothing important. They didn't have to rush all the highs and lows of a week into a thirty minute phone call.

It wasn't long until they arrived at the main building of the University of Ghana. The white exterior reminded him of Elmira slave castle, but it was kept in pristine condition. In contrast, the clay tile roof resembled a building Rainey thought he would only see in Japan with its multi-level steeple design.

Once they had parked and stood outside her car, Rainey took the pleasure of scanning her from head to toe—perfection! Thank you, Lord. "This is impressive."

Taking the attention off of her, she boasted, "My employer is one of the largest and oldest of the thirteen Ghanaian universities. Come on." Walking backwards, she teased him into joining her along a pathway. He did, playfully whirling her around so they were side by side.

The plush greenery, mature palm trees and meticulous landscape presented an idyllic backdrop. To add to the serenity, birds called out to them from the trees. Again, this was not an Africa he had imagined.

During their stride across the campus, Rainey was surprised to see an American icon honored far away from home—the W.E.B Du Bois Memorial Center. If he didn't watch himself,

Rainey would confuse it with a campus back in St. Louis like Washington University.

Rainey toured inside Balme Library, the university bookstore, and visited the Great Hall and the Legon tower of Learning.

Once he had had enough, from there Josephine suggested grabbing a bite to eat in the dining hall.

As they stood in the food line, most dishes seemed recognizable, but Rainey didn't take any chances selecting something that looked delicious, only to pay for it later. His stomach had barely recovered from some of the seasonings ingested on his first trip.

Sitting near a window that gave a picturesque view of the campus, Rainey quietly listened to Josephine's excitement about the university. "Do I get to see the building where you work?"

Once they finished eating, Josephine guided him in that direction, sometimes speaking and introducing him to her colleagues.

"The Graduate School of Nuclear and Applied Sciences at the Ghana Atomic Energy Commission employ hundreds of engineers, scientists, and researchers," she said, still in her tour guide mode although they had entered her workplace.

Although a few areas were restricted from visitors, Rainey was able to get a good sense of her job demands. She introduced him to more people, including the researchers she assisted and a female coworker who watched them intently.

"Kim, this is my friend from the United States, Dr. Rainey Reynolds."

As he shook her hand, he corrected Josephine. "I'm her very significant other."

The woman giggled. "I like him!" She squinted at Josephine as if there were secrets between them about him. Kim pulled Josephine aside and the two engaged in a hushed conversation where it appeared Josephine received some type of scolding. When their talk ended, Kim waved goodbye.

Stuffing his hands in his pockets, he pivoted on one heel. "Am I'm going to be privy to what you two discussed?"

"You," was all Josephine said, before announcing that was enough for one day. "I have worked despite taking a vacation day. If we don't head toward Kanda, it will take us more than an hour to get home. This is why I don't drive and prefer the trotros."

The punishing heat greeted them outside. All Rainey wanted was a shower and bed, but he had learned his lesson before. Once Josephine's family had extended a dinner invitation, it was not to be ignored or postponed. So after they settled in her car, he prepared for the unknown.

&⤫

As Josephine drove away from the campus, Rainey began to doze. She grinned. He was becoming predictable. Content with his presence, she left him undisturbed until they inched closer to downtown Accra. The horns and hawkers stirred him from his nap.

"Welcome back," she teased.

Rainey stretched his legs, then covered a yawn with his hand. "How could I forget about this?" Digging into his pocket, he pulled out cedis and appeared eager to make a purchase.

Josephine's heart warmed. God had already converted him to salvation. Maybe she was converting him into a true Ghanaian. At her home, the Amoahs and other extended family members welcomed Rainey back as an old friend.

Her father extended his hand in a welcome handshake and they had a festive time around the dinner table. "Dr. Reynolds, you have given me much to reconsider when I visit your country in the coming months. I will try and see America through African American eyes."

Rainey nodded. "I appreciate that, sir. Please let me know when you are coming."

Josephine was pleased and judging from the look Rainey gave her, he was, too. When the newest member of their family, baby Beatrice woke, Rainey had a chance to hold her.

"She's beautiful," he complimented as Beatrice seemed content to cuddle in his arms. Josephine sighed. Quickly her mind played a rude trick on her; being three years older than Rose, her time clock was ticking faster.

The night ended on a good note. Rainey refused her offer to drive him back to the Highgate Hotel and called a taxi. That impressed her father. Whispering goodnight, Josephine negotiated his fare and sent him off.

The next four days raced in a blur until it was time to say goodbye—again. Rainey had asked her a couple of times had she started the visa application and each time she reluctantly told him no.

Rainey had no choice but to wrap his arms around her while she released her tears of sorrow in his chest. She felt foolish for her display of weakness, but her heart was breaking.

"Baby, shh," Rainey cooed in her ear. "You're making this hard for me to leave. If you will come to America, I will pay for your flight and put you up in a hotel, although Cheney wouldn't hear of it, then Grandma BB would try to pull rank. Everybody wants to see you. What's holding you back from applying for a visa? What is it?"

"I'm scared that if I go to the States again, because of my feelings for you I won't want to come home." She hiccupped.

"And how is that a bad thing?"

"Ghana is my home." She held her head up. Through blurred vision, his face came into a fuzzy view as she sniffed. "I don't want to live any other place, but Africa."

When she felt his body stiffen, her heart plummeted. That was not a good sign.

His voice was low, but his response determined. "I'm not relocating, Josephine. We need time to cultivate our relationship. You have to come to America with open eyes."

Shaking her head, Josephine disentangled herself from his security and stepped back. He hinted of an ultimatum and she was not one to be pressured. "We have a stalemate, Dr. Reynolds. Why must I yield?" Taking a deep breath, Josephine had to say it. "So I guess this is…" she swallowed and exhaled. "I guess this is over between us."

Josephine held her breath as she waited for his reply. His flight called for boarding. This was not a time for cliffhangers. If he stated they could no longer be a couple, she wanted to hear it now, face-to-face.

Reaching down, Rainey lifted his bag. "Josephine Abena Yaa Amoah, this is not over between us. I'm just as stubborn as you." He placed a hard kiss on her lips, leaving her stunned.

"God did not put you in my path to take you back." When the second boarding was announced, he seemed just as frustrated as her. "I'll be in touch." Without another word, in his signature swagger, Rainey walked away. Josephine was as Abigail sometimes said—a hot mess. Her heart was in limbo while her lips tingled from his touch. Regardless of what he said, it was over because she wasn't going anywhere but back to her bed again.

Chapter 22

The days had turned into weeks since Rainey's departure. Outside, Josephine maintained a cheerful disposition while her heart bled on the inside. The statement that 'love hurts' was accurate. Secretly, she had hoped Rainey would call her bluff and prove his undying love.

"But he already has," Abigail would remind her. "I don't know if I would have stood my ground so fiercely, because love is soft, but I admire your strength, sister."

Cheney emailed her to say a cheer up contingency force was en route.

So here Josephine was déjà vu at Kotoka airport, waiting for incomparable Grandma BB and her neighbor, Imani Segall, to clear Customs. In all honesty, Josephine welcomed the distraction, even if it did come from the United States and in Stacey Adams shoes.

Reflecting on her last evening in the States, Josephine, Cheney, and Imani were relaxing on Grandma BB's patio. They were exhausted after treating her to a girls' day out shopping spree. Stretched out in a rocking recliner, Josephine's stillness had alarmed Grandma BB when she had drifted off to sleep.

"Hey, I say we call 9-1-1," Grandma BB said as Josephine felt the woman's peppermint breathing over her body, but the warmth from the sun was too intoxicating for her to stir.

"I think she's fine, Grandma BB. The paramedics have your address on speed dial anyway," Cheney had tried reasoning with her god-grandmother.

Josephine could have ended the charade by opening an eye or saying something, but she figured why bother. It was her last day in St. Louis, and she should have some fun at Grandma BB's expense.

When she arrived in St. Louis, it didn't take her long to learn that Benton Street was the focal point of neighborhood commotion. As a self-appointed neighborhood watch captain and one-woman militia, Mrs. Beacon had single-handedly beaten down more than one questionable suspect, using her walking cane as an assault weapon and her attack dog, Silent Killer, to corner burglars.

The widow's antics were legendary. She had stolen two crooks' get-away van while they were in the process of burglarizing a nearby home. Grandma BB had escaped—or that's what she called her covert actions—from a nursing home and rumor had it that she had a boyfriend in a virtual world. Colorful didn't begin to describe the loveable childless widow, Mrs. Beatrice Tilly Beacon aka Grandma BB—a name only a few privileged friends were allowed to call her.

"Hmm. I think Josie done had a sun stroke," Grandma BB continued.

"We haven't been outside thirty minutes," Imani argued. *"I barely caught one sun ray. If she's out, it's probably from that rich pasta you made. Humph. You always were heavy handed on the seasoning."*

"Listen, repo girl, she's used to spicy dishes," Grandma said, clearly annoyed. She began to take digs at her neighbor's profession. *"It doesn't take long—"*

Imani, the former diva airline attendant, oddly developed a fear of flying, so she switched to a more challenging, competitive and lucrative career as a repo woman.

Josephine secretly had dubbed the sassy Grandmother B as Hatfield, and the elegant diva Imani as McCoy. The seventy-something widow and thirty-five-year-old archrivals were no match, and at the end of the day they laughed, hugged, and retreated to their respective corners—homes. If they weren't feuding with each other, they were wreaking havoc in some unfortunate souls' lives.

Before their harmless bickering escalated, Josephine's lids fluttered open and she scooted up on her elbows. They all chuckled. Grandma BB argued she knew all along that she was fine, then Josephine extended an invitation for them to visit her. Until now, they hadn't been able to come.

"With Ghana bordering Cote d' Ivoire, Parke's ancestral homeland, we won't need a second invitation," Cheney said without hesitation.

"That's what I'm talking about. We can leave Grandma BB behind to guard the city," Imani teased.

"Hold it, Mani," Grandma BB, known for creating nicknames. "If you're going, then I'm going." Then she turned to Josephine. "I hope you have enough room at your place for my wardrobe, Josie."

"Are you kiddin'? Watch out. Grandma BB is coordination queen. Her undergarments, clothes, shoes, and nail polish have to match. I thought she had a body in her luggage when we went on a weekend ski trip years ago," Cheney spoke up.

Grandma BB shrugged indignantly. "It has been done. Runaway slave, Henry Boxcar Brown shipped himself to freedom from Virginia to Philly. Don't give me any ideas," she huffed and rested a fist on her hip.

"Just pack your Stacy Adams, and you'll be fine," Imani baited, *referring to Grandma BB's unusual fashion attire that included her trademark men's shoes. She had yet to understand the reason behind that one.*

The memories vanished as her two American friends headed toward her. Tall, shapely and a fashionable dresser for any occasion, Imani looked stunning in her two-piece outfit. Grandma BB was just as stylish in a colorful sundress and shawl, and to round out her signature look—white Stacy Adams Belmont sling-back sandals.

Grandma BB's eyes brightened and a smile stretched across her face once she recognized Josephine after clearing Customs. Within minutes, the friends were hugging, laughing and complimenting one another, but upon further inspection, Josephine noted that Grandma BB's pedicure included three corns polished the same color as her toenails.

She stifled a belly-curling laugh. Before Josephine could relieve Grandma BB of her large suitcase on wheels, a stranger approached them and asked if they needed help with the luggage.

"Touch me or my stuff and I'll give you a royal American beat down." She snarled and stomped her foot as if she was about to deliver.

The man scurried away, mumbling, "Insane Obruni."

"Grandmother B you may not come into a foreign country and threatened to do bodily harm. The U.S. Embassy may not wish to intervene on your behalf," Josephine advised.

Imani shrugged. "As you can see, the neighborhood terror has no boundaries. Can't take her anywhere." Imani tee-hee'd despite Grandma BB's indignation.

Her friends had been there less than thirty minutes and already they were creating havoc or comedic relief. Outside the airport, Josephine haggled with the taxi driver over a fair price to their hotel.

In the back seat, Imani closed her eyes, apparently exhausted after their flight. On the other hand, Grandma BB was as alert as a kindergartener after a morning nap.

"So when is the first party?" Grandma BB asked as she scanned the passing scenery.

"It's only Wednesday—"

"And your point is, Josie?" Grandma BB shrugged. "I want my money back. The New York Times reported Accra as one of the top five places to visit. *Umph.* I thought your country had some kind of national celebration every month about anything—National Chocolate or Cocoa Day festivities, so I'm ready to dance."

"Neither one is underway at the moment," Josephine said from the front seat where she sat with the driver.

"Exercise is good for the body after a stroke. That's what my private duty nurse, Dino, says."

"Dino," Imani repeated with a moan. Her eyes remained closed. "I was willing to pay out of my pocket for his physical therapy services, but he informed me he only worked with Medicare and Medicaid patients. How Grandma BB qualified, I don't know. That woman has a bankroll." Imani pouted and shook her head. "And there is no way I'm going to let you out-dance me. We both need some beauty rest first."

"Speak for yourself. My beauty has been regenerating for decades. You're the one who needs to start your beauty regime now. I already saw one wrinkle."

Imani gasped. Fully alert, she rummaged through her bag and pulled out a compact and inspected her face.

Even their driver snickered. Josephine had missed them. They were part of the landscape that made her St. Louis stay enjoyable. "Don't you want to visit some popular tourist spots?" She could never get enough of showing off her country.

"I'll make my own hot spots, thank you very much, if it doesn't include those slave castles. I've lived through the civil rights era and prejudice against our first Black president; I've seen enough hatred. It may make me want to go home and hurt somebody."

God forbid. Josephine definitely had to get her in somebody's church for prayer before she left.

"Wait a minute, Grandma," Imani argued. "Don't let my olive skin tone, hazel eyes, auburn hair and great body fool you. If Black folks got White in their blood, there are a lot of folks passing as White with African blood in their veins. I don't care how many generations I have to go back, but I'm ready to embrace my Blackness...You know renowned genealogist Dr. Henry Gates has found a lot of African descendants of famous White people and—"

Grandma BB cut her off. "Well, I came to party and have a good time."

"Let us compromise. We can take a short visit to Elmira castle for Imani. Grandmother B, you might enjoy Big Milly's Backyard."

"I don't care if the woman is big or small, I didn't cross the ocean to attend her backyard barbecue."

"No. You have the wrong idea. Your backyard doesn't have hotel rooms and coconut trees on a beach like Big Milly's Backyard. The *Guardian News* voted it as the top Boutique Hostel in Africa."

"If there's dancing at this *hostel*, then I'm in and we can leave this senior citizen with her Geritol back in the *hotel* room," Imani teased, adding a wink.

Josephine suspected the pair would be heartbroken without the other. Once they reached their hotel, the driver carried in their luggage under Grandma BB's supervision.

"I will return later in the afternoon to pick you up for dinner with my family at our house," Josephine advised getting back in the taxi as Grandma BB yawned.

Many hours later, Josephine returned to the hotel to get her guests to learn that Grandma BB had only recently awakened and was getting dressed.

"The woman snores like a frog. The next time I'm getting a separate room," Imani complained, then snorted before giving Grandma BB a tight squeeze.

Grandma BB cut her eyes at her roommate. "If word gets out about my sleeping habits, I'll let people know you stuck your thumb in your sleep."

Josephine laughed until they reached the beehive of downtown Accra. They were in awe of the number of hawkers. That grabbed Imani's attention immediately. "Let's get something," she pleaded with Josephine at a stoplight.

Unfortunately, she also had to cater to Grandma BB and stop two more times. "Tourists!"

Her family was waiting at the door when Josephine arrived with her guests. *"Awkaaba!"*

Grandma BB nodded while Imani repeated the Twi greeting with ease.

"Showoff," Grandma BB said as they were shown to the living room where other relatives were waiting to meet Josephine's former American host family and friends.

Once they sat to eat, Grandma BB was in rare form as she decided to regale Josephine's family with tales of how she tackled a neighborhood boy who was trying to steal cars. "I whipped out my belt from my purse and gave him a whipping he should have been got when he started walking."

"Oh my," her mother said, placing her hand over her mouth. "Such violence."

"I'm sorry your husband is not alive to protect you. You must have been devastated upon his death," her father said.

Josephine stilled her body and bowed her head. Calling on Jesus was her only prayer. She looked up and Grandma BB cast a faraway look. "Yes, it was so long ago when the drunk driver hit him and left the scene," she said just above a whisper and sighed. The next instant, Grandma BB rebounded with a shrug. "But I got revenge on the perpetrator."

Josephine attempted to change the subject before Rainey's name came up. "Grandmother B would you like to try—"

"How so?" Her mother interrupted Josephine.

"When that coward finally came forward and admitted his guilt, I shot him," Grandma BB stated with such ease and no remorse.

The stunned expressions and gasps around the table said it all. Josephine buried her face in her hands and took a deep calming breath. Regaining composure, she tried to talk about something more pleasant. Grandma BB cut her off.

"Oh, I didn't kill him." Grandma BB waved her hand in the air while angling her body in her seat. "It was target practice on Rainey's father."

"Rainey's father?" Her father stiffened and gave his guest a pointed look. "You mean to tell me Rainey's father killed your husband?"

"Yep, the scoundrel." Grandma BB nodded as if they were discussing a recipe or decorating tip.

Her father immediately eyed Josephine for verification. Again, Josephine bowed her head in shame. If the Reynolds and Grandma BB were Ghanaians, her father would have forbidden any association with them. "And my daughter lodged at your home?"

"That played out before Josie came." Grandma BB winked at Josephine, which only made her tense.

Feigning the lateness of the hour, Josephine had to get her former host out of the house, so she could repair the damage. Although she and Rainey weren't actively building a relationship, it didn't mean she would allow anyone to slander his name. Besides loving him, she knew that Rainey was a good man, despite their stalemate.

Imani seemed to pick up on the hint and suggested they go. "We have big plans for tomorrow." Jingling her keys, Josephine couldn't get rid of her friends fast enough. Since Imani and Abigail hit it off, her sister wanted to accompany them. While keeping her thoughts private, Josephine was cordial during the drive to the hotel and wished them a blessed night.

"Enjoy yourselves as tourists on tomorrow. Sorry I have to work on Friday, but that night we'll go to Big Milly's," Josephine assured them.

When she and Abigail were back on the road toward home, her sister spoke first. "Papa will be unforgiving not to have heard about this from you. This is why Rainey didn't say more about his father."

"Yes." She gripped the wheel tighter than necessary. "It is a moot point at this time. Rainey and I will never see each other again. It's too painful." Being a great sister, Abigail had the foresight not to comment.

Much too soon, the sisters arrived back home. Josephine drove through the gate and parked. Together they walked in the house in a somber mood.

"Goodnight, Abigail. Josephine, have a seat here with me," their father called out as soon as they cleared the front door. Abigail gave her a sorrowful expression.

"Yes, Papa?" Josephine said tentatively, stepping farther into the living room. She mentally prepared for the dialogue that was about to take place.

"Daughter." He reached for her hand. "I am mortified that I put you in such a volatile situation so far away from home. You never once shared during your stay in St. Louis or after your return that your safety was in question."

"Their discord occurred before my arrival. I never felt threatened or afraid. Since that time, Rainey's father has repented, been baptized in Jesus' name and filled with the power of the Holy Ghost. As you know, recently Rainey received the promise of the Holy Ghost."

"What about this Grandmother B. Where is she in her walk with the Lord?"

"She has a stubborn spirit, but God can deliver her. Cheney says she's on several prayer lists across America."

After a few moments of silence, her father seemed to have come to a satisfying conclusion. Patting her hand, he placed a kiss on it. "Very well. Americans are a strange breed." Standing up, her father walked down the hall to his bedroom.

That was simple, she thought—until he returned.

"Is there no any animosity between Grandmother B and Dr. Reynolds, the son?" Frowns marred his forehead.

"No." Josephine refrained from stating Grandma BB either liked a person or put them on her "stay out of my way or else" list.

"Does the younger Dr. Reynolds have any skeletons that might resurface, such as this horrifying incident?"

She shook her head before answering, "No, papa." Whatever skeletons he had, Josephine was convinced they were buried when he was baptized in Jesus' name.

His intimidating expression let her know he had reached another verdict. "Not only am I a man who watches and prays, I'm an avid listener even when nothing is said. Goodnight."

Falling back on the sofa emotionally drained, Josephine imagined strangling Grandma BB. Then her mind flashed to Rainey. Josephine imagined hugging him.

రాుక్

Thursday morning, Josephine had recovered from the previous night's debacle. After spending more time in prayer, Josephine had a clear heart to enjoy her American guests and act as their tour guide to the slave castle and shopping. Grandma BB never mentioned the discussion at her house the previous day. By the end of the night, Josephine was reminded there was no such thing as uneventful when it came to a day in the life of Grandma BB.

On Friday, Josephine left Grandma BB and Imani to their own devices to shop and sightsee while she reported to her employer. Later, she and Abigail would accompany them to Big Molly's Backyard.

Once at her workstation, Josephine logged onto her computer. She quickly checked her personal email, hoping, praying for something from Rainey. Even a one-line message would make her day. He stated it wasn't over between them, yet he did nothing to prove his word as their communication evaporated into air.

Deep down inside, she had hoped Rainey would reconsider. Josephine shrugged and managed a slight chuckle, although nothing was witty. "He probably hoped I would cave in to my emotions and would lead to the same conclusion." *How can two stubborn hearts beat as one?* she wondered.

Her demands at work kept her busy almost until it was time to leave, but that didn't stop Kim from interrupting her on more than two occasions.

"Love is hard to find, friend. Take a chance at happiness."

"Distance did not separate you before you married," Josephine tried to reason with her coworker.

"And it would not have, if I had a choice between love and a little bit of happiness; I would choose love." Kim said, then hurried out the door to have dinner with her husband. "

Kim's words were still floating in Josephine's head when she arrived home. She was about to shower, but the water service was interrupted. Josephine simply freshened up. With Abigail tagging along, they headed to Frankie's Hotel to pick up their tourists.

Grandma BB and Imani were waiting in the lobby, excited and charged with energy. Both women were sporting Ghanaian waist jewelry—thin, slinky and colorful beads. They were popular keepsakes many female tourists liked to take away as souvenirs. Josephine squinted. Grandma BB had a belly ring?

"They are custom-fit," Grandma modeled, showcasing the handcrafted jewelry on a firm body for a woman in her seventies or teetering on her eighties. One never knew for sure, since Grandma neither acted nor looked her age.

Abigail laughed. "We know. We should have worn ours."

Josephine agreed, ushering them to her car.

"The beads are a great touch, but I came for some authentic African Kente cloth," Imani chimed in.

Once they were strapped in their seatbelts, Josephine began the hour drive to Kokrobite, a small fishing village where Big Milly's Backyard was located, right on the beach's edge. Josephine *tsk*ed. "The imitations in the U.S. are insulting. There are two distinct types of Kente cloth."

"Since I had a hard time deciding, I got both. I think the woman tried to rip me off with the price, but I wasn't having it. I'm the queen of haggling, still I probably over paid." Imani shrugged.

"Any price is well worth it. My mum is from the Ewe tribe and they weave cloth with animals, human and symbol designs. The Ashanti from my father's Akan tribe strictly use geometrical shapes. Mostly kings and people of importance wear them, the Ashanti cloth is more expensive."

"Ooh, I can't wait to get something made when I get home." Imani rocked from side to side. "I'll be like royalty."

"Humph. A royal pest," Grandma BB said.

Their conversation bounced from their slave castle visits to Cheney's pregnancy to Grandma BB's latest fiasco. "We have selected a good night to come. I thought we would have to go tomorrow night to see the mesmerizing African Showboyz at Next Door Beach Resort, but they will be performing at Big Milly's tonight. Excellent."

Grandma BB shook her head. "Next Door—I guess the owners couldn't come up with a catchier name."

"We are simple-and-to-the-point people. Plus, Ghana is a religious country. It is not uncommon to see Bible text as the name of a business, like To God Be the Glory store Number 150, or His Grace Cosmetics and Boutique, or Anointed Fast Food, No Jesus No Life Supermarket or—"

"Chile, you better stop there before God strikes me dead," Grandma BB warned, snickering. "But somehow I don't see anointed and fast food together in the same sentence."

"Very well." Josephine nodded. "You will enjoy the African Showboyz tribal quintet. The Sabbah brothers will mesmerize you as they dance to African drums."

"Ooh." Imani snapped her fingers. "As long as I can shake my body along with them."

"Yes, they want all to enjoy. Their performance includes glass eating, mystical fire twirling, and comic routines," Abigail added. "They have enchanted audiences throughout Africa, France, and Germany with their youthful energy. They have even toured the U.S. and were nominated for two Grammys after being featured in 1GiantLeap, a documentary on world culture."

Josephine smiled. Abigail was just as proud of Ghana's beauty and accomplishments as Josephine. Then Abigail asked about American dating. While Imani and Grandma BB had plenty to say, Josephine remained quiet. Evidently, she had a lot to learn.

They made it to Kokrobite Beach. She could tell by Grandma BB's expression, so far, she was not impressed. Hand painted letters against a loud blue background posted on a tall white wall marked the entrance to Big Milly's Backyard.

More than one hundred mature coconut trees bowed as the entered along the trail. The light shined brighter in Grandma BB's eyes as she took in the scenery. Tropical plants and trees strategically placed created a garden effect inviting a laid back atmosphere.

Grandma BB nodded. "Hmm-mm. We should've stayed here, Imani. They have little huts." She pointed.

"Actually, Big Milly's Backyard is a budget hostel with thatched roof double huts to keep the rooms cool, plus suites and cottages. But it's limited to twenty," Josephine said, leading them to the music.

"Hey, the granny and I took some anti-malaria medicine. We should be okay, right?" Imani thought to ask.

"Yes." Josephine grinned—*tourists.* "When the bats in the trees start chirping at dusk, they will scare away many of the mosquitoes."

"Bats?" Imani turned up her nose.

"They're harmless," Abigail assured their guests.

They detoured to the bar under a thatched roof. Josephine ordered everyone juice drinks. It didn't take long before the African drum beat enticed Imani to the dance floor on the beach.

Grandma BB joined her. Josephine was content to listen to the waves and be part of the landscape until Abigail dragged her off her stool to dance. Josephine didn't sit down until the African Showboyz took center stage. They were as much a part of her culture as the hawkers. By the time they left, the energy was just as charged on the ride to their hotel, but Josephine was exhausted.

A few days later, it was back to the airport to say goodbye to Josephine and Abigail's American guests. Despite her best efforts, Josephine had been unsuccessful in enticing the pair to Sunday church services.

"Did we cheer you up, baby?" Gone was the sassy, troublesome woman as Grandma BB's concern was etched on her brows. "I was on my best behavior."

"That's debatable," Imani mumbled. Abigail giggled. Josephine shook her head.

"I didn't mention Rainey's name one time like Cheney told me not to," Grandma BB continued.

"You just did," Imani said dryly.

Grandma BB snarled at her traveling companion. "Keep it up and when we get home, I will set your lawn on fire."

Imani shrugged. "You've already done that, and if you do it again, you'll pay for it again."

"I was simply trying to kill the weeds and it got out of control." Grandma BB spat, then turned back to Josephine and took her hand in her soft one. "I wish you would come back to visit me once again. I have truly missed your company. Those visas sure can mess up a good thing. Maybe you can apply for one of those purple cards, so you can become a citizen."

Maybe in another country, but not the United States. "It's a green card, Grandmother B. I would have to marry an American citizen," Josephine corrected.

"An offer might be waiting on the table," Abigail murmured.

"Sister!" Josephine stomped her foot.

"Listen, sugar. Whatever the differences are with Cheney's twin, work them out. He seems to be decent enough...unlike his dad," Grandma BB stated. "He's handsome and you might as well say rich, with his fancy car."

Imani cleared her throat, which seemed to alert Grandma BB to stick to some sort of script. "For me, love came once and it was short. All the other men I've dated since Henry's death have been boy toys."

A tear slid from Josephine's eyes. "I'd have to give up so much," she whispered.

"But how much will you gain?" Grandma BB gave her a tight hug. "Well, as Cheney says, 'Pray on it'. I love you, baby."

"Come on, Granny, we have to catch a flight. I have a list of repos I've got to chase down when I get back to work," Imani advised.

After the final group hug and kisses, Josephine and Abigail returned to the car. *How much would I gain by giving up so much?*

Chapter 23

"Are you all right?" Janae asked Rainey as they lounged in his condo's lower level. Sipping on fruit juices, they were watching his niece and nephew's poor attempts at winning a game of pool.

It was a Friday night, and Janae had dropped by his place unannounced. She had just picked up her children from after school activities.

Crossing one bare foot over the other, Rainey stared ahead, debating if he should answer. After all, it had been a while since the two had a normal conversation that didn't involve her finding fault with the family.

"Not at this moment."

Janae leaned closer. "What's going on, Rainey? Does it have anything to do with that woman in Africa?"

"Josephine is off limits and not up for discussion." Rainey gave her a deadpan look to back up his statement.

With pursed lips and slanted brown eyes, Janae physically restrained herself.

"Mom, Uncle Rainey, I beat Natalie!" Alex grinned.

"He cheated," Natalie replied, sparking an argument.

Rainey stood. "That's enough, you two. Play fairly or don't play."

"Yes, sir," they mumbled in unison while casting accusatory frowns at each other.

Resettling in his seat, Rainey had no answers as to his next move, since he had turned it over to the Lord. Any other time, he would have given a woman the ultimatum and walked away—like he did his ex-girlfriend many years ago and he saw how badly that ended.

Rainey couldn't do that this time because he loved Josephine and no other woman could compare with her beauty, wit and charm. So God had him in a holding pattern.

"What's going on with you?" Rainey turned the tables on her. Janae was the one stalling now. "Hey," he lowered his voice. "Maybe you and Bryce should get away."

"That's what he says, but someone needs to keep an eye on things while Daddy is..." she swallowed and stuttered, "away." Janae frowned.

"I just don't get it. Why did this have to happen to us? I've lost business at some of my salon chains and friends..." she ranted and Rainey had no choice but to listen. The entire family was hurting emotionally without their dad's presence. "I have a problem forgiving people. I just can't strut through the church doors like you and be a changed person," Janae admitted.

So some of the truth was coming out and Janae accused him of defecting. More than once, Rainey wondered why it didn't bother her to continue holding onto the past like super glue.

"Well, you better solve it, because one day you're going to need someone to forgive you."

As the silence seemed to stretch between them, Rainey tapped her hand. "Come on, sis. Let's show these two kiddies how to really shoot pool." After two games, Rainey and Janae were tied one win each, the same as his love life—tied, but with no real winners.

Josephine had been on Rainey's mind more than usual lately. For the past few weeks, he had used all his restraint not to call or email her. He wanted her to stew and to realize what she was giving up as a lesson. Only, he was the one who was sulking and whose heart was breaking, but he kept up the charade around others as if he was in control. How far was that from the truth?

If Josephine returned to St. Louis, she would be in need of nothing. Rainey would make sure of that. If only she would take one more trip, then she could see everything through the "eyes of love"—that old cliché.

A few days earlier, Rainey vented his frustration to Cheney who had sat on the sidelines and not interfered. He appreciated that, but now he was about to go crazy over Josephine's excuses not to visit.

"It's called instant intercession," she explained when he finished. She had said a brief prayer for him on the spot, then topped it off with a hug.

Still nothing seemed to change instantly. Rainey needed fast results. Where Janae had issues with forgiving people for the slightest indiscretion, he struggled with maintaining a patient spirit.

The next morning after reading his Bible before he left for his practice, Rainey wondered at 2 Peter 3:9: *The Lord is not slack concerning his promise, as some men count slackness; but is longsuffering to us-ward, not willing that any should perish, but that all should come to repentance.* Clearly, the scripture applied to salvation, but Rainey sought a scripture about God not being slack concerning another request—Josephine.

Do not pray amiss. Your thoughts are not My thoughts, neither are your ways My ways, the Lord forcefully spoke like lightning from Isaiah 55:8, *I am not a man, I am God.*

Rainey shivered from the reprimand and repented quickly. He really had no reason to complain. Despite taking two trips that should have hurt his bottom line, his practice had seen an increase in the number of new patient referrals. So he was blessed in spite of his reckless actions.

There was no explanation except God. Who was really learning a lesson here, him or Josephine? But enough was enough.

While his office staff was at lunch, Rainey closed the door and pulled out his international calling card. His heart pounded as he tapped in her number; he wondered if Josephine would accept his call.

"Hello," Josephine said in the sultry manner, which he enjoyed.

Momentarily speechless, Rainey was clueless about what to say first—an apology, I miss you or I love you. He exhaled. "There is so much I want to say. I...I just wanted to hear your—"

"I'm sorry for my stubbornness and unwillingness to compromise. This emotion is new to me, but I do love you so much."

Instant forgiveness, a man couldn't ask for anything better. "My apology was coming." Rainey grunted. "I love you, too, babe."

"I want to be happy and I'm most happy with you. I will make arrangements to come for a visit."

Yes! Rainey pumped a fist in the air. Then he stood from behind his desk and did a jog in place. "You tell me what date and I will purchase your airline ticket."

"Dr. Reynolds," Josephine began. Rainey smirked, having missed her tongue-lashings. "Your country has not relaxed restrictions on travel. Our ambassador's trip to the U.S. was delayed a week because someone in his office misfiled paperwork, and he is a diplomat. So in two weeks, the ambassador and my father—his assistant—will arrive in the States for a week-long conference."

So that was the trip Gyasi mentioned when Rainey visited last. "Will my lovely Ghanaian woman be accompanying them, too?" His heart pounded wildly. That would be a welcome surprise!

"I'm an ambassador's employee's daughter. I'm non-essential," she said slowly.

"You're most essential to me," Rainey cooed at the same time his assistant knocked and opened his door.

Caught in the act of a happy dance, she eyed him. Rainey froze. "Your one o'clock appointment has arrived," she mouthed and backed out in a hurry. He nodded, but was in no hurry to break their reconnection. "We'll talk again?"

"Yes. Tomorrow or the day after. My family and I are attending a celebration tonight."

"For what now?" Some things never changed.

"Adae Kese," Josephine explained. "The forty day celebration—"

"Okay, sweetheart, I get the point. I have to go. I'll call tomorrow as soon as I get home." They said, "Love you," in unison and disconnected.

Whistling, Rainey left his office in a good mood. *Lord, I will never accuse You of being a slacker again.*

As if to make up for the time they lost, Rainey called Josephine twice a day for a week. They Skyped more often, and Rainey couldn't be any happier, knowing that Josephine was making preparations to visit.

"Hey, babe. Don't forget to email me your father's itinerary, including his hotel and cell numbers. I would like to see him while he's in the States next week."

"He's going to be in New York, not St. Louis," she reminded him.

"If I can fly to Accra, then I think I have enough frequent flyer miles to fly to New York."

"I'm sure he would be glad to see you. He's asked about you."

That was encouraging. "That's good to know. Well, I better go. *Med wo papaapa.*"

"I love you, too, Dr. Reynolds." After they disconnected, Rainey sat in his kitchen and stared out the bay window, looking toward the common pond he shared with others in the gated community.

His trip to New York would have a purpose. There was only one reason why he or any man in love wanted to meet with his woman's father. Was he sure he wanted to take the big step? Would Mr. Yaw Amoah welcome him with open arms as a lost member of an African tribe and give his stamp of approval?

He clued Cheney in on his plans. "I'll be praying God's favor," she said excitedly. Rainey didn't have to tell Shane. His friend knew Josephine had his heart. Next, he typed a long letter to his father, revealing his intentions.

Finally, Rainey contacted Josephine's father the day he arrived in New York. "*Akwaaba*, Mr. Yaw Amoah, I would like to speak with you if you have time during this trip."

"Hello, Dr. Reynolds. It would be good to see you again. I have free time at the end of the week."

"*Meda wo ase.*" Rainey said thank you in Twi for brownie points and ended the call.

His father's response came two days before Rainey's flight to New York.

Dear Son,

I am a happy man. I reread your letter several times. I imagined that we were relaxing on the terrace or out to dinner, but it was just the two of us men—father-to-son—face-to-face. First I would tell you how proud I am of the man you became, how you've made your mark and that I've been on the sidelines rooting for you.

I would let you know the responsibilities of a good husband and great father. I would remind you that a wife is a life-long partner and to share everything and not keep secrets. I am the example of making a mistake and keeping secrets until the Lord showed me my sin right in front of my face when Cheney moved next door to Mr. Beacon's widow.

I'm sure your lady is beautiful inside and out, and that she challenges your heart. I accept my absence at important events, but my heart is with you. If the Lord's wills, I hope to see you in a few weeks when you come to visit. I'm counting down four months, one week, one day until I see everyone at one time, including your bride. Give her my love.

I love you, son—my only son. I'm proud of the man you've become.

Your father.

Rainey choked. The words lifted off the page. He definitely could hear his father's voice as if they were sitting in the same room. "God, please continue to bless my father and keep him safe. Thank You. In Jesus' name. Amen."

The next morning, Rainey's plane landed at LaGuardia airport. He secured a limo to the St. Giles Hotel-The Court where the diplomats' staffers and other personnel were staying.

During the ride, he reviewed his spiel to win Gyasi's approval. In no time, the driver parked on 39th Street near Lexington. Rainey tipped him and stepped out confidently.

Granted, Rainey had survived the first dinner at Gyasi's home. Shame couldn't begin to describe how Rainey felt every time he had to explain his father's absence. Yet, he was still a part of Dr. Roland Reynolds' fan club. He had no problem losing a friend or a client who badmouthed his dad. Yes, he had lost some clients, but most understood what his father did so long ago had nothing to do with Dr. Rainey Reynolds.

The hotel lobby buzzed with people from everywhere. It was as if the United Nations was holding a meeting. Searching faces, Rainey recognized Gyasi among other men dressed in their African garb.

Why was he nervous? In America, a Black man with money, status, and a solid career was a prize. Hopefully that would translate in Ghana to Josephine's father.

Gyasi noticed him and waved, then excused himself from his group. *"Akwaaba."*

Josephine's father returned the greeting. "It's good to see you again, Dr. Reynolds. Since it's a nice day here, how about we walk? Friends say Fagiolini is a nice restaurant for a meal."

"Sure."

Gyasi's walk was more of an irritating foot-dragging task. Not a good pace on the streets of the Big Apple. "Are you enjoying New York?" Rainey asked, since it appeared that Gyasi wasn't going to initiate a conversation.

"Yes, I have accompanied my employer here several times." He stepped aside to allow a pedestrian the right of way. "I have not been to St. Louis. Is it this busy, *yo?*" He made a sweeping wave with his arm in the air.

"Nothing like this," Rainey was glad to say. "We walk slower and have a tendency to smile and speak. The closest metropolitan city in the Midwest with this pace would be Chicago."

"I see."

After crossing several blocks, they arrived at Fagiolini. The staff greeted them and they were promptly seated without a reservation. After Paul, their waiter, handed them their menus, he suggested dishes based on their likes and dislikes and different seasonings.

Rainey noted Gyasi's expressions as he ordered. He was ready to get this over with so he and Josephine could start planning their wedding. Before Christ saved him, a long engagement wouldn't bother him. Now walking with Christ and loving Josephine, he found the scripture that said it was better to marry than burn. And the big bonus, according to the Bible, they were equally yoked.

Once Paul disappeared, Rainey cleared his voice. "Mr. Yaw Amoah, I'm sure you're aware of why—"

"Our food has not arrived," Gyasi stopped him.

Drumming his fingers on the table, Rainey nodded and backed off. He checked out the restaurant that seemed to cater to the business crowd. Stalling wasn't one of his strong points. Either the food better get there soon, or Rainey would personally drag the chef to their table to prepare it in front of them.

Paul returned with their drinks and salad. Gyasi offered prayer, and Rainey Amen'd it, ready to talk. Before they finished their salads, their main dishes arrived. After a few more bites, chews, wiping his mouth with his napkin, slow sips of his drink, Gyasi sat back and seemed ready to give Rainey an audience.

Of course, it was imperfect timing. Rainey had a mouth full of food. Dabbing his mouth, Rainey began his spiel, forcing himself not to make eye contact as a sign of respect. "Mr. Yaw Amoah, I'm sure you know why I asked to see you while you are here in New York."

When Rainey peeped up, Gyasi's blank stare wasn't encouraging.

Pushing his food aside, Rainey folded his hands and leaned forward. As Paul headed their way, Rainey gave him a fierce look. He detoured to another table.

"I love Josephine. She has a part of my heart and I need her. I can provide for her and our children." Rainey rambled on, hoping at any time, Gyasi would put him out of his misery and consent. Instead the man picked up his fork and continued to eat, never taking his eyes off Rainey.

"I'm asking for your daughter's hand in marriage," Rainey concluded.

Gyasi took his time in responding. "In America, you have customs and traditions. Dr. Reynolds, I am insulted that you would take advantage of my visit to ask for my daughter's hand in marriage. You come to me on my soil in our traditional custom and I might entertain you."

Stunned, Rainey stuttered, "I apologize, sir. I was unaware of the Ghanaian tradition."

"That is most unfortunate." Finishing his meal, Gyasi summoned the waiter for dessert. Rainey had lost his appetite.

Disappointed that his meeting with Gyasi did not go as planned, Rainey escorted him back to the St. Giles Hotel and handed him an envelope tied with a red satin bow. It was meant to be a pre-proposal note and it still was. Rainey just didn't know how much of a delay there would be.

"This is for your *woho yε fεw* daughter." Rainey was sure his pronunciation of beautiful was right this time.

Gyasi hinted a smile of approval. "She will receive it."

Stuffing his hands in his pants pockets, Rainey thanked him. With an hour to waste before heading to LaGuardia, Rainey wandered down Fifth Avenue. Eying the skyscrapers, including the Empire State Building, the lyrics from the Temptations' "Runaway Child Running Wild" taunted him to go back home where he belonged.

The rejection stung. The name Reynolds opened doors—or used to—not closed them. Then Diana Ross's song, "Ain't No Mountain High Enough" gave him a boost.

Rainey wouldn't be a Reynolds if he didn't have a plan B to get what he wanted. He hailed a cab. "Lord, I need You in on this, too. I know I should have acknowledged You beforehand, then You would have directed my words and path. It's better late than never, right? Here I am, Lord."

Once he was en route back home, Rainey replayed the long lunch, but short conversation with Gyasi. Rainey's slip-up had been not putting God in the mix and that was where he kept having problems. At least no other person besides his father and Cheney knew his mission that morning, not even Shane. Being the voice of reason, Shane would have reminded him that Josephine was putting a blow to his manhood and to throw in the towel.

Love bears all things, believes all things, hopes all things, and endures all things, God whispered 1 Corinthians 13:7.

Rainey closed his eyes. *God, how much am I to bear in a lifetime?*

By the time Rainey's plane touched down in St. Louis, God hadn't answered. But for some unknown reason, Parke came to mind as he walked through the airport terminal.

Although Rainey knew more about the Ghanaian culture now than when he first started dating Josephine, he would be the first to admit he lacked knowledge. Maybe his brother-in-law could give him a quick review of Africa Wikipedia. He whipped out his smartphone and tapped in his sister's name to call.

He heard the noise in the background before she said hello. It wasn't unusual for the Jamieson household to sound like a party with three children.

"I'm back and wanted to stop by."

"You never need an invitation. I can't wait to hear about your 'meeting'. Come on over. It's family game night. The more the merrier," Cheney said. Rainey would have preferred privacy, but he was a man on a mission and he had wasted enough time.

Suddenly, she released a hearty laugh that caused Rainey to abruptly remove his ear to safeguard it from hearing loss.

Cheney stuttered her way back into the conversation. "I'm sorry, twin. When you get all these little Jamieson cousins together, they're a ball of energy."

His sister seemed to be the happiest person he knew. "Okay, I'll see you in a few."

Twenty minutes later, Rainey parked behind a row of vehicles in front of a three story historic home. The mouse gray house with large paned windows was an imposing structure.

Getting out of his car, Rainey hiked up the steps. With all the noise on the other side, he doubted they could hear him knock, so he tested the door. The chiming sound alerted them an intruder had entered the premises.

He became the center of attention. His niece, Kami, hugged him. She was Cheney and Parke's only daughter, and she, amazingly, resembled Parke as if she was his biological child rather than being adopted. Next his oldest nephew, followed by the little ones, acknowledged his presence with a smile or wave, but that was the extent of their greeting. They were not huggers.

Glowing, Cheney's eyes sparkled as she engulfed Rainey with a rocking hug and then a loud squeaky kiss. Rainey patted her stomach. "How are mother and child?"

Cheney beamed. "We are blessed."

"How far along are you again?"

"Umph. Not far enough. Six months." She rubbed her stomach. "So am I about to have a Ghanaian sister-in-law?" she whispered with an angelic hopeful expression.

"Sadly, no."

Cheney gasped and covered her mouth. "What happened?" Parke walked behind his wife suddenly in a panic-stricken state.

"I ran into a problem. I don't know if my sister told you, but I was in New Yor—"

"Yes, in confidence," Parke acknowledged in a low voice, shaking his hand. He tilted his head. "Let's go to the back where we can talk in quiet. These Jamiesons sure are a loud clan."

Cheney elbowed him. "We are Jamiesons, sweetie."

"Right." He winked and swatted her backside. "And don't you forget it, Momma."

Rainey greeted everyone as he made his way across the gleaming hardwood floor of the living and dining rooms where more of Cheney's in-laws camped out. Even Grandma BB and Imani were present. Both still boasted a fading tan from the Ghana sun.

Knowing the role his father played in her tragedy of becoming an early widow; Rainey never knew what to say around the woman. He kept his distance. However, since his father's imprisonment, Grandma BB had warmed to him with kind eyes and a friendly smile. No doubt, it was because of his being Cheney's twin.

They passed the enormous kitchen that usually sparkled, but not today. Parke helped Cheney step down into a sunken room. The back walls were lined with books. The front wall had every electronic play toy a man could ask for. With a sectional sofa, love seat, ottoman, and two recliners, Rainey estimated the size to be what could easily be two bedrooms put together.

"Have a seat, bro," Parke offered as he claimed a spot and dragged his wife down with him. As Cheney snuggled up next to her husband, Rainey recapped his conversation with Gyasi.

"He said no?" Parke looked perplexed. "Whew."

"In so many words. The blow to my ego took me down," Rainey hated to admit.

Parke seemed thoughtful before he responded. "Every culture has different traditions. Did he give you a hint at all?"

"No."

Screams of laughter echoed throughout the house. "I'm so sorry to interrupt you two while you're entertaining."

"You don't entertain family, you tolerate the knuckleheads." Parke joked, then became quiet. "Look at this as a test. Hold on a sec." Parke shifted and nudged Cheney aside. He got up to leave the room.

"Have you talked to Josephine?" Cheney asked.

"Not yet."

"So, when is the wedding?" Grandma BB asked, barging into the room.

"Excuse me?" Rainey didn't know if he was more shocked that someone knew his business or that it was Grandma BB who knew it.

"I was eavesdropping." She made no effort to apologize.

Cheney squinted at the woman until she shrugged and went back to the others.

Parke returned with the laptop and his younger brother, Malcolm. The man didn't say too much, but he watched everything. He could easily be a bouncer. Rainey pitied the man who crossed Malcolm's path.

Malcolm got their youngest brother, Cameron, on the phone who was considered the lead genealogist. How did a simple plea for help turn into a family conference call? Rainey rested his head in his hands. "This is so embarrassing."

"We're all in this together." Parke sat and booted up his computer. Malcolm relayed Cameron's instructions to navigate to a few websites.

After checking out a few sites, Parke tilted his monitor toward Rainey. "Man, look at this. There is actually an engagement process." He read aloud, "The kokooko ceremony begins with the elders and men in the groom's family knocking on the bride's family door. That's called an introduction...blah, blah..." He scanned the page. "Get this. The bride's family gives you a list of demands—or gifts for the bride-to-be like jewelry, a dowry, plus liquor, other stuff, plus liquor..."

Barking out a laugh, Malcolm held his stomach. "Her old man is going to make a killing off of you. I hope your dollar is worth more than Ghanaian cedis."

Peering closer at the website, Rainey didn't share in the entertainment. It read as if the groom-to-be was bringing the party with him. There was an endless list. He practically had to dress Josephine from head to toe. And what was up with all the liquor?

Rainey had money—investments, his practice and a trust fund his late grandfather set up. His first and only withdrawal had been for buying out his practice from a retiring orthodontist.

"I'm not worried about the money. What I can't make good on are the men in my family. That's what happens with being the only son." Rainey huffed. I have some distant cousins, but I doubt they would want to go to Ghana. Janae would never let Bryce leave the country, and Parke I know you can't leave Cheney's side. Maybe I can buy a family," he joked.

Parke stood abruptly and yelled for his cousins. "Ace, Kidd, you got a sec?" Within a few minutes the brothers from Boston stood in the doorway.

"What's up?" Ace, the younger one, asked.

Kidd just folded his arms and leaned against the door post. "Cuz."

"We have a situation. My brother-in-law needs help. I've got his back on this."

"We're in as long as it's spiritually legal. My illegal activity days are over," Kidd said, resembling a linebacker.

Rainey swallowed. He couldn't believe what he was hearing. None of the Jamiesons were kin to him in any way, and Parke, the eldest of the bunch, was an in-law. Getting onto his feet, he shook each Jamieson's hand. "Thanks, man."

"We can accompany you to Ghana. You name the day and time and we'll be on that flight," Parke seemed to speak for everyone. "And don't count Bryce out, yet. I think our brother-in-law may welcome a trip."

"Don't get too many ideas, dear." Cheney twisted her mouth. "I don't care how close you are to Cote d'Ivoire. No detours, dude. Help my brother and come straight back home," she said as if she was scolding a kindergartener.

What was comical was his brother-in-law's response. "Yes, wifey."

Rainey felt back in control. "Be prepared to leave as soon as your passports and visas are ready. No later than a month."

He forgot about Shane. His best friend would go if for no other reason, than to talk him out of it.

"Consider it done."

"Hold up! Hold on and wait a minute," Cameron shouted. Malcolm had put him on the loud speaker. "I'm still on my honeymoon. Even the Bible gives newlyweds a year before the husband goes off to battle."

Parke barked. "Man, this isn't war, Mr. Deuteronomy 24:5."

Rainey interrupted Parke. "I'm fighting for my woman and that's war to me!"

"Enough said," Cameron agreed. "But after we vouch for you, I'm out of there."

"Count me in, too," Grandma BB announced as she returned, clunking in her oversized Stacy Adams shoes. "I'm the god-grandmother of the bride-to-be. After all, if it weren't for me bringing you two together in the first place, you wouldn't be looking like a puppy dog that lost his favorite toy. But it'll cost you."

Rainey didn't even want to know, so he wasn't about to ask.

"You'll have to name your first born after me." Grandma BB folded her arms.

Was the woman serious? Ain't no way. "What if we don't have any girls? Are we exempt," he tried to string her along. Rainey didn't need any enemies in this.

If I am for you, there is no man who can stand against you, God spoke Romans 8:31.

Nodding, Rainey addressed the woman in a kind tone. "I'll pass."

The room was quiet, waiting for the little tornado to react. Grandma BB seemed to give him an appreciative smile. "You'll do. Can't have any pushovers in this family." She hugged him, then that embrace enticed the Jamieson wives into a group hug.

Soon the men joined their wives and before Rainey knew it, they were engaged in a group prayer. Grandma BB tried to squirm her way out of the circle; everyone blocked her path, especially Parke who was doing the praying. Watching with one eye open, Rainey smirked.

"Jesus, we acknowledge that You are a God of blessings and there are no failures in You. Go before us in Jesus' name. Let him find favor and let Your perfect will be done in Rainey and Josephine's lives..." In unison, everyone said, "Amen."

"Unfortunately, twin, we can't come in our state," Cheney said, pointing to her belly and Malcolm's wife Hallison. "But we have no problem having another kiddie party and spending money while our husbands are away."

Parke teasingly snarled and then winked. Cheney wrapped her arms around Parke's neck and kissed him. "Thank you for being there for my brother. I love you."

Rainey left to head home. It had been a long day and he longed for Josephine's voice. First thing in the morning, Rainey would go over his financial portfolio. Malcolm was right. Gyasi was taking him to the bank.

Chapter 24

Josephine suspected something had happened between Rainey and her father while they were in New York. The brief conversation with Rainey Saturday evening lacked the enthusiasm that normally filled their brief phone calls. It was like pulling teeth getting him to mention it.

"So you made it to New York." She had hoped her father wouldn't judge Rainey by his father's transgressions.

"I did." Rainey was quiet.

"And…" Josephine prompted, waiting for him to fill in the blank. Rainey didn't. She sighed. "Did you have dinner, go sightseeing…" Again, she was helping him along with the conversation—nothing.

"Sweetheart, your father and I enjoyed lunch. We were both cordial and genuinely glad to see each other."

That's it? Josephine frowned. From Rainey's dry tone, she wouldn't deduce that a warm and cozy tête-à-tête had transpired. When she mentioned her visit to the immigration office, Rainey perked up.

His mood tumbled when she informed him what happened. "They had been having computer problems and now their system is down and they said they didn't know how long it would be before it would come back up."

With their agreed time for international calls coming to a close, they talked scriptures and love. She sang an African lullaby and ended the call.

Now the next day, she eagerly awaited her father's return from traveling abroad, hoping to better understand what transpired between the men she loved and respected.

She recalled Pastor Ted's Sunday morning message on 'Why are you anxious if you trust in Jesus?'; it was starting to take root as she meditated on Philippians 4:6: *Be careful for nothing; but in everything by prayer and supplication with thanksgiving let your requests be made known unto God.*

Her family was about to eat dinner when her father walked through the door, hours earlier than expected. Everyone scrambled from the table to envelope him in a hero's welcome home.

Josephine was especially excited to see him. After the hugs and kisses, they washed their hands and prepared to enjoy Sunday dinner with friends and a few more extended family members who came by after church.

After he said grace, everyone helped themselves to tilapia, *waakye*—a mixture of rice and peas and other starchy dishes. Eating with gusto, her father enjoyed the dried roasted cassava of *gari*. The evidence was his moan after soaking the *gari* in a milk based juice with sugar and groundnut peanuts.

Although the meal was tasty, Josephine waited for any clues on the meeting with Rainey. When her father patted his stomach, Josephine took that as a sign he was ready for dialogue.

"I had a wonderful time visiting with my eldest daughter and Dennis while in London. Madeline sends her love and good news. She is expecting." He grinned boastfully. "It appears I will be an *impaa* soon."

Cheers, laughter, and applause circulated around the table. Josephine and Abigail hugged each other. If the Lord willed the baby to live past eight days, they would have a niece.

"How was New York, papa?" Josephine dared to ask.

His expression gave nothing away. "The ambassador says the meetings were positive and the flight to London was without incident..."

Soon her mother suggested her husband rest. Everyone pitched in to clear the table and restored the kitchen and dining room back to order. Before their guests left, Josephine held her baby cousin, Beatrice, who was growing even more beautiful, then she hugged her other cousins.

While her mother unpacked his suitcase, Josephine pulled him aside. "Papa, were you able to meet with Rainey."

"Yes." He nodded.

Not again? Josephine exhaled slowly to mask her frustration. She was about to give up and walk away when he stopped her. He went into his bedroom and returned with an envelope tied with a red ribbon. "Your young man sent this."

She accepted it with a smile. That's why Rainey was so hushed and her father had not mentioned it in front of the others. He sent her a keepsake. She welcomed the letter as if it was a large gift.

In the privacy of her own bedroom, Josephine carefully untied the ribbon and opened the small envelope. As she unfolded the letter, rose petals fell out. She fingered their delicate texture and waved one under her nose, then proceeded to read her missive.

Hi Baby,

When I gave this letter to your father, the petals were fresh. That's how we are when we are together—fresh, new and so alive. As these traveled, they began to die and that's how I feel every time I leave you, a part of me aches and seems to die.

I miss you, I love you, and together, we become a rose.

Rainey

After reading it a second time, she folded it up. The power failed just as she was about to log on the computer. Josephine was too happy to care. The letter was worth the wait. Opening her curtain, she watched the night sky and dreamed, recalling the scripture: *All thing work together for the good to those who love the Lord and are called to his purpose.* "Jesus, please let Rainey and me be Your purpose." Closing her eyes, she said, "Amen."

Chapter 25

Three weeks later, Rainey checked in at Lambert airport with his 'posse'. His mother was excited about going to Ghana and meeting Josephine officially. Bryce acted liberated to be traveling without Janae and Shane was quiet in his own thoughts.

Rainey glanced at the time on his iPhone. The others should be there shortly. He silently asked that God would grant him the desire of his heart and that it was His will that Josephine and he marry.

Scanning the terminal, Rainey got a glimpse of the Jamieson men, all five of them: Parke, Malcolm, Kidd, Ace, and even Cameron had torn himself away from his wife to be there for him.

It was comical watching others, especially the women, check them out. Not surprisingly, Malcolm and Kidd had identical menacing looks as if they were bodyguards with their bulkiness.

No wonder Cheney had nicknamed Kidd and his brother, Ace, the bad boys from Boston when they first relocated to St. Louis. Only the loves of their lives—their wives, Eva and Talise, were able to tame them.

Rainey didn't want to know how the two had earned the name, but he was glad for their presence. Not that they all looked alike, their common thread was the gold band around their left ring finger. At thirty-six, he was ready to join their club.

Seeing the pack made Rainey wish he had brothers, or even close cousins. That was the downside to being the only son. The upside was every woman was at his beck and call, beginning with sisters who adored him and his mother who spoiled him, but it was his father who taught him how to be a man.

He and Bryce had been close since he married Janae, but Rainey was closer to his childhood friend Shane—Dr. Maxwell. Maybe, it was worth looking into setting aside some time to delve into the male side of genealogy to find cousins. He would talk to Parke about the 23andme DNA test.

Rainey squinted. Sure enough, Grandma BB and Imani strolled among them, reveling in the fact that the men were with them and that they were probably the envy of every woman in the terminal. Shaking his head, Rainey knew the trip would truly be interesting.

"Is that your sister's friend?" Shane asked.

"Which one?" Rainey asked.

"The white one in the tight jeans, black biker jacket, long hair, riding boots...wow."

"Oh, that's Imani Segall." Rainey had known her for so long, he considered her as another sister.

"Nice." Shane didn't take his eyes off of her.

"I wouldn't get too excited. Some women take your money, Imani will take your car." Rainey said at Shane's bewildered expression, "She's a repo woman and she's been known to tow away the wrong vehicle."

The pair laughed, then his friend frowned. Rainey knew what was coming next.

"Has the other woman been diagnosed with dementia or Alzheimer's?" Shane asked with concern as he pointed to Grandma BB who was dolled up in her authentic-looking African garb, but the outfit was outshined by her Stacy Adams shoes.

Although Shane was aware of the history between Grandma BB and Rainey's father, he had never met her in person. "That's Grandma BB."

Shane blinked. "What is she doing here, sabotaging your shindig?

Rainey stretched out his legs. "Actually, no. She's coming to support me." He shrugged. "I'm taking it at face value and counting my blessings. As far as her egocentric taste in attire, I suspect she was born bourgeois."

Standing, Rainey shook hands with his in-laws then traded a pat or two on the back. Bryce and Shane also got to their feet and exchanged greetings. "I appreciate you all for coming." They nodded as one by one, each Jamieson acknowledged his mother with a kiss on her cheek. She glowed from the attention.

Parke relayed that Cheney was beside herself that she couldn't tag along and that she would miss the fun. At seven months along, Rainey wouldn't advise it and Parke wouldn't hear of it—and his dad would argue against it. Through his letters, Roland asked about his baby girl's condition when Cheney wasn't up to traveling to see him. The best Cheney would get was for Imani to videotape it.

Once they boarded the plane and settled in, Grandma BB dozed off and her snoring kicked in. Imani would nudge her and Grandma BB threatened her neighbor with bodily harm. It was a comical cycle.

After two stops and twenty-five hours later, Rainey and his entourage landed at the Kotoka airport. "My third trip," he mumbled, stepping off the plane onto the tarmac. "And hopefully my last for a long time."

Josephine knew he was coming. He led her to believe it was a regular visit because he couldn't stay away any longer, which he couldn't. Rainey doubted she knew his intention. He came to impress her father. After he and Parke had researched the elaborate and odd custom required to propose, Rainey was ready.

Once his weary group debarked, they dragged their bodies across the tarmac and boarded the shuttle to the terminal. Next their passports were scrutinized. Everyone passed Customs without their luggage being inspected, except Ace.

Cheney had said he pulled some stunt years earlier that landed him on the no-fly list. Rainey wondered if that had anything to do with it. When Ace was given the okay, Rainey led them through the terminal and outside to taxi drivers. He negotiated the fare for three taxis like a local to Highgate Hotel, where he had stayed on his last trip.

While the others climbed inside, Parke seemed distracted as he scanned the area and shook his head. "You have no idea how badly I want to forego sleep and head to the Elmira castle."

Gayle stuck her head out the cab and teased her son-in-law, "Then it would be my pleasure to inform my daughter that you disobeyed her orders."

That got a few laughs as his brother-in-law shivered as if he feared the repercussions. Rainey wasn't worried about his twin and Parke's marriage. Theirs was solid. Anyone could see they really loved and respected each other.

"Never mind, Mom Reynolds. After we get some rest, we'll head to the Amoahs to start this ritual.

As a group, they would initiate Kokooko—the knocking on their door. As the fiancé-to-be, Rainey had to rely on the elder members of his family to plead his case and make his intentions known. Rainey would not be allowed to utter a word.

"This is definitely a shot-gun proposal," Shane mumbled, shaking his head as he looked out the window.

Shane wasn't exactly sold on the custom or Rainey's rush to get married. His friend had said, before agreeing to come along, *"I still think it's too much trouble for one woman."*

Regardless of his feelings, the most important gesture was Shane was there with him. That said a lot about their friendship and brotherhood.

"My options are limited on this, Shane." Rainey shrugged. "The Kokooko is supposed to happen a week or two before the wedding, so I'm going for a two-for-one—the proposal and marriage ceremony. When I leave here, I will be a married man."

His mother sniffed from her front seat post. "I wish your father was here to see this."

"Me, too, Mother. Me, too." He had given Rainey his blessings, so he had peace in his father's absence.

"Well, we're going to wrap this shindig up in four days. Two, if we pray hard enough," Parke stated.

Rainey huffed. "Then we better add fasting to the mix, because Mr. Gyasi Yaw Amoah doesn't come across as a man to tolerate any mis-steps."

By the time they arrived at their hotel, Rainey had seen a welcome sight—hawkers. Not as many as in downtown Accra, but they were there, capturing his party with their wares balanced on their heads. As Rainey had been at first, Shane, Parke, and his mother were in awe.

Everyone checked in and went their separate ways. In his suite, it didn't take long before Rainey appeared comatose.

By four o'clock, Ghana time, everyone was awake and refreshed. They dressed as if they were going to a wedding—his.

Rainey patted the engagement ring and wedding band tucked away in his pants pocket.

They took taxis to the nearby Accra mall, pulling out the long list with plenty of things left to purchase. Suggested options for the mother-in-law were sandals or cash. Earlier in the week, he and his mother shopped at Neiman-Marcus for as many items as they could pack in their suitcases. While there she purchased Fafa's sandals.

For the father of the bride, Rainey had the bribe money, known as the bride's dowry. He had five thousand dollars in travelers' cheques, plus, the additional two thousand dollars for Gyasi.

Inside the mall, Rainey asked everyone to get the non-personal items on the list. He offered to pay for them, but everyone declined, saying they would be their wedding gifts. Their generosity touched him. Then as if someone activated a time clock, everyone dispersed for gift hunting that quickly turned into a shopping expedition.

In addition to bearing presents, the custom called for plenty of liquor. Since Rainey no longer drank and neither did Josephine's father, he purchased premium non-alcoholic drink for the celebrations.

They met back at the entrance at the designated time with purchases, which included souvenirs for their families. Hailing taxis, Rainey and the others got in and began the bumpy ride to the Amoahs.

Once they arrived in Kanda, they got out of their taxis with shopping bags. Standing right outside the gate, Parke suggested a quick prayer.

Rainey didn't wait for the others as he bowed his head. "Father God in the name of Jesus, this is the woman I chose to be my wife and helpmate. Jesus, please intercede on my behalf. Lead us and we will follow."

A chorus of Amens ended the impromptu prayer meeting. Bryce and Shane patted Rainey on the shoulder. "We've got your back," they said, almost in unison.

It was a solemn assembly as the group, with Rainey bringing up the rear, stopped at the front door.

Parke knocked. Although Josephine knew he was coming, she wasn't expecting him until the next day. Gyasi opened the door within seconds. Seemingly not intimidated by the number of imposing figures, Gyasi searched the crowd until his eyes connected with Rainey. Nodding, he then gave his attention to Parke who bowed his head slightly so as not to make direct eye contact.

His brother-in-law had done his homework. "Mr. Yaw Amoah, I bring you greetings from the Reynolds and Jamieson families in the United States." He presented a basket with four large bottles of sparkling favored water.

Gyasi accepted the offering.

"We have traveled across the world to have an audience with you and your family concerning a pressing matter regarding our intentions."

Extending his hand, Gyasi welcomed them into his home. Fafa came to his side and greeted her guests, ushering them into the living room. She excused herself to bring refreshments.

Gyasi offered a seat to Grandma BB, Rainey's mother, and Imani, then took his seat before allowing the men to relax on the sofa and available chairs. During the formalities, Rainey craved seeing Josephine, but he dared not speak through this Ghanaian custom.

Parke fumbled inside his pocket for Rainey's poem to re-cite as the proposal. Gyasi folded his hands. He darted his eyes around the crowd, but paused and scrutinized Rainey. The man had the most intimidating face, that Rainey was glad he had switched his deodorant to Old Spice. There was nothing worse than letting this man see him sweat.

Clearing his throat, Parke made a boastful presentation, reading it word for word. "My brother-in-law has peeped through your garden and a magnificent flower beckoned to him. Majestic and delicate Josephine is that flower and her roots are deep."

Rainey shrugged when Parke shook his head. Yes, it was corny, but it was from a boilerplate example Rainey found on the Internet. Shane would never let him live down this part of ceremony.

"He asks for your family's permission to uproot that flower for his garden to admire her beauty until God closes his eyes. Dr. Rainey Reynolds is asking for your daughter, Josephine Abena Amoah's hand in marriage." Parke paused as all eyes focused on Gyasi instead of the refreshing drink Fafa was passing around.

"We come prepared, sir, to meet the requirements for your permission to uproot your beautiful flower."

Again the room was silent. Either Josephine was not home or she was hidden from his sight. If only he could just touch her finger as a point of contact.

Gyasi and Fafa spoke softly in Twi. Rainey had memorized the playbook, so he knew what was coming next.

"Can you come back in a week while I consult the other elders in my family?"

"We cannot," Parke answered, playing his role as an elder most convincingly. "We're prepared to meet your demands. Although Rainey can stay longer, we have families and two pregnant wives at home."

"Make that three. Eva is expecting again." Grinning, Kidd broke protocol to add that tidbit. And that opened the floodgate.

"Mr. Amoah, my son loves Josephine. Really loves her. I look forward to embracing your daughter as my own, not as an outsider." Gayle capped her pitch with a gentle smile. Fafa smiled back even if Gyasi remained expressionless.

Grandma BB stood—oh boy. That was not a good sign. Rainey closed his eyes. He couldn't watch.

"Mr. Amoah, as you are probably aware, I tell it like it is and Dr. Reynolds is a proud man, yet he's putting everything on the line for Josie. With me around, you don't have to worry about a thing. He has my vote."

Opening his eyes, Rainey watched as Grandma BB smoothed out her dress and retook her seat. At least she left her Stacy Adams shoes at the hotel.

One by one, his extended family—because that's what they were at the moment, vouched for him.

"I see." Gyasi stood and left the room. Everyone faced Rainey as if he knew what to expect after a second consultation. He didn't. Soon enough, Gyasi returned with a list and handed it to Parke. "Two days."

Chapter 26

Josephine had just returned home late after attending a program at the university. She was in a good mood, knowing Rainey would arrive the following day.

"Rainey was here?" Josephine asked her father again when he called her into the living room not long after she walked through the door. Her heart pounded with excitement.

"He arrived with many family members and friends," he stated.

What was going on? What was her father alluding to? Folding her hands, she waited for him to continue.

"But the father is the head of the family and he is in prison for a cowardly crime. That dishonor does not sit well with me, Josephine, to entertain an engagement ceremony." Her father frowned.

Josephine gasped. *Oh my Jesus, he came to Ghana to initiate a Kokooko?* Her eyes blurred and her heart warmed that he was so endearing. She wondered who accompanied him. While she was excited, her father's concerned look didn't go away.

"Most fascinating is Grandmother B's character assessment of the son of the man who killed her husband. She has no ill feelings toward him. That's God. Your young man has some strong family and friend ties."

If only Grandma BB would make a vow with God and honor it, Josephine thought. Cheney had told her how her host had attended church and received salvation through the water baptism in Jesus' name and the gift of the Holy Ghost.

Yet, the woman seemed to turn her back on Jesus. God was still giving her His grace to come back. Despite all her misgivings, she found kindness in her heart to speak highly of Rainey. Josephine would be forever grateful.

Gyasi drew her mind back into the conversation. "Daughter, I've seen you happy and sad. In two days, your young man's family will return. As is our custom, I will ask you, then, your answer. Marriage is a commitment, not a test-drive—as Americans say. If there is something troubling you about your doctor, then consider that carefully. A vow before God is written in stone."

Like the gospel song, "My Soul Says Yes," Josephine's heart screamed yes, but the practical, methodical side said it would never work. After the bliss faded away, would Rainey's love replace her love for Ghana?

Unlike Madeline who wanted to see the world; Josephine had seen it and couldn't wait to get back home. The most she had promised Rainey was to visit him in the U.S. That was progress for her, but marriage? Would he be willing to live half the year in America, or at least spend the winter months in Ghana?

Her father stood and kissed her cheek then stared at her. "As you know, your mum and I expect great things from our daughters of the Akan people. The heritage is passed down to you. In two days, choose wisely, Josephine. Have no regrets." Walking out the room, he continued to his bedroom and closed the door behind him.

Josephine blinked back her tears as she turned off the light and entered her own room. She loved him immensely, and he loved her. "Jesus, I'm acknowledging You. You know my heart as well as my future. Lord, I want to give back to my people, my country…"

When she could no longer form the words, the power of the Holy Ghost spoke through her. She let the tongues flow as she welcomed the intercession. She didn't know what else to pray, but the Holy Ghost was actively uttering those things to be done in her life. Shutting out her problems, Josephine worshipped Him.

Once Josephine composed herself, she sensed she was not alone. Opening her eyes, she saw her faithful sister standing by. If there was any type of prayer or praise going on, Abigail was drawn to it. If Josephine moved away, who would be her prayer partner then?

ॐॐ

The next morning, Josephine checked her email before heading off to work. As expected, Rainey had emailed her three times. *Did she dare open them?* She debated before signing off. Not yet, she needed that day to commune with God on what He wanted her to do.

Since Abigail had class that morning, they rode the trotro into Legon together. Walking across campus, Josephine's mind drifted back to the day she had given Rainey a tour of her work-place. She was proud to be a part of such a prestigious institution. When she sniffed, Abigail reached out and squeezed her hand.

"Love should never make you sad. If Rainey loves you, he will keep you smiling." They hugged. "See you at home." She hurried in the opposite direction to her business class.

Throughout the day, when Josephine thought about Rainey, she prayed and asked her coworker Kim to do the same. Without questions, Kim happily complied. By the time she retired for bed later that night, Josephine had resisted all temptation to open any of his emails.

The next evening, at the appointed time, the doorbell rang. Unlike a few days ago, Josephine's house was quiet. Tonight, many of her extended family had been summoned to witness the Kokooko.

She was not permitted to be in on the "negotiations" until it was time to give her decision. Abigail and two cousins waited inside her bedroom with her.

When there was a knock at the door, Abigail opened it and her grandmother, mother, and a few more female cousins hurried in carrying larges boxes, small ones and bags. They contained her bridal clothes handpicked by her husband-to-be, as well as gifts for Abigail, Fafa, and a few cousins. *Jesus, I should be happy because I love him, but I'm scared,* she prayed silently.

"I'm not sure," she whispered as her mother embraced her.

"When you look into his eyes, you will have your answer," her mother advised. "Now, let's get you dressed."

The room was giddy with excitement as they *ooh*ed and *ahh*ed over one item after another. Abigail dusted her face with shimmering power and blush. Her bridal gown was the most beautiful one she had ever seen in African garb. Everyone helped her dress, fussing with each detail as they admired Rainey's gifts.

A cousin arranged an elaborate head wrap with splashes of red and gold interwoven with other colors. Next, Josephine slipped her slender feet into exquisite beaded heeled sandals.

"You are breathtaking, Josephine," her mother choked, patting her chest as a jeweled necklace was draped around Josephine's neck to match the dangling earrings, all compliments of Rainey. The final touch was a dash of perfume.

The knock at the door signaled that Josephine was being summoned for her answer. Since this was a festive occasion, sometimes the bride teased her husband-to-be with a decoy. Josephine had consented that Abigail could be her temporary stand-in. It was all in jest. Nothing meant to be deceptive as in Genesis 29 where Laban tricked Jacob into marrying the wrong sister, Leah, instead of Rachel, whom he loved.

When Abigail slipped out of the room, everyone put their ear to the door. They giggled when they heard Rainey gasp when asked if this was his intended bride. Their laughter eased some of the tension.

Josephine took a deep breath. Would she betray her heart or herself? "God, I don't know what is best for me. Your Word says in Luke, 'out of the abundance of the heart, my mouth speaks.' Let me have no regrets with my words," she whispered. Those who heard her mumbled, "Amen."

Abigail raced back in the room near hysteria. "Marry him!"

"Why?" Josephine panicked.

"Because you love him, silly." Abigail gave her a gap-toothed grin.

Counting to three, her cousins walked out in front of her, shielding her from view. Taking deep breaths, Josephine trailed them. When she turned the corner of the hall, her eyes immediately locked with Rainey's. She had to keep from drooling.

He stood at her entrance as did all the other Jamieson men and someone in the mix was taping it. Although she appreciated the others' unexpected presence, Josephine hardly took the time to register who was there as she joined her family on the other side of the room. It was like opposing families in a game show. Rainey retook his seat and the other men followed suit.

She glanced at Rainey's mother who was teary-eyed. Gayle Reynolds' smile was genuine.

The awestruck look on Rainey's face was priceless. She felt beautiful. Josephine hoped she was the vision he saw when he chose her attire. Her father and maternal grandfather and older uncles stood. Parke took the lead and stood with the others.

It was déjà vu. Not long ago, Madeline had been in the position where Josephine now was.

"Dr. Rainey Reynolds, is this the bride you seek as your wife?" Her grandfather asked.

"Yes."

Her grandfather turned to her. "Josephine Abena Yaa Amoah, do you voluntarily want to enter into a union with this man?"

With one word, her life would change. She swallowed, then opened her mouth as Rainey broke protocol and got up. Staying behind the imaginary line between both families, he knelt on one knee, never taking his eyes off hers.

Her heart fluttered. "Yes," she whispered and exhaled. She didn't realize she was shaking until her grandfather asked her a second time.

"Josephine Abena Yaa Amoah, do you love this man enough to become his wife?"

She exhaled again and nodded before uttering, "Yes."

Josephine had one last chance to bow out with a yes, no, or wait—we need more time—but the look of love on Rainey's face made her surrender by the third time. With more conviction in her voice, she answered with a resounding, "Yes!"

Low cheers surfaced around her. Rainey appeared the most relieved. Reaching in his pocket, he displayed and then slid her engagement ring on her finger. The diamonds glistened, or maybe it came from the glaze in her eyes. She didn't realize she was shaking until Rainey engulfed her in a hug.

Josephine practically collapsed in his arms right after the kiss. It was art. He had perfected how to kiss her with record speed, making every second count.

Fluttering her lids, Rainey was waiting to give her a wink. As Rainey's spokesman, Parke stepped forward and presented them with his and her Bibles.

Hers was a deep burgundy with *My Beloved Mrs. Reynolds* engraved on the cover. He was confident she would say yes. His Bible was a rich navy with engraving on the front.

"This is a symbol of how important it is for the scriptures to be applied in your married life. Honor God by loving each other," Parke spoke as if he was ordained or from experience. Josephine honestly didn't know which was true.

Next, Josephine's grandfather prayed for a shower of blessings over their lives and for those generations to come. That concluded their wedding ceremony. Josephine and Rainey were whirled into an informal receiving line. That was the cue for every elder to offer advice for a budding marriage. It just so happened there were twelve elders in attendance.

With a smack on the drum, the festivities got underway. The beat encouraged everyone young and old to celebrate their union. The laughs and food were plentiful and her new husband's affectionate hugs were constant.

Before the celebration ended, Grandma BB upstaged the bride and groom with her interpretation of what seemed like every dance step known to man from the twist to the wobble and then made a quick study of the African beat.

Chapter 27

The glow from the red moon in the African night sky served as a spotlight outside the window of Dr. and Mrs. Rainey Reynolds' honeymoon suite. Josephine opened her eyes, wondering if she had been dreaming. An arm secured around her waist and the ring sparkling on her finger, were proof she was not.

She smiled as she peeked at the moon through the sheer curtains. The wedding was beautiful. Everyone said she looked like an African princess. She had felt like an African doll.

When they left her now "former" home, the celebration was in high gear. Grandma BB and Imani were dancing down a Soul Train Line. She couldn't believe all the Jamieson men that had accompanied Rainey on his behalf. She wiggled her ring finger.

"I did it! I said yes to the husband," Josephine whispered, mimicking the popular TV show for brides when they find that perfect wedding dress, "Say Yes to the Dress."

"For a moment, I thought you might not." Startled, she felt Rainey's warm breath tickle her neck until she giggled. "What was going on in that beautiful head to cause you to hesitate?"

"Oh, did I wake you?" she quietly asked as if others could hear them.

Gently squeezing her, Rainey kissed the top of her hair. "How can a man sleep when he has a treasure such as you?"

Rolling over she faced him, Josephine blushed at the compliment. She reached out and stroked Rainey's jaw. He watched her intently without saying a word. She would enjoy the many pillow talks they would share. "I was thinking about how all this happened."

Rainey chuckled. "Ah, I admit this whole getting engaged and married in one night was foreign to me, but no one would have had to ask me twice about marrying you." He toyed with her braids, wrapping the curls around his finger.

"What's wrong, baby, are you having regrets?" The moonlight shone on his eyes. Josephine read his concern.

Josephine loved him, but she was not either of her sisters. Madeline's love for Dennis assuaged her original issues about not marrying a Ghanaian man and Abigail was itching to leave the continent to explore her options. Josephine always envisioned her future with her immediate and extended family on African soil, and making a contribution to her nation's education and wealth.

Then Dr. Rainey Reynolds walked into her life and she could barely breathe normally. Josephine knew she was getting in over her head by falling in love without a concise plan on how this was going to work.

Shaking her head, a tear escaped. "My father asked me three times if I wanted to marry you and I answered yes."

Rainey made it clear that he could not make a decent living in Accra, so as an African woman married to an African-American man, Josephine's vow meant consenting to being uprooted as any good wife would.

"But?" Rainey, fully alert, rose up on an elbow. "You know I will move mountains to give you your heart's desire."

She wanted to boo-hoo for the love this man—her husband—had for her. She had to be truthful, so there would be no secrets between them. "I miss home already, not knowing when I will see Ghana again."

Rainey stroked her cheek and then outlined her lips. "Baby, you have my word that you can return to Accra any time you want—no restrictions."

His nostrils flared as he inched his lips closer to hers. "And because I love you so much and don't want you out of my sight, I will re-arrange my patients to accompany you." His declaration was seductive.

"That's love," she whispered. What more could she ask for? Josephine smiled and returned his affection by placing a kiss on his eyes and nose and mouth.

"Keep that up and there will be no more pillow talk tonight, but I want you to know that your home is now my home."

"Meda wo ase."

Rainey winked. "You are welcome, Mrs. Reynolds." He grinned.

"What I will miss most is the naming ceremony we will have when our child is born." Josephine sniffed as her eyes blurred.

"I expect you to teach me your customs for us to incorporate into our marriage. Now, I'm sure the bride crying on her honeymoon night is not one of them."

Jesus, thank You for fighting fear with faith or I would have missed my blessing with this man, Josephine thought as she admitted not many men would put aside physical desires to ensure their wives' comfort. "Sorry to worry you. I'm not even a day old bride. I guess I have newlywed jitters."

"Close your eyes," he coaxed and then showered her with pure love until she drifted back to sleep.

Three days later, Josephine Reynolds fought off another crying spell while she bid her husband goodbye at the Kotoka Airport. Rainey looked just as torn to leave her.

"Wife, I don't want to leave you. God knows I don't, but I have to get back and prepare things for the new Mrs. Reynolds."

Josephine exhaled. She liked the sound of that. The Jamieson men had already returned home to their families the day after the celebration. Only Grandma BB and Imani remained an extra day to shop off the beaten path open markets and pick up more waist beads.

"Hopefully, our separation wouldn't be long," Josephine said through her tears.

Sitting in the restaurant, the couple waited for Rainey's flight to be called. "I don't understand. You have the documents of my sponsorship, I submitted the fee, and you scheduled your appointment with the Bureau of Consular Affairs. Of all the times to have another computer glitch, why now?"

Neither she nor Rainey could believe the sign on the door: *An unexpected computer virus has hampered our ability to honor visa appointments, walk-ins, and renewals. We appreciate your patience and understanding and will keep the public updated.*

Rainey's nostrils had flared. He lacked patience and he didn't understand the complexities of her government.

Josephine had been on a nonimmigrant visa as an exchange student when she first traveled to America. Now that she was married to a U.S. citizen, they both thought applying for an immigrant visa for permanent residency wouldn't be as much of a hassle.

"As a newlywed, I'm not happy. I had hoped they would have finished the reviewing process by now...I've been here a week and a half so I could escort my bride home. I don't like the idea of you traveling alone."

"I'll be there as soon as I can, husband, I promise. I've requested my birth certificate, and they have checked into my background to prove I haven't a police record." Josephine still didn't want to leave her homeland, but everything was waiting for her: Cheney and the rest of her in-laws, possibly a part-time position as an archivist and researcher at a non-profit organization and most importantly, her husband.

When his flight was announced, Josephine shed the real tears as Rainey cupped her chin in his hand. She thrived on his touches of possession. She was about to say something when Rainey *shh*ed her. "Hold still. I'm memorizing every angle of your face to visualize at night when you're not there."

Josephine never cried so much as she waved goodbye.

Chapter 28

It was the second consecutive Saturday family dinner at Rainey's mother's home where, as a married man, Rainey had come alone. He definitely wasn't happy and had no problem letting everybody know it. The disappointment mixed with pity on everyone's faces continued to break his already fractured heart. He had no good news about when his wife would join him.

"This is when your faith kicks in, Twin," Cheney said softly, then added, "Look at what Jesus did for me. I wasn't even supposed to have a child or become pregnant, but I did. I wasn't supposed to carry a baby to full term. Again, I did. That was God."

"I'm not trying to take anything away from God....but look at what you had to suffer before having a house full of rugrats." Rainey pointed out that after she married Parke, she had miscarried and delivered a stillborn. *How was God in that?* He no longer threw the abortion that started her woes in her face.

The discussion resurfaced after dinner while reclining in the living room. Cheney lifted her chin. "Since without faith it's impossible to please God, I, along with the other Jamieson wives, actually Eva Jamieson—Kidd's wife who is a closet wedding planner extraordinaire—have come up with great ideas for your American wedding. Of course, we have gotten Josephine's input, my poor sister-in-law."

While in Africa, Kidd had mentioned that his wife was expecting. Rainey wondered how all these pregnant women were going to manage that. He didn't comment.

"And poor daughter-in-law." Gayle sighed and shook her head. "I wish you had seen her...Josephine was so beautiful."

"Imani videotaped it. I cried..." Cheney said.

I'm still crying, Rainey pouted inside. In an attempt to comfort him, Rainey's family shared their best memories of his life, starting from childhood to the present. They were careful not to mention Josephine's name, which made him miss her more. He was about to advise them of that, too.

"Bryce described the ceremony and how much money you dished out." Janae *tsk*ed.

"And your point is? I don't believe mother and father gave you a budget when you married Bryce." He cut his eye at his brother-in-law with a "thanks big mouth" expression.

"I'm sorry, man. Janae wanted details."

"It's all right, man. She's your problem," Rainey said, then announced he was heading home. He was finished with this conversation, or at least he thought he was until Janae showed up at his office the next day, bearing gifts of an apology and a hot boxed lunch.

He truly loved both of his sisters, but something was going on with Janae. He asked if she was suffering from depression, diagnosed with cancer or anything else to make her be suspicious of mankind.

"I'm just guarded. I just don't take things at face value like I used to." Janae dipped a corner of her roast beef sandwich in sauce. "I don't really know Josephine, but is there a possibility that she's..." she frowned, "that she's not trying hard enough to get here? I'm just putting it out there."

Rainey calmly released the remains of his pastrami sandwich and sat back at his table in his office. He chose his words carefully. "Janae, watch what you say about my wife's character.

Don't even think about mistreating or acting snooty around her. I don't have a problem cutting you off as a relative, not in retaliation, but in love.

"Humph." She rolled her eyes.

"And speaking of character," Rainey pointed at her, "I think you're wearing down my brother-in-law. Don't chase him away, J. He is by far the best thing you've got going because he puts up with your 'tude. You need Jesus."

Janae's posture straightened as she displayed a smile most people paid him to duplicate. Too bad it was a fake—front caps. "Aren't you saved now and not supposed to be acting like that?"

Rainey wasn't in the mood to play games. "The Bible says a man shall leave his mother and father. I left this country for that woman and will do so again."

Picking up her purse, Janae stormed out of his office. Although he admitted he was a bit harsh, Rainey didn't try to stop her. He boasted defending his wife, but his wife was not a push over. Josephine would get Janae in check with her sweet spirit and sassy mouth. Shaking their conversation from his mind, Rainey put on his own fake smile until it felt genuine as he saw his patients for the rest of the afternoon.

Later that night at home, Rainey sent her a simple email: *I miss you, baby. Come home.*

Josephine's response was rather lengthy, but through all the words of 'I miss you too' and 'Love you', only one thing stuck with him. "The only delay now is my medical exam by their authorized doctor. When I canceled and tried to reschedule it, the appointment was pushed back ten days."

"Baby, why did you have to cancel?" Rainey asked himself. Realizing he was becoming frustrated, He closed his eyes and

prayed before responding. He didn't want to have an argument with his new wife via email.

Rainey replied: *I love you and my family and I are praying. Dad sends his love through his letters, Mrs. Reynolds,* then he signed out.

"Jesus, please don't let me have to back up my argument with Janae and go get my wife. Please."

The weeks turned into thirty-two days and Rainey was beside himself. "God, why did You let me go through all this only to take my wife away?" That seemed to have become his constant petition to God, and God never answered back. His mother's and Cheney's calls of reassurance did nothing to sweeten his sour mood.

When Shane called to get the latest on Josephine's trip, he ordered Rainey to meet him at the gym after his last appointment. Afterwards, they would get something to eat. "This is not negotiable, Dr. Reynolds."

He agreed, needing to vent anyway. Plus, Rainey was beyond tired of coming home to a house void of his wife. After working out, they dined at one of Shane's favorite places.

Throughout their meal, Rainey could tell his friend had been biting his tongue. So Rainey gave his permission to release it. "What?"

"Hear me out, Dr. Reynolds. Have you ever considered that all this was a scam? We hear about them all the time with "mail order" brides trying to get into the U.S. Then the other day on the news, agents uncovered an identity theft ring that originated out of Africa. Yesterday, two Nigerians tried to board a plane in London with—"

Squinting at his longtime friend, Rainey wondered where this was going.

Shane continued as if he had been taking notes for a home-work assignment. "Don't you think it's ironic after all you've done to woo Josephine with two international flights, one reli-gious conversion, not to mention the money you doled out for the African bash, that she's still there and you're here. It's almost like a sca—"

Jesus, keep me from falling. Jesus keep me from falling, Rainey prayed to keep from getting ghetto and punching Shane in the mouth. He and Shane may have disagreed about things in the past, but neither one had ever considered boxing each other.

Holding up his hand, Rainey issued a warning. Why was Shane thinking the worst about his wife? "Say it, Shane, and this will end our friendship. You're trying to insinuate that my wife, whose reputation I will not let you taint, is doing something scandalous.

"One flight changed me—the mission trip, the people, God and Josephine. The gifts were part of her tradition—I didn't question it because I love her. You were there—surprisingly—and saw for yourself how beautiful she was and could see how much she loves me."

"Yes, to all of that." Shane didn't back down. "One fact remains. You're wearing a wedding band and there's no wife by your side." He pointed to Rainey's finger. "I'm just worried about you. Have you considered Josephine might have changed her mind? You mentioned that she seemed torn, and she was hesitant in answering yes. I saw that with my own eyes." Shane thumped his chest.

It served Rainey right for letting everybody get into his head. Rainey should have kept his concerns regarding his rela-tionship with Josephine to himself. As if sensing he had crossed the line, Shane lightened the mood and talked shop.

Although Rainey accepted the subject change, one thing Shane said echoed in his mind: Did Josephine really want to come, or was she satisfied with him making a couple trips a year to be with his wife?

No, he refused to entertain that. His wife was the most honest and straightforward woman he knew. Josephine wouldn't deceive him—would she? If there was ever reason to pray, it was now because more than his marriage was at stake, so was his sanity.

When Rainey left the restaurant, he drove around the city and its landmarks, not ready to go home again to another empty house.

ॐॐ

Back in Accra, Josephine was in tears as she admired her wedding ring. Her mother and sister couldn't console her. If Josephine ever had any doubts in her mind that she would miss her country more than her husband, this was the deciding factor.

"Rainey has not returned my calls all week. I placed an international call to Cheney, but I did not want to upset her in her condition. We prayed, but she's concerned about her twin, too, since he missed the last couple of family dinners." Her heart was breaking. Since she resigned from the university, Josephine had no job and, it seemed, no husband.

"Cheney called me back. Parke and the other Jamieson men were heading over there to check on him..." Josephine hiccupped. "And Grandmother B, too."

"Oh, that's good," her mother cooed, rubbing Josephine's back.

"No it is not. Grandmother B has a license to carry a firearm. She brags she has never missed because she was a sharp shooter in a past life or some type of foolishness. She didn't hesitate at shooting Rainey's father. Cheney said Grandmother B mumbled something about Rainey needing a little lead in his behind."

Josephine balled harder. "She is trying to make me a widow before I'm a good wife."

A heavy hand squeezed her shoulder. Josephine looked up and met her father's soulful eyes. "Papa, can you get the ambassador to do anything?"

Her father shook his head sadly. "With the two Nigerians taken into custody for trying to bring weapons into New York a few months ago, all visa requests are on hold until further notice. It's time to pray."

Was God trying to tell her something with one roadblock after another in her life and marriage? Josephine was so close to going to her new home after passing her medical exam for her permanent residency visa. All her paperwork was finally in order. She sighed. "I love Rainey, but I fear that he believes I am not coming." She sniffed.

"Would you like for me to speak with him?"

"Yes, papa, please," Josephine pleaded. That gave her hope as her mother ushered everyone out her bedroom so Josephine could get some rest.

"All things—not some things—work together for good to those who love the Lord, Josephine. Now is not the time to stop loving the Lord when things get tough," her mother whispered before closing her door.

Chapter 29

The next day, Gyasi was outraged. He barely enjoyed his favorite dish of fried yams with chofi—turkey tail. Josephine had never seen her father so angry.

"I'm insulted! I have placed two calls in to Dr. Reynolds and they have not been returned. I will not be disrespected! Already your husband has betrayed my trust."

Jesus, I'm loving You as my situation deteriorates, Josephine prayed as her father paced the living room floor. Sitting between Abigail and her mother, they each held her hands.

Her mother wrapped her arm around Josephine's shoulder. "Husband, you are upsetting our daughter."

He acted as if her mother had not spoken. "Under Ghanaian law, Josephine has grounds for a divorce. In sections one and two of the matrimonial clause, this is evidence of an irrevocable marriage breakdown. He's guilty of sections four and five: unreasonable behavior and desertion..." he rambled on.

Josephine sniffed; her father was accusing her husband of the awful things that Rainey would probably blame on her. He didn't want to leave her in the first place, but she assured Rainey she would follow soon. That had almost been two months earlier—almost. Gyasi's employer—the ambassador—did his best to get her visa granted, but even his hands were tied.

"If you can't go to him—through no fault of your own—then it is his responsibility as the husband to return to Ghana and fulfill section seven, which is to live together as husband and wife."

Closing her eyes, Josephine bowed her head, praying her father would not recite all the sections and articles for filing for a divorce.

Standing, her mother tried to reason with her husband. "Dear, men are a prideful species. Maybe Dr. Reynolds is handling the absence of his wife just as badly as you. He needs time."

"Time." He grunted. "Ecclesiastes 3 states there is a time and place for everything. I hope that young man does not run out of time as my son-in-law. The clock is ticking."

I hope not either, Josephine prayed.

⇛⇝

A few days later, all the elders and other family members met at Josephine's house for prayer on behalf of Josephine's situation. Without employment to keep her distracted, she welcomed it.

Her grandfather commanded everyone's attention. "As on the night of your wedding, Josephine, we celebrated life and love. Tonight is also cause for celebration. We gathered here by faith. We know of the Lord's acts of kindness."

"Amen," murmured around the room among her loved ones.

"We will praise God as if He has already moved all the paperwork in your favor. And if we have to do this all night, we will," he advised.

"Thank you, *Impaa,*" Josephine said softly to her grandfather.

"Yes, like in the Book of Acts when the saints basically prayed Paul out of prison," her mother added.

⸗ us draw our minds in and petition God in the ...." Her grandfather led his family.

⸗urs, Josephine's family members prayed, moaned, sang, mumbled, and shouted. The Lord made His presence known as many of her family spoke in other tongues. It seemed when one person ran out of steam, another picked up the prayer chain.

Josephine's loud prayers faded until her eyes drifted. She felt someone tap her on her shoulder. Stirring, Josephine opened her eyes and looked around. She blinked. Those close to her had dozed off as well. The hand on her shoulder was firm. She was perplexed who could have woke her.

Men everywhere should lift up holy hands and pray without ceasing, God spoke from 1Timothy 2.

Immediately Josephine felt ashamed that while her family continued to utter prayers from their lips, albeit softly for her benefit, she had fallen asleep.

"Jesus, please give me strength..." before she finished asking, a fire seemed to begin to churn within her until it ushered out a power for her to pray harder, stronger, longer and more determined than she had ever remembered in her life.

You cry unto me day and night. Increase your faith and see if I do not act quickly, God spoke from Luke 18.

A while later when the elder said, Amen, parents gathered their children to go home. It was sunrise Saturday morning and the Amoahs and family had prayed all night. Josephine headed to the shower. Hoping that the prayer had changed her circumstances, beginning with her husband, she checked her email— nothing from him.

Let patience have her perfect work, God spoke James 1:4.

Nodding, Josephine took a deep breath, said a quick prayer and composed an email. She didn't know if Rainey would open it, delete it, or respond.

Good morning my beloved husband. I am coming home to you soon. Please keep a place warm for me in your heart.

Love,

Your loving wife.

Her own heart was too full to say more, so Josephine hit SEND, and said another prayer, "Jesus, please make sure he reads this, please, in Your name, Jesus, I ask this. Amen." Grabbing her Bible, she began to read, searching the scriptures until she got an answer from the Lord.

Josephine felt confident she was going home. She hoped she didn't get mixed signals and God was telling her to get ready for her home going instead of going home to her husband.

Chapter 30

As far as Rainey was concerned, he was prayed out. Yet, when he walked through the garage door of his condo, he felt an urge to pray—again. But a battle stirred in his body as his stomach growled.

Cheney had once told him that when they refuse their bodies food when fasting, the Spirit grew stronger. Setting his keys on the counter, Rainey dragged himself to his bedroom while his stomach protested each step.

Sliding to his knees, Rainey began to pray in a weary voice until the Lord's presence filled the room. He listened in awe as his spirit spoke to the Lord in an unlearned language. Energized, Rainey elevated his praise.

While in the spirit of worship, someone rang his doorbell. Deciding to ignore it and stay in tune with God, Rainey clapped louder. He even added a little dance to his praise, but the ringer was persistent.

Annoyed, Rainey wiped his face of any residue of tears. He stormed out of his bedroom, rebuking the devil. "It ain't nothing, but Satan interrupting my prayer time."

Opening the door, Rainey froze as he stared unbelievingly at his visitors. Protocol called for Rainey to speak, hug and kiss his mother first, but he couldn't. It was as if Rainey was starstruck.

Choked with so much emotion, he stepped outside in the chilly night and engulfed his father in a bear hug. The tears he shed earlier in prayer were nothing to compare with his current floodgate.

"Dad, you're home early…..you're free…" Rainey pulled back from their embrace and patted his father's shoulders to make sure he wasn't dreaming.

Still in shock, Rainey finally acknowledged his tearful, sniffing and beaming mother. Remembering his manners, he ushered them inside. "Dad, when…"

Filling the foyer with a hearty laugh, Roland's presence warmed the room. Rainey could barely contain his joy as his father's larger than life voice echoed through his place. He guided them to the kitchen as his suppressed hunger resurfaced.

Like old times, not so long ago, the two doctors walked together with their hands on each other's backs. Although his father wasn't a short man, Rainey had him beat by a couple of inches. For good measure, his father squeezed the back of Rainey's neck. Once they were in the kitchen, Rainey couldn't think straight to put together a peanut butter sandwich, so his mother took charge of selecting one of Miss Hazel's meals she had prepared and frozen for Rainey.

He couldn't take his eyes or hands off of his father. "I thought you still had a month or so to go. How?"

"Praise God for overcrowding." His mother answered instead. "When Roland informed me of the possibility of early parole, we decided to keep it quiet, praying nothing would happen to spoil the blessings." For good measure, she stopped what she was doing, walked to the table and squeezed her husband.

Within a half hour, they had blessed their meatloaf, pinto beans, cabbage and cornbread dinner. It was like old times as they joked and chatted about family.

"So now what, Dad?" Rainey wiped his mouth.

"The first thing is Roland is getting a physical, then I'm going to fatten him up." His mother gave his father a worshipful glance. "Then we're going shopping for new clothes, and—"

"Have a celebration," Rainey said caught up in the moment.

They gave him a deadpan look. "What?"

Rainey grunted and shook his head. "Sorry, that's something Josephine would have said."

"Speaking of my new daughter-in-law, any word on when she is coming?" His father asked with a hopeful expression.

Stalling, Rainey was ashamed to answer.

"Son?"

"We aren't exactly on speaking terms." Rainey avoided eye contact as he rubbed the back of his nape. "I couldn't bear to hear any more excuses. The ball is in her court to make it happen... Maybe I've been played." Rainey used Shane's phrase.

His mother stood abruptly. She was furious. "How dare you speak so badly about Josephine! No woman wants to be separated from the man she loves and she does love you. I saw it in her eyes the night you two were married."

Once his mother finished chewing him out, his father picked up the pieces and lit into him. "Do you think I could have survived in prison without the love of my family? I gave you every reason to turn your back on me, but none of you did," toning down his stern voice, he added, "Keep hope alive. Don't turn your back on her."

Chastened, Rainey assured them he wouldn't as they prepared to leave and pay a visit to his sisters.

The next morning while sitting in his office, Rainey thought long and hard about the things his parents said. It wasn't that easy to keep hope alive. They definitely were standing on the outside looking in. They didn't know how each email from Josephine was ripping out his heart. He didn't think it was possible to invest in so many excuses.

Believe all things, God spoke.

What things? Rainey asked as he closed his eyes in frustration and exhaled. At least his next appointment would provide him some comedic relief. They were a set of twin boys, Peter and Paul. After two years of wearing braces, Rainey would remove them today and complete their care.

He chuckled, recalling one of their pranks. On their first visit, the boys tried the switching-their-identities trick on him. It didn't work. Rainey always reminded them, a twin could always tell another twin apart. Of course it was a myth, but they didn't know that, and neither did that keep them from trying repeatedly.

Suddenly, visions of his and Josephine's Ghanaian wedding knocked everything else out of his mind. She looked so beautiful. He had loved her so much that night and the love grew stronger, even in her absence. Ring or no ring, love was not going to make a fool out of him again.

Despite his resolve, Rainey was tempted to check his Gmail account, if for no other reason than to have the satisfaction of knowing she was emailing and he was ignoring her. Hmmmm. Josephine had sent another one—good!

Then "believe all things", "Don't turn your back on her", "I saw love in her eyes" reminders flooded his mind. Mixed emotions battled within him whether to open it or send it into a folder labeled "J" with the others. He clicked before he changed his mind.

My beloved husband…

Rainey glanced away. The words were already invading his heart. He refused to soften. He took a deep breath to stay in control.

His traitorous heart forced his eyes to finish, then there was a knock on his office door, alerting him that the comedy twins had arrived. He didn't want to smile, but he did, imagining Josephine's clipped British accent as she asked him to keep a warm place in his heart. "Lord, something has to change in a hurry because I have needs and I need my wife."

৵৶

Three months and counting. That's how long Josephine had been Mrs. Rainey Reynolds. The thought saddened her, but the prayer vigil hadn't stopped. As a matter of fact, it increased as her friends and a few former coworkers added her and Rainey to their prayer lists. Madeline and Dennis, and a group of Ghanaians who lived in Britain that understood her plight, began to seek the Lord on her behalf.

Across the waters in America, Cheney had a Jamieson prayer line going among her family, friends and church.

Then three days after Josephine prayed and sent her last email to her husband, he called. Her heart pounded as she answered, "Rainey?"

"Mrs. Reynolds?"

Closing her eyes, Josephine smiled. She liked the sound of that. "Yes, I'm sorry that I am upsetting you, but I really am trying to get there."

"I know, babe, but before we continue, may I speak with your father."

Josephine didn't argue. As expected, her parents were lounging in the living room, watching a show, starring Joselyn Canfor Dumas.

"Papa, Rainey would like to speak with you." She grinned and handed him the phone. The scowl face showed he didn't appreciate the interruption during his favorite program. Her mother nudged him.

To give them privacy, her mother looped her arm through Josephine's and guided her to the kitchen. "They will learn to understand each other. Our ways are not like Americans' ways, neither are Americans' ways like ours and the world's ways are not like God's ways,"

Excitement mixed with curiosity about Rainey's phone call kept Josephine from fully receiving her mother's pearls of wisdom. "Hmm-mm."

As Josephine sat at the table, her mother hummed while preparing them chocolate banana shakes.

Five minutes later, Josephine still hadn't taken a sip. She was too nervous, waiting to speak with her husband. Her father was taking up a lot of phone time. There would be none left for her.

Finally, her father's footsteps grew louder as he approached the kitchen. With a huge grin, he handed her the phone. Josephine exhaled with a sigh of relief. That was a good sign.

Excusing herself, she hurried into her bedroom and closed the door. "Is everything all right between you and papa?" Josephine wanted to make sure that her father wasn't happy because he forced Rainey to grant her a divorce.

"Yes, babe. I took Gyasi's reprimand like a man, but I had to apologize for my actions when I refused his call. I honor him as I would my father and I would never have treated him like that."

"Meda wo ase."

"I'm sorry, baby, for disrespecting you and your situation. I have a lot to understand about things outside the United States."

"What happened for you to have a change of heart?" Getting comfortable in her bed, she brought her knees to her chest. She was in pure bliss.

"Well..." Rainey dragged out the word as if something big had happened. "Let's just say I received uninvited, unwanted, and unexpected guests."

"You're teasing me. Tell me," Josephine pleaded, giddy with bliss.

"First, Parke and his cousins made a special visit to encourage me with their testimonies about rough patches that plagued their relationships before they were married—they were my unexpected guests."

"And your unwanted company?"

"Grandma BB. She is downright scary. Although Cheney came along to chaperone, the woman kept patting her purse. Since Missouri is a conceal-and-carry state, I started praying."

Josephine giggled until a tear dropped. Then she praised God for protecting her husband because her former host was unpredictable. "I'm glad you are safe. That leaves one more. Who else visited you?"

Silence. Josephine wondered if he was going to tell her.

He mimicked a drum roll and exhaled. "A few days later while in prayer, someone at my door interrupted me—my father!"

Josephine gasped and immediately began to praise God. Seconds later, Rainey joined her. "That is wonderful news, dear husband."

Rainey described in detail what happened. Full of joy, Josephine chuckled. She didn't care what her husband talked about she just enjoyed hearing his voice and happiness—now if only she was there to share in his joy. "This calls for a celebration!"

"And that's what I told them." Rainey chuckled, then became quiet. "Stubbornness is draining. It seemed like God kept telling me to 'believe all things'. I didn't know what that meant exactly until I opened that email. After reading your latest words, I knew in my heart that you were suffering like me."

This was what Josephine had been waiting to hear. Rainey acknowledging that she was miserable without him. She frowned, debating whether she wanted to hear the answer to her question. "How much time do we have?"

"Thirty minutes. I used twenty getting on Gyasi's good side."

Josephine giggled. They crammed as many 'I love yous' and 'miss yous' as they could before praying together and sharing a scripture. When they reluctantly disconnected, Josephine had a smile on her lips and praise in her heart.

The next day, her father's employer increased the efforts within his power to influence the U.S. Embassy in Accra, Ghana, to increase the priority of Josephine's paperwork. But two weeks had come and gone—nothing. Rainey didn't hide his frustration; neither did Josephine hide her disappointment, but the phone calls didn't stop coming.

Josephine continued to occupy her time with volunteer work at a girls' school, then she received the exciting news. Cheney had delivered a healthy baby—another boy. In an email,

Cheney wrote there would be no more 'p names" in the Jamieson house.

Praise the Lord, sister-in-law,

I can't wait until you see him. He's beautiful. His name is Chase Alexander Rainey Jamieson. I got carried away with the extra name, but if his African aunt could have all those names, so can he.

Wait on God. I know the distance is trying Rainey's and your faith, but trust me. The Lord is faithful. When man says no, God says, "Under whose authority? I didn't say no."

"Yes, God is faithful." Josephine replied back:

I am honored that you have selected my husband's name. In Ghana, since Chase was born on a Friday, he would first be named Kofi. Like former United Nations Secretary General Kofi Atta Annan.

It's October. Hopefully, I'll be home for Christmas, as the American song says, but while I wait for patience to have her perfect work in me, at least I can look forward to the Akwasidae Festival. We call it a celebration of reflection in the lives of Ashanti's.

Kiss Chase for me,

Aunt Josie

Not long after that, Josephine had a breakthrough. Her father's employer advised that America had marginally opened its door, but with limited access and they didn't know for how long.

"You must prepare to leave immediately. We never know when a turn of events will shut the door again," her father said, his words accompanied by a sorrowful smile. Within minutes, she emailed Rainey and typed "Urgent" in the subject line, and then "Call me" in the body of the text.

It was early morning in Ghana when Rainey phoned. She was alert immediately. "I'm coming home." Josephine could hardly wait to feel her husband's arms.

"When?"

"I'll be there in about ten days. I miss you."

"Then I'll see you in about eight. There is no way I'm letting my wife travel home alone. I love you."

"*Me Dor wo.*" She softly made a kissing sound. His response was a deafening smack that made Josephine's grin brighter. She was going home.

Chapter 31

Rainey boarded his flight to Accra to accompany his wife back to the States—finally. *Come on*, he wanted to tell the pilots once they were airborne, *let's get this flight over with.*

Just think, no more phone minute rations or interrupted internet connections. No more Skype where Rainey strained to see every feature of his wife, but couldn't touch her. In essence, no more torture. He smirked, recalling their last phone call a few days earlier.

"Make sure you're wearing that rock on your third finger when you greet me at the airport."

"Of course, dear husband. Why?"

"You'll find out." They disconnected, but he had a smile on his face.

Their life was just beginning. Rainey sighed, closing his eyes at the same time his ears began to pop, indicating the plane was descending.

"The captain has asked that you remain seated with your seatbelt fastened," the flight attendant announced.

What was wrong? They had just taken off, maybe fifteen, twenty minutes earlier. He sat straighter. *Lord, please, no more delays in Jesus' name. Amen.*

"What's the problem?" Rainey whispered, stopping the attendant as he made his way to the front.

"Nothing to be alarmed about. One of our pilots has taken ill; we're returning to the terminal, so he can receive medical attention. The airline has been alerted and another pilot should be en route," he explained and hurried to get strapped in.

Nothing to be alarmed about? This man held the life of every passenger in his incapable hands.

I cause the wind to cease, the waves to roll, the sun to shine. I hold this plane in the palm of My hand, God chastened Rainey. *Pray in My name for him.*

Ashamed that he had selfishly dismissed the man's needs for his own, Rainey repented and bowed his head to silently pray, *Lord, I know I read in Your Word that men should pray everywhere. Please forgive my insensitive thoughts. Your will be done. Lord, in Your name, Jesus, please restore that pilot's condition wherever it has deteriorated...in Jesus' name. Amen.*

Once the plane landed, passengers were instructed to stay on the plane as the airline switched crews. When the door opened, paramedics rushed in. Rainey overheard someone say the man had initially passed out, then regained consciousness, but complained of shortness of breath.

Déjà vu kicked in as the second flight crew took charge within the hour. This time around, Rainey pushed back his desire to see his wife, and he prayed off and on for the pilot and his family.

As soon as the flight attendants cleared passengers to use electronic devices, Rainey tapped his Bible icon on his smartphone to find the scripture with 'men should pray everywhere'. He found it in 1Timothy 2:8. He mediated on it, and then continued reading until he dozed off.

After twenty-six hours, including one layover, Rainey's Ghana International airplane landed at Kotoka airport. He grabbed his toiletry bag. With a moist wipe, Rainey dabbed his face and made quick use of a floss pick before popping a breath mint in his mouth.

When his aircraft came to a stop on the tarmac, Rainey stood, stretched and checked his shirt and pants for excessive wrinkles. He couldn't believe it. His wife was finally coming home. Rainey prayed for patience as his visa was checked and cleared through Customs. The steep ramp to the terminal and into the lobby quickened his steps.

Rainey rounded the corner and there she was—Josephine Reynolds—his wife. Smiling and waving, she hurried toward him. Rainey focused on getting to her, and when she was within reach, he dropped his bags. With ease, Rainey swept her off of her feet, then kissed her without a protest. Since she was wearing her ring, he had every right to show a little public show of affection—or a lot.

The kiss might have been over, but Rainey refused to break their connection. With an arm around her waist, Rainey scooped up his two carryon bags in one motion. Every time the realization hit that he hadn't seen his wife in seventeen weeks, he squeezed her.

"How is your father?"

He loved her more for asking. "He's happy to be sleeping in a real bed with his wife like I will be beginning tonight!"

"You should have had a celebration for his homecoming."

Rainey rubbed her back. "Wait a minute, Mrs. Reynolds. Some things are worth celebrating. Other things you'd rather forget."

"You're married to a Ghanaian, which makes you a Ghanaian citizen once you complete the paperwork. It's a tradition that we celebrate the good things God has done for us, including deliverance, renewal and second chances."

Rainey shook his head. His Ghanaian wife had a lot to learn about the American way. "A prison homecoming was definitely out." This wasn't one of Tyler Perry's Madea movies.

కోను

The next morning in the honeymoon suite at the Mövenpick Ambassador Hotel, Josephine cuddled against her husband. If she was dreaming, there was no way she was about to open her eyes. She inhaled the lingering scent of Rainey's cologne. Yes, her husband was beside her. Smiling, she said a quick prayer of thanks to Jesus and then drifted off to sleep.

Much later in the day, they reluctantly ended their brief second honeymoon to check out and get to her parents' house before it was late. Rainey still had a concern about female mosquitoes.

Family members had come together to celebrate Rainey's return and bless Josephine's departure that would take place the following day.

Rainey seemed overwhelmed. "They are all here for us?"

"Yes." Josephine said as she had him sample more Ghanaian dishes. They danced and rejoiced until her father and other elders pulled Rainey aside for private discussions, aka a tongue lashing. Her husband took it in stride.

Rainey arranged for a driver to take them to the airport since it would be early. What she couldn't take on the plane, Josephine's family would ship.

That night—the last night in Accra for a long time—the couple slept in the Amoahs' guest bedroom cuddled inside a mosquito tent—per Rainey's request. She humored him. It was a bittersweet moment. Although Rainey promised she could return home whenever she wanted, in the back of her mind she wondered if they would go through the same headache when it was time for her to return.

"Are you happy?" Rainey whispered.

"I pray that I will be a good wife."

Turning her around to face him, Rainey smiled. "If you want to make me happy, then be yourself. I married you because I love you like I have never loved another woman."

"As I, or I never would have married you."

"You did have me sweating there for a moment," Rainey confessed, then the rest of their night was indescribable.

The next morning, Abigail boohooed more than Josephine as Rainey tried to console the sisters.

"Be happy. You are coming into a phase most women envy. Be a good wife and God will reward you with many babies." Her mother blushed before her daughter.

Rainey escorted Josephine away from her family when their car arrived for the airport. "Can we drive past the university at Legon?" Josephine asked once they were settled in the back seat.

Rainey nodded to the driver. Josephine cataloged the early bird hawkers, the trotros, and the dawning of the craziness of downtown that gave way to the serenity of the university. When she became homesick, she would pull from the memories of her native land to comfort her.

"Honey," he whispered. Josephine didn't realize he had called her. She leaned into him. As her vision blurred, she cried softly in the comfort of her husband's arms.

"I am a man with everything, but now I'm a husband who needs his wife. God help me not to ever cause you to second guess my love or regret leaving your world for mine. When you want to come back, I hope the longing in your eyes will be because you will be leaving me," Rainey said softly.

"Yes, I'm sad to leave Ghana," Josephine choked, "but it will be harder to leave you, dear husband."

"That's good to hear." Rainey rubbed a kiss in her hair. Retreating to their own thoughts, neither said another word until they arrived at the airport.

Chapter 32

Rainey didn't relax until their plane was flying over the Atlantic Ocean. He felt like he had just undertaken a rescue mission, getting his wife out of the country before anybody knew she was missing. How did spies do it for a living with such finesse?

With a three-hour layover in London, Josephine's sister and husband would meet them there. Rainey and Josephine would change planes in New York and then finally arrive home in St. Louis. Content with Josephine sleeping next to him, Rainey rested his head on top of her African head garb and dozed, too.

Five hours later at Heathrow's Gatwick Airport, they walked hand-in-hand through the terminal to the lobby. Rainey identified Madeline afar off. Not because of a similar African garb, but the smile—yes, it was as perfect as Josephine's. As the two sisters embraced, Rainey introduced himself and shook hands with Dennis.

Next, he welcomed Madeline's hug. "Please keep my sister happy. She's very special."

Rainey stared into Josephine's eyes. "I will."

While they grabbed something to eat, Rainey took the opportunity to ask Dennis' insight about marrying a Ghanaian when the sisters went to the restroom.

Dennis shrugged. "Every woman is a delicate creature. I have to remind myself when I feel Madeline is being difficult that it's me who is lacking the understanding. God instructs us husbands to love and understand our wives."

Agreeing, Rainey nodded.

"Some things we do in London would not be acceptable in Ghana, so at times, my wife has a hard time biting her tongue." Dennis grinned.

Rainey barked out a laugh. They definitely would get along. They placed their orders and had a lively discussion about their cultures over sumptuous food. The hardest thing was pulling the sisters away to say goodbye.

Rainey prepared himself for the tears. Surprisingly, Josephine had a brighter smile than when she left Ghana. He couldn't help but squeeze her tighter. "Still happy that you married me?"

Josephine blinked. "Ecstatic."

By the time they touched down at Lambert airport in St. Louis, the only thing Rainey and Josephine wanted was a bed for sleeping. Exiting the terminal to the lobby, he almost stumbled at the unexpected welcoming party. "Whoa."

There had to be more than thirty people, mostly the Jamiesons and his family, there to greet them. They held signs and balloons that read, *"Akwaaba* Home", "Congratulations Newlyweds!" "Hi Aunt Josie". The smaller children waved homemade signs. Their claps and whistles drew bystanders' attention.

"Where is this African princess you described in your letters?" his father boasted.

Rainey tried to get Josephine's attention, but Cheney's new baby had captured her attention. "The new Mrs. Reynolds."

She twirled around in response. Her African attire's bright colors gave her a glow against the backdrop of his family. Rainey reached out his hand and she came.

"This is my lovely wife, Josephine Reynolds." Grinning, he watched his father's reaction as he made the introductions.

"You've done good, son. She is beautiful."

"I thought so, too, the moment I laid eyes on her." Rainey's nostrils flared.

Josephine bowed slightly as a sign of respect, but Roland hugged her. "Welcome home, Dr. Reynolds."

"Welcome home to you, daughter," his father said. "Please call me whatever makes you comfortable. Doctor is too formal for family."

"Thank you, Dad." Everybody laughed, including the small ones as they made their way downstairs to claim their baggage.

☙❧

Josephine felt right at home as she surveyed her new extended family: the babes, brothers, sisters, and cousins.

Once they were in Rainey's car, Josephine scrutinized each passing building and street. It had been two years since she last visited. Caught up in reminiscing, Josephine didn't realize they had reached their destination until Rainey squeezed her hand.

"This is our home, baby—for now. We can go house hunting anytime you're ready, Mrs. Reynolds."

Her husband had described his condo as small, but the large front window and entryway said otherwise. Another welcome home sign hung from the door. She smiled.

"This is it—the beginning of our life as husband and wife," she said in awe. She would be a legitimate wife with no ocean or time zone to separate them. "Thank You, God."

"Yes, thank You, Jesus, for my wife that I adore," he mumbled as he teased her lips, which made her heart flutter. "Come on my African queen. I've been waiting to pamper you for months. The only thing I want you to do is absolutely nothing," Rainey said as he struggled to grab every piece of their luggage in one swoop. It didn't work. Smothering a laugh, Josephine came to his aid.

"I'm your helpmate, Dr. Reynolds, and from my observation, you need assistance."

"Well, thank you, Mrs. Reynolds, for lightening my load—my heart."

Opening the door, Rainey deactivated the alarm. Turning on the foyer chandelier, they set their bags on the hardwood floor landing.

Josephine screamed and held on to Rainey's neck as he swept her into his arms. He closed the door with his foot. Massaging his clean-shaven jaw, Josephine was thankful there was no limit on how many times a woman could tell her husband she loved him and she did.

Rainey turned her hand to the inside and placed a kiss on her palm. "I know. I see it in your eyes."

"I didn't realize the intensity until I couldn't see you." She closed her eyes. "I want to be a good wife and never leave your side again."

"You won't. Believe me, where you go, I'll be right behind you." Still carrying her in his arms, he bypassed rooms and headed down a hall toward what Josephine guessed was their bedroom. "I'll give you a house tour later."

Chapter 33

That weekend, Josephine and Rainey were invited to their first party at Parke and Cheney's home. She was excited to be surrounded by family.

During the drive from West County to North County, Josephine couldn't get enough of Rainey's touches. She never thought she would be a clingy woman, but she wanted to make up for all their time apart and Rainey wasn't complaining.

At the Jamiesons' house, there were balloons and welcome home signs everywhere. There were even more people than at the airport days earlier. "Surprise!"

"A celebration!" She twirled in Rainey's arms and planted a kiss of gratitude on his lips.

Josephine was reintroduced to Parke's cousins and their wives, Rainey's friends, and a re-introduction to Shane and his date. Plus staffers and church members. The number of guests seemed endless.

"We know you're already married, but consider this your wedding shower, welcome home and housewarming party," Cheney explained.

"Where is Grandmother B?" Josephine had spoken to her former host the day after she arrived, but had yet to see her.

Cheney sighed and shook her head. "At home with a full blown attitude. She and Daddy can't be in the same space, or it will violate his parole and her probation since they both were each other's victims and assailants."

The news saddened Josephine. Few people thought about the consequences of sin. Cheney wrapped her arm around Josephine's shoulder. "We'll go shopping together."

"I would like that."

Rainey's laughter caught Josephine's attention as he talked with his father. "I told my dear husband that we should celebrate Dr. Reynolds coming home. He is free."

"Bad idea," Janae walked up behind her. "It's disgraceful. Do we have to remind the world what he was accused of?" Janae twisted her lips.

Josephine sensed the discord. "Dear sister. A celebration is a joyous occasion, a time of renewal, praising God for deliverance. The shame is gone. May I suggest an invitation for loved ones and friends?"

Cheney gnawed on her lips and made eye contact with someone over Josephine's shoulder. Pivoting on a heel, Josephine looked into her new father-in-law's eyes. Gayle stood next to him frowning. *Uh-oh*. Not good. The room seemed quiet as if everyone had overheard their private conversation. Rainey was at her side immediately. "What's wrong?"

Roland seemed to be considering her proposal. "Josephine, I like the way you think. I'm not the same man. My true friends will wish me well."

"Daddy, you can't be serious!!" Janae was beside herself. "Maybe some thug would have a barbecue with fellow gang-bangers..." She lifted her chin. "We do not entertain such nonsense."

Parke joined the debate. "Let's give Pop Reynolds some time to think about it." Others around the room nodded. "And Janae, I'm sure even Donald Trump has barbecues."

Josephine learned America 101: There is no freedom of speech. *God, I'm not in Ghana anymore, help me to make friends and not enemies with my sister-in-law,* she prayed silently, swallowing the hurt of rejection.

With loving kindness, you can draw her, Jesus spoke gently in her ear from Jeremiah 31:3.

Accepting her mission, Josephine was determined to love Janae Reynolds Allen despite the rocky start. Although the woman was cordial at the airport. One thing for sure, prayer warriors outnumbered her sister-in-law. She and Cheney would stay on one accord to lead her to Christ.

At that moment, Josephine's new nieces, Janae and Cheney's daughters, Natalie and Kami pulled Josephine aside with a zillion questions about Africa.

"Aunt Josie, how do the women carry the platters? Can you show us?" Natalie asked. Her eyes were bright with excitement.

"It's simple. One day when we're by ourselves, *yo?*"

"We can go in the kitchen," Kami pleaded and tugged her toward the buffet table where there was enough food for all the guests plus more.

"Food is to be eaten. Plus, the trays are filled with food," Josephine tried to use as an excuse. Ghanaians could balance a lot of weight on their heads. However the girls didn't need to know what.

Kami pointed to a small cheese platter that was almost empty and grabbed it. "C'mon, Aunt Josie. You can show us in the kitchen where no one is around."

Josephine consented to her determined nieces. She asked for a clean hand towel and wrapped it on top of her head. Then placed the platter on top and began to parade around the spacious kitchen to the girls' delight.

Rainey peeked his head inside the door, looking for her. "*Woho yɛ fɛw.* My beautiful wife on the runaway." Leaning against the doorpost, he folded his arms and watched her demonstration.

Within minutes, she had a small audience. Josephine removed it and set it on the counter to applause. Some seemed impressed; others were in awe. Janae was neither.

ॐ∾ॐ

"Barbaric," Janae snapped and left the kitchen.

Rainey was sixty seconds from making a scene. Instead of confronting his sister, he pulled Bryce aside. "Josephine is my wife now. Your wife, who happens to be my sister, has issues," he hissed as Parke joined them, not knowing the nature of their discussion. "Deal with Janae, man. I won't let her cross the line and insult my wife. I mean it, Bryce."

Parke chuckled. "Something tells me Josephine won't need backup."

"Hey, that's my wife you're talking about," Bryce defended, it seemed, more out of obligation.

"Seriously, bro. She is out of control and you need to do something."

Bryce seemed frustrated as he looked over his shoulder at Janae who was amused by whatever their dad was telling her. "I'll handle my wife."

For the rest of the evening, Rainey kept Josephine close to his side while Janae avoided Bryce.

Chapter 34

On Rainey and Josephine's sixth month wedding anniversary, what started out as a small vow renewal ceremony turned into a major production, compliments of one Jamieson wife, Eva, who was a closet wedding planner, always on the hunt to put her skills to work.

Then Gyasi, Fafa and Josephine's sisters demanded to be in attendance. Even his father and Grandma BB's parole and probation officers cleared the two to be at the same function under supervision. Rainey smirked. One thing for sure—well ninety-eight percent sure—Grandma BB wouldn't try anything crazy. It was the two percent that could be dangerous.

Something else crossed Rainey's mind. How would Gyasi receive his father with a tainted reputation? From day one of meeting Josephine's father, Rainey had to work hard to earn his respect. Of course, refusing to speak with Gyasi during Rainey's pity party didn't help either.

They had just finished eating one of Josephine's Ghanaian dishes. Rainey reached across the table and took one of her hands in his.

"What is it?" Josephine frowned. "Please tell me," she coaxed him.

"I'm just wondering if our fathers will get along, considering what my father has done in his past."

Josephine seemed thoughtful. "Our fathers are good men. Their common interest is our happiness."

"But do you think they will become genuine friends?" Rainey wanted a more definitive answer.

"Husband." Josephine placed her free hand on top of his. "My father will not shun Dr. Reynolds—my new dad."

Hmm-mm. Rainey would make sure of it as he lured his wife closer for a kiss.

A few days later, Rainey accompanied his wife to the airport to welcome her family to St. Louis. His parents insisted on being part of the welcoming committee since most would stay at their mansion where there was plenty of room.

Rainey wasn't worried about his father, who refused pity. Thanks to a small scale celebration spearheaded by his beautiful wife, he reconnected with a circle of his friends.

As far as his father's medical profession, that decision was in the hands of God and the medical review board.

His African guests were exiting the terminal; Rainey swallowed. *God, please let this go over well*, he prayed.

Josephine hurried to them. His mother greeted Fafa. His father extended his hand to Gyasi.

No, dad, Rainey cringed, *no, no no.* That was Gyasi's privilege in the Ghanaian culture. While Josephine was pre-occupied with hugs and kisses, Rainey watched the two father's interaction.

Gyasi accepted the shake and bowed slightly.

Okay. Rainey exhaled. *So far, so good.*

"Let's get your luggage. I've had Miss Hattie, our cook, prepare a feast," Rainey's mother said as she and Fafa walked in front. As the group headed to claim their baggage, Rainey trailed closely behind the fathers.

Because of the number of Ghanaian visitors, the Reynolds secured a limo to bring them to their palatial mansion in the Central West End.

In no time, the limo and cars pulled into the circular driveway in the private neighborhood near Forest Park. Miss Hattie had the food ready to serve once they got settled.

Later, most pardoned themselves for naps. Not Gyasi, so his father requested a private talk in the study.

Oh boy. Since he was not invited, Rainey paced the hall, trying to overhear the tone of their conversation.

"Gyasi, I want to apologize for my absence at our children's wedding ceremony, but Rainey assured me he was well represented by the men in the family."

"I have to admit, Roland, it was regretful that you missed one of the most celebrated moments in their lives. Under the circumstances, it could not be helped."

Silence. Rainey imagined Gyasi's scowl.

"It is not my place to judge you…"

That's right, Rainey said to himself.

"Your past actions hold a shameful mark against any man's character."

Don't take that, Dad. Give him a scripture or a hook…I repent, I repent, God, Rainey waited for his father's response.

"Thank God for the Blood of Jesus that washes my past white as snow. That is my defense."

Gyasi chuckled. "Then I guess you are starting off with a clean slate. Welcome to the Amoah family."

Rainey thought he was about to collapse from relief. There was no need for him to stick around. When he turned, Rainey bumped into Josephine whose arms were folded as her foot tapped softly. His eyes widened in surprise. He brought his finger to his lips to *shh* her.

"Eavesdropping is bad manners," she whispered, then pulled him away.

"Goodbye, son," his father yelled as he and Gyasi laughed heartily.

EPILOGUE

The day had come for the renewal ceremony. As Rainey and the groomsmen dressed at the church, he doubted his wife could look more beautiful than the night they married in Ghana. For the rest of his life, nothing could outshine that moment.

His father crossed the room to assist Rainey as he fought with his bow tie. Regaining a healthy weight, his dad looked good. The medical board did grant him obstetrician privileges at three hospitals for emergency calls only, but he could no longer have a private practice. His dad was okay with that as he contemplated reinventing his career.

Roland's eyes sparkled with humor as he took control and manipulated Rainey's tie with ease. They both chuckled.

"I praise the Lord that I didn't miss this day, son."

"I could only have one best man," Rainey said. Everything had worked itself out as James 1:4 said, *But let patience have her perfect work, that ye may be perfect and entire, wanting nothing.*

He glanced around the room at his other groomsmen: Shane, Parke, Bryce and even Dennis, Madeline's husband, accepted his invitation. That gesture made Josephine ecstatic. He did aim to please. Gyasi left the room minutes earlier, raving about how happy his daughter appeared to be.

Shane walked up to him. "No hard feelings. You really do have a beautiful wife."

"Thank you, man. We've always been each other's voice of reason, so I know you'll always have my back. Let me know if you ever need heavenly intervention. I know how to get a prayer through now."

Shane backed up. "Don't start."

"Dad Reynolds, will you lead us in a short prayer?" Parke asked his father-in-law. Everyone encircled Rainey.

"Father, in the name of Jesus, we come to Your throne where we not only receive mercy, but healing, blessings and wisdom. I ask that you teach my son to love his wife unselfishly as You have loved us. Bless their marriage and the babies to come. We thank You in the name of Jesus. Amen."

"Amen," the others said in unison as a knock at the door indicated it was time to start.

Rainey and his father took their places in front of the altar as Parke, Dennis, Bryce, and Shane stood behind them. It just so happened that Abigail and Shane were the only single people in the wedding party.

He smiled at his nieces marching down the aisle; his three nephews followed. When it was Josephine's turn to grace the "runway", Rainey became weak in the knees at the sight of his wife. Her rich brown skin glowed in the off white gown that reminded him of a fairy with the same type of crown on her head.

Having removed her braids, Josephine's hair flowed down her back. The look of love on her face reminded him of when she first beckoned him to 'Come to Africa.' And Rainey did just that and returned home with a jewel.

The reaffirmation of their vows was simple, but powerful. At the reception, his father stood to make a toast with the sparkling white grape juice that all were served. "To my lovely daughter who has showered my son with blessed happiness."

Cheers and applause roared throughout the banquet room.

Josephine stood and countered his toast. "To my husband who will get another tiny blessing in about seven months."

More cheers erupted as Rainey sat stunned. When it sunk in, Rainey stood and cupped Josephine's face in hands.

"We're having a baby?"

"Yes." Josephine nodded, stroking his jaw.

Turning to his guests, Rainey lifted his glass. "You're all invited back to our firstborn's naming ceremony in seven months and eight days."

Rainey kissed his wife and didn't let her out of his sight for the remainder of the night.

BOOK CLUB DISCUSSION QUESTIONS

1. How do you feel about Josephine's unwillingness to leave Africa to find happiness?
2. Why was Josephine so willing to celebrate Dr. Reynolds' return home?
3. Do you agree with Rainey that Josephine should be the one to move to America?
4. Did The Acquittal dispel any myths or stereotypes you had about Africa or Africans?
5. What was your favorite scene in the story?
6. Do you have a desire to visit one of the slave castles?
7. Why was Janae against Rainey going to Africa?
8. Do you believe a person can pick up the pieces after prison?
9. Did Rainey put Josephine on the spot to marry him?
10. Which was your favorite character and why?

THANK YOU FOR READING!

More From The Author

Coming winter 2013, *The Appeal* (A Guilty Parties novel): Janae and Bryce's fallout: No one could ever accuse Janae Reynolds Allen of trying to keep up with the Joneses. In her circle of elite friends, she was the "Joneses." Born into money and married into money, Janae continued to prosper with a chain of beauty spas. What she doesn't have in her life is Christ. When everyone around her begins to embrace God's salvation, Janae is determined to be the lone man—woman—standing until her husband, Bryce, commits to Christ. Begrudgingly, she begins to attend church, but is it for the right reason, for show or salvation? *The Appeal* is about the power struggle within a marriage when one spouse is ready to surrender to Jesus, and the other refuses to yield.

In spring 2014, look for *The Confession* (A Guilty Parties novel): Sandra Nicholson's story (Kidd & Ace's mother)

Coming June 2014, a new series with Whitaker House: *A Strike at Love.*

About The Author

Pat Simmons is a self-proclaimed genealogy sleuth. She is passionate about researching her ancestors, then casting them in starring roles in her novels. She hopes her off-beat method will track down distant relatives who happen to pick up her books. She has been a genealogy enthusiast since her great-grandmother died at the young age of ninety-seven years old in 1988.

She describes the evidence of the gift of the Holy Ghost as an amazing, unforgettable, life-altering experience. She believes God is the author who advances the stories she writes.

Pat has a B.S. in mass communications from Emerson College in Boston, Massachusetts. She has worked in various media positions in radio, television, and print for more than twenty years. Currently, she oversees the media publicity for the annual RT Booklovers Conventions.

She is the author of nine single titles and several eBook novellas. Her awards include *Talk to Me,* ranked #14 of Top Books in 2008 that Changed Lives by *Black Pearls Magazine.* She is a two-time recipient of the Romance Slam Jam Emma Rodgers Award for Best Inspirational Romance for *Still Guilty* (2010) and *Crowning Glory* (2011). Her bestselling novels include *Guilty of Love* and the Jamieson Legacy series: *Guilty by Association, The Guilt Trip,* and *Free from Guilt. The Acquittal* (A Guilty Parties novel) is her first of two 2013 releases.

Pat has converted her sofa-strapped, sports-fanatical husband into an amateur travel agent, untrained bodyguard, and GPS-guided chauffeur. They have a son and daughter.

Pat's interviews include numerous appearances on radio, television, blogtalk radio, blogs, and feature articles.

Please visit Pat at www.patsimmons.net

Or contact her at authorpatsimmons@gmail.com or

P.O. Box 1077

Florissant, MO 63031

Made in the USA
Lexington, KY
28 August 2013